£15

CELIBATE LIVES

George Moore

CHATTO & WINDUS

LONDON

Published by
Chatto & Windus Ltd.
London
*
Clarke, Irwin & Co. Ltd.
Toronto

First published 1927
This edition first published 1968
© *J. C. Medley & R. G. Medley 1927*

SBN 7011 1295 6

Printed in Great Britain
by William Lewis (Printers) Limited
Cardiff

CONTENTS

WILFRID HOLMES

WILFRID HOLMES was by many years younger than his brothers
and sisters, all of whom were making their way in the world,
the girls marrying and the boys doing well in different pro-
fessions ; the Army had claimed one, the Law another, and
as a Civil Servant the third was helping to run the Empire
in India.

The Holmes were tall men with long faces and small eyes.
Wilfrid, the last, was larger-framed, more heavily built than
his brothers ; his long, oval face was fuller, and in him the
family eyes were not less intelligent than his brothers' eyes,
but weaker, announcing an indolence of mind and body so
inveterate that he had just grown up in it without struggle,
passing from childhood into boyhood and from boyhood into
manhood clinging to the widow's skirts. Mrs. Holmes's
husband having died when Wilfrid was a small child, Wilfrid
had known a father's influence and authority only derivatively
through his eldest brother, whom he dreaded, for every time
Hector returned to pay his mother a visit at Bushfield, the
family place, the question was asked : What is Wilfrid going
to do with himself ?   Has he not yet decided on a profession ?

Mrs. Holmes tried to soften criticisms of her spoilt child
with stories of Wilfrid's different aspirations, and she told
these with a gentle humour.   Wilfrid, she said, is thinking of
entering the Consular Service, and if you could get a letter
from your old friend—— But, said the brother, who was
staying at Bushfield at the moment, will Wilfrid try to pass
the examination, for there is one ?   Mrs. Holmes parried the
question, and when Hector returned six months or a year
later and Wilfrid's future was again discussed, she told with

the same gentle humour that he was now thinking of astronomy as a profession, and had gone so far as to purchase a telescope. Every uncloudy night, she said, he has it out on the steps ; Jupiter's Satellites can be seen through it, and Saturn's Ring. He knows the names of most of the stars, and speaks of the different ascensions. But, mother, what you tell me is mere star-gazing, otherwise idleness. Modern astronomy is little more than mathematics, and Wilfrid never showed any interest in mathematics at school, nor in classical studies, nor in games. Mrs. Holmes defended her yoe lamb, and spoke of a cricketing suit she had bought for Wilfrid—bats and wickets, shoes and gloves. Oh, he may have liked all these things, Hector answered, but not the game itself ! And now that he has left school and come here to live with you, has he taken to riding or shooting ? When you go to London does he attend dancing classes ? You would like to know, Hector, if he wastes his time with young women ? I am glad to say he does not.

A man—— It was on Hector's lips to say that a man who is indifferent to women is indifferent to all things, but he felt that words were unavailing and that Wilfrid would have to follow the course of his life like another. And to make his last days at home a pleasant thought for his mother—Hector was returning to India—he spoke kindly to Wilfrid, saying : I shall always remember, Wilfrid, your showing me your telescope. In the train (his mother and brother were accompanying him to Portsmouth) he spoke of the canals in Mars, his words awakening certain qualms of conscience in him lest they should influence Wilfrid to worry his mother to buy him another telescope ; but that night at the Theatre Royal, Portsmouth, one of the Gilbert and Sullivan operettes swept the firmament for ever from Wilfrid's mind, and his last words to Hector, whom he accompanied on board, were : I think I shall sell that telescope and buy a flute, words that darkened Hector's face. The cry : All ashore, however, enabled Wilfrid to escape without rebuke, and all that day and the next and till the end of the week Wilfrid could talk of nothing but flutes, and many and long were the walks that he and his mother took from instrument-maker to instrument-maker, Wilfrid never satisfied, till at last she said : Now, Wilfrid, you must make up your mind what flute you want. And it was after the purchase of two flutes and a piccolo that mother and son returned to Bushfield Park, Wilfrid with the intention of devoting his life to musical composition.

As there was no teacher in the neighbourhood of whom he approved, he sent to London for the score of the opera he had heard at Portsmouth, and by comparing the notes that his flute uttered with those upon paper he learnt their values, approximately, as he confessed to his mother one day on her asking him if he was reading or playing by ear. I can read at sight now, mother, for I have discovered that it makes a great deal of difference if the note is black or white. Yes, Wilfrid, it does ; but you are giving yourself a great deal of trouble trying to learn by yourself what anybody could teach you in a few weeks. She spoke to him of her old governess, whom she would like to ask to Bushfield for her holidays. A music-master, he said, could teach him better than a woman ; all the same, he learnt from Miss McCabe how to play the piano a little ; and he continued his studies afterwards in London with an ancient bandmaster selected by himself, reaching within a year the stage of being able to write down a tune when it was dictated to him, without asking that it should be repeated unduly —three or four times were enough, if it was repeated slowly, and if he gave his ear, which was a slow one, wholly to the capture of it. His mother allowed him three pounds a week, one of which went to pay for his music lessons ; and when his mother climbed the five flights that led to him one morning between ten and eleven (Wilfrid was rarely able to persuade himself out of the bedclothes before eleven) he came to the door, in answer to her repeated knocking, in his shirt and

trousers, asking in an aggrieved tone who was there. Oh,
mother, I didn't know it was you ! he said, recognising her
voice. Come in quickly, for I am making my cocoa, and if
the milk boils over it will be spoilt. And the milk happening
to boil over during his absence at the door, Mrs. Holmes
expressed her regret. You will take an hour to dress yourself. Let me go and fetch the milk for you. It was my
fault. She often spoke of this visit afterwards, mildly amused
at his solicitude for his cocoa, imitating very well the tone
of his voice when he said : I must go at once to fetch some
more milk. And she told how she had sat watching Wilfrid
stirring his cocoa, hearing him say that it took a long time
to find out when the cocoa was properly mixed, and that it
was hardly less difficult to make tea. To make tea properly,
he said, the water has to be really boiling. And he told a
long story of what he had suffered from a charwoman, who
not only forgot to pour his tea into a second teapot within
two minutes (anything over two minutes made the tea worth-
less, undrinkable), but left it on the hob, to keep it 'ot, she
said ; and when she did remember to put it into the second
teapot she forgot to heat the pot first, and hotted it up upon
the hob. I will make your tea for you in the future when you
leave this garret and return with me to Bushfield, the mother
answered. But she could not persuade her son to leave his
garret. He was still attached to music, and had composed
a number of airs which he played to her on his flute whenever
she called to see him. She listened to him patiently, like
a mother, and after each tune she said : I like that ; that 's
very pretty, a very pretty tune indeed ; sometimes venturing
upon a criticism : But is not the last tune somewhat like the
first that you played to me ? Wilfrid played the two tunes
over again and thought his mother fastidious, and she re-
strained herself always from saying : But, Wilfrid, the top
line is not enough. Modern music is in the harmony.

Harmony was a word that rarely came into Wilfrid's talk
about music, he being of the opinion that, whereas there

were many harmonists, there were few melodists. Mrs. Holmes consulted the music-master, from whom she learnt that Wilfrid's ear was slow ; he could not hear simultaneously the different parts of a fugue ; and on being pressed still further, the bandmaster gave it as his opinion that Wilfrid should never look upon music as anything more than a hobby, a verdict that Mrs. Holmes received without surprise, the bandmaster's opinion having long been her opinion. But she loved her son too dearly to utter a word of discouragement. Instead she made provision for him in her will, confiding him to the care of her younger sister, who, when Wilfrid's mother passed away, did not forget to send her nephew a cheque for fifty pounds each half-year. And upon this money Wilfrid lived his lonely life, trying always to make both ends meet, living aloof, avoiding his relations instinctively. If one of these called, Wilfrid welcomed him, begged of him to stay to tea ; and after tea he accompanied his relative, sometimes a brother, sometimes a cousin, to the station, and parted from him with such a show of courtesy and friendliness that he was surprised that Wilfrid did not return to supper, as he had promised that he would, next Sunday.

But months, sometimes years passed, without their seeing him, and again somebody would go forth and return with the truant from family life, who would again disappear, leaving them to their gentle disputations round the fire, seeking reasons for Wilfrid's aloofness, the true reason never spoken, everybody keeping it hidden away almost from himself. To speak it, or even to allow it a place in their thoughts, would be to impugn their own conduct towards Wilfrid, to set themselves above him, to make it plain to him that he was their inferior. Whosoever cannot get his living dreads his relations, dreads their eyes and words, and of all their coming to bring him back to supper, for as they pass out of the squalor of his neighbourhood into fashionable London the windows and doorways begin to reproach him, and he detects a sneer in the eyes of the servant who opens the door to him. The pictures on the walls, the carpets under his feet, the food he eats, the wine he drinks, remind him of his inferiority; and one night on returning from Hampstead Wilfrid said: Never again will they walk me round their drawing-rooms, showing off their wealth! and he lay awake, attributing motives, and asking himself why they troubled to come to see him and to pester him with invitations. The answer to his questions came: That they may better discuss me and pity me and gloat over my poverty. But I never apply to them for help. Perhaps if I did they would not be so eager to see me! In these thoughts he lay awake, passing into sleep towards morning, awakening out of sleep a happier man than when he lay down, for about him was the familiar room in which he read and wrote and played his flute.

As soon as he was out of bed his first task was the brushing of his clothes. A button to which he attached his braces hung by a single thread, but there was no need for Wilfrid to ask the landlady's help—he could sew on a button. He could clean his boots, too, and very often did, for there were other lodgers besides him in the house in which he lived, and the landlady and her drudge could not attend upon them all. If the relations of overnight could see me now! Wilfrid said to himself as he brushed. I wish they could, for they would see that I can do many things that they cannot. If I cannot get my own living, I can at least get my own breakfast. I can light a fire, and not one of them would know how to do that. Whereupon he opened the oven (the grate was an old one, with convenient hobs), took out some dry sticks, and very soon a fire was blazing. And, still thinking of his relations, he went to the cupboard, cut his bacon, melted the butter in the pan before dropping in the eggs; and before the landlady knocked to ask if she might do his room Wilfrid had finished his breakfast and was nearly dressed. Yes, Mrs. Plowden, he answered, you can come in; I have only to tie my neck-tie and slip on my coat. And they fell to talking of the present prices of sausages, steak, and mutton chops. I think I shall treat myself to-day, Mrs. Plowden, to a little custard pudding. If you are busy with your music to-day, Mr. Holmes, I shall be glad to make your pudding for you—an offer which Wilfrid accepted, though he would have preferred to make his own pudding and cook it in his own room. But he knew that a lodger such as he was must become a friend of the landlady, and that he could do this by accepting and rendering services, by courtesy and by conversation ; for Mrs. Plowden wearied of her servant's talk, which was always, she confided to Wilfrid, about men, and was glad to come upstairs, to listen, as she put it, to a toon on the flute.

He was, however, careful not to enter into conversation with Emma, for he was aware that in Mrs. Plowden's eyes he was a big, fine-looking man ; and he had also learnt by experience that women are jealous, and that the pleasure Mrs. Plowden took in coming upstairs for little private talks with him would be embittered if more than three words at a time were exchanged between him and Emma, and of all if he were to entertain Emma to an air on the flute ; so he never played to her, and, by reticence, tact, and courtesy, and by never playing the flute late at night or when other lodgers were in the house, he had managed to obtain a position in No. 31 Goldhawk Road, Shepherd's Bush, that seemed unassailable. But tact and reticence and courtesy give way sometimes under sudden stress of circumstance, and one day Wilfrid discovered the score of a French operette that he had sought vainly for years, in a rag-and-bone shop, and, bringing it home, he spent a great part of the night playing it over softly, so softly that he believed no one could hear him. In this he was mistaken, however, for next morning the landlady, when she came to do his room, wore a look of weariness upon her face, and not many words were exchanged between them before she told him that his room would be wanted at the end of the week. He begged her not to be so brief with him, and his promise not to play again after twelve o'clock, and never to play, morning or evening, till the lady on the drawing-room floor had left the house, softened Mrs. Plowden's resolution.   You see, Mrs. Plowden, I had been trying for years to get the score of Hervé's *La Reine de Navarre*, and came upon it by chance in an old rag-and-bone shop, the only score in existence, perhaps, certainly one of the very few, for the opera was only played three times—it was a complete failure in Paris. I have been seeking it for years. I shouldn't have played last night, I know, but, Mrs. Plowden, I assure you I played so softly that I did not think anyone in the house could have heard. I will call upon the lady on the drawing-room floor, and if you would not like me to do that, I will apologise to her when I meet her on the stairs. I can assure her that, so far as I am concerned, she will never know another troubled night.

Mrs. Plowden's face darkened, and as she tossed the bedclothes hither and thither she muttered that she was not sure that the drawing-room floor piano was not much more noisy in the house than Mr. Holmes's flute, words that encouraged Wilfrid to believe that he had only to propitiate the lady on the drawing-room floor. And, meeting her on the staircase some five minutes after his interview with Mrs. Plowden, he told her how sorry he was his flute-playing had disturbed her rest, speaking with such courtesy that she regretted having made the complaint, and to make amends for it she invited him to her piano, saying that she would like to run through the score with him. Wilfrid accepted her invitation, and, when the slight interest of *La Reine de Navarre* was exhausted, their talk turned on composition, Wilfrid admitting that he had been engaged on an opera for some time. The lady urged him to run upstairs and fetch it, saying that it would interest her to play the accompaniments. But they are not written, he answered, only the top line.

For a moment this seemed a serious difficulty, but the lady offered to improvise ; and Wilfrid came in in such excellent time and tune that she began to foresee a possible combination—Wilfrid supplying the melodies and she the accompaniments, in this way writing an opera between them, a hope that might have been fulfilled had not an unexpected and cruel accident caused Wilfrid to seek another lodging, and one as far as possible from Shepherd's Bush. He went to Notting Hill overcome with shame, unable to understand how it was that Mrs. Plowden had declined to accept his word or Edith's, her daughter, who had returned to Shepherd's Bush unexpectedly. He had intended to ask Mrs. Plowden for another blanket, but forgot to do so (the slight misunderstanding that had occurred between him and Mrs. Plowden on account of his flute put everything else out of his mind), and, finding sleep impossible, he had bethought himself of a blanket from the spare room, never dreaming that Miss Plowden had returned home. To make matters worse, it so happened that Mrs. Plowden was pressing her daughter to tell the whole story of her betrayal when Wilfrid appeared in his nightshirt on the threshold.

Good God, who would have thought it ! cried Mrs. Plowden.

Mother, he 's not the one, Edith answered without hesitation.

Mrs. Plowden, I beg you to believe that I came here for an extra blanket, interjected Wilfrid, and knew nothing of your daughter's return.

Mother, you are wronging an innocent man, Edith implored.

But their assurances did not deflect Mrs. Plowden from her purpose, and for many months Wilfrid heard in his thoughts the unfortunate voices still raging—Mrs. Plowden asking intermittently if it wasn't he who was it, and Edith always refusing to give up the name of her betrayer. The last words that passed between Wilfrid and Edith were : Mother would have believed you if it had not been——

Wilfrid had not heard the end of the sentence, Mrs. Plowden
having hustled him off her doorstep. And now Wilfrid rose
from his chair, asking himself what purpose might be served
by recalling unpleasant memories. But memories are often
very insistent and will not be repelled, and he sat terrified
at the thought of his escape. If Edith had not been an
honourable girl Mrs. Plowden might have taken him into
court, and the magistrate might have made out a mainten-
ance order against him—five shillings a week, which he could
not have paid. And his aunt! He had stood on the brink
of ruin, but had escaped the worst. All the same, he had lost
his very comfortable lodging. For the house in Notting
Hill was not nearly so well suited to his needs as the house
in Shepherd's Bush. He missed the hobs and the oven,
Mrs. Plowden's attendance, and the accompaniments, which
threw light on his melodies, inspiring new versions. If
Edith had only told the name of the blackguard who——
But she hadn't. Such is life, he muttered, and continued
to work at his opera, *The Mulberry Tree*, till the story he was
illustrating began to seem disjointed, broken-backed. Any
one of the professional librettists could put it right in a
minute by a trick, he said, but I should like to have it un-
disfigured by artifices, and only time will be able to do that
for me.

So he turned to the second interest in his life, the legend
of *Tristan and Isolde*, which, in his opinion, had never yet
been traced to its source. His researches brought him so
often to the British Museum that he felt it would be a saving
for him to live in Bloomsbury ; and he went thither, hoping
to find a grate with an oven like the one in Shepherd's Bush.
But the hob grate seemed to have disappeared from the
neighbourhood, old though it was, and in his search he did
not come upon one of those small mending tailors who can
turn an old suit of clothes into what looks like a new one.
These were grave disadvantages, but he was nearer his work,
and he had been much encouraged lately by the discovery

that he could work out Isolde's history by means of place-names. Nothing is more lasting than the names of places; in the course of ages a letter or two may be omitted or transposed, but the name remains practically the same. And the art of the imaginative historian lies in the divination of missing letters; the moment they are restored light breaks, and very soon Wilfrid was in possession of the names of certain minor chiefs who had accepted Isolde's father as Overlord. Another week, another month at most, he said, rising from his desk one day, and my case will be complete. And so absorbed was he in his conjectures that he did not hear one of the librarians ask him if he had succeeded in carrying Isolde's family history further back than the fifth century. The librarian had to repeat his question, and, awaking from his reverie, Wilfrid answered: I think the facts show that the family history can be traced back to Tara. One of her ancestors ruled there, I believe. In another month I shall be able to tell you for certain. Well, the reason I spoke, said the librarian, is that there is some talk now that the story came to the French chronicler, Chrétien de Troyes, from Brittany, and that the Bretons got it from the Celts of Cornwall, who in turn got it from the Welsh. It is being pointed out that the old Welsh pedigrees tell of an Arthur, a king of the district round Chester, who had a cousin, King March, a minor king, who married a lady called Eisylt. As you can see the Irish coast easily, Lleyn—— The librarian did not finish his sentence, so busy was he gathering in the books that readers were thrusting upon him. A hurried time, not one for prolonged talk, and while Wilfrid stood among the jostling crowd, dumbfounded, the bell rang, and the last readers were roused from their books by weary attendants.

A small rain was falling; umbrellas were opened in the pillared portico; and this crowd, comprising a thousand different interests and intellects, always brought the same thought into his mind—that it was strange that so many

B

people should have a small sum of money in their pockets ;
and he never failed to think that if these trickles of the
world's wealth stopped for a week the world would split
and fall to pieces—a ship wrenched apart by waves, each
carrying a spar, a mast, a part of the hull away. But to-day
as he stood admiring the crowd he remembered suddenly
that his aunt's fifty pounds had failed to trickle into his pocket
that morning. For the first time there had been a delay,
and it seemed to him ominous that the delay should have
coincided with the news that a new theory regarding the
legend of *Tristan and Isolde* was being considered. He had
looked forward to receiving his aunt's cheque, but that
morning his head was so full of his work at the British Museum
that he had hardly given the matter a thought ; and he might
not have done so now if the librarian had not mentioned the
possible Welsh origin of the story. Two misfortunes on the
same day seemed to predict trouble for him, mayhap a break
in his life. His aunt had never failed before. But has she
even failed to-day ? he said, almost angry with himself.
A letter is often delayed in the post, and on my return home
I shall find hers. Has any letter come for me ? he asked.

No letter has come this afternoon, sir. Were you expecting one ?

Yes, he answered, and ran upstairs. Now what would
happen to him, and what would happen to the Isolde legend,
if his aunt failed to send her fifty pounds ?

At that moment he heard a knock far away in the street,
and as the postman approached the house that Wilfrid lived
in each knock became louder, clearer. The knocking stopped
at last, and Wilfrid asked himself what the cause of the delay
might be. He had never known the postman loiter as he
loitered this evening. Was there an undue number of regis-
tered letters to be signed for ? Were they all out at 54 ?
The knocking began again ; once more it stopped, and this
time the man was kept waiting on the opposite side of the
street not many doors away. He knocked again and again,

but nobody came to the door, and it was all Wilfrid could do to keep himself from running across to ask him if he had a letter for No. 45. As he was about to start the man moved away from the door to come over to deliver letters. He passed 45, and Wilfrid was driven to consider how it was that his aunt's cheque had failed to arrive on the appointed day. He was on the last flight of stairs in his nightshirt and trousers in the morning when the landlady opened the door. No, Mr. Holmes, there 's nothing for you this morning.

The day passed in watching for the postman, and every time he went by without delivering a letter, or delivered letters for the other lodgers, Wilfrid pondered anew the fact that for the last twenty years his cheque had arrived to the very day. Was his aunt dead ? The thought was a terrible one, and it was followed by a hardly less terrible thought—that her last cheque was the end of her bounty ! But that could not be—she would have written to tell him. He began to count her years, and, giving up the count in despair, he remembered that in the case of her death (which must come sooner or later) he would have to apply to another relation, to his brother in India, who would give him his choice between Bushfield Park and the workhouse, and with hard words, saying : You have never earned five shillings in your life. You shall go to Bushfield as caretaker at three pounds a week. What answer would he make ? All the world would side with his brother. Nobody would understand why he could not live at Bushfield ; nobody would understand that he could not earn his living. Nobody had ever understood this except his mother, and nobody ever would. He laid no blame on anybody ; he did not understand it himself. He was healthy, strong, educated, and more intelligent than many of the men he met at the museum. But he could not earn his living, and, worst of all, he could not tell why. There seemed to be no excuse for refusing to live at Bushfield. Nobody would understand—he did

not understand. A frightened look came into his face, for
he saw in that instant a lonely figure, a confessed failure,
amid sad shrubberies and dismal woods. I have always lived
in London, he said, and will die in London, come what may.
But he could not live in London without some money, and
only one sovereign remained to him. A sovereign between
me and the streets, he said to himself, and fell to thinking
how much life for him it represented if he restricted his
diet to bread-and-margarine. Three weeks, quite that; a
month, perhaps, he continued, with bread at its present
rate. But his rent—six shillings a week! His landlady
would give him a week's credit, no doubt, but she might
not. And in his dire necessity he wrote to one of his brothers
for five pounds, a thing he had never done, it being his pride
to live apart and to owe them nothing. He did not hate
them, but——

His thoughts melted into memories of his youth, memories
of slights received from them all. Some were kinder than
others, but he knew he was looked upon as the family fool,
and his pride had been to show them that he did not need
their help. But this last barrier of self-respect was broken
down. He had had to write to his brother for five pounds !
The five pounds came by the next post, and now he would
be able to live for quite a long while, with care. As he sat
working out how much he might spend daily he stopped to
think what his aunt's death would mean to him when she
died. He did not believe she was dead ; but she would
have to die sooner or later. He might die before her ; life
is good in this, that it provides us with a way out of our difficulties ; and he fell to thinking that he had not been feeling
very well lately—his doctor had even spoken to him of the
possible necessity of an operation, for which he would have
to go into a hospital. If his aunt were to live, she might
pay for the operation, but he would not like to ask her for
any more money than she gave him ; so it behoved him to
strive for some employment that would bring him in two

pounds a week. If he could find some editorial work that would bring him in two-pounds-ten a week !

The thought of an extra ten shillings a week and what it would buy for him awoke him from the dazed stupor into which he had fallen, the consequence of an empty stomach ; for he had lived on bread-and-margarine and drunk only water for more than a week, and was beginning to feel that if this diet were to continue uninterrupted his strength to resist his ill might leave him. So with his stomach turned resolutely against his daily fare he went out to buy himself a couple of ounces of tea and an egg, and as he sat stirring his tea he bethought himself of his many attempts to earn a little money by journalism. He had once paid a provincial newspaper a part of his small inheritance for permission to write leading articles, and when he had written fifty-one he had cut his contributions from the different numbers of the paper in which they had appeared. After correction they were sent to a printer to be reset, and the proofs were forwarded to a London editor with a letter requesting the latter to read the articles, and, if he approved of them, to invite Mr. Holmes to join the staff of the London daily. He enclosed stamps for the return of these samples, and they came back to him with a printed form saying that owing to lack of space the editor was unable to avail himself of the contributions, which he returned with thanks. But after a little while he forgot to enclose the postage-stamps, and his articles were not returned to him ; and in answer to questions addressed to the editor he received a printed form telling him that the editor could not undertake to correspond with the authors of rejected manuscripts. As an earnest of his will to work, several sets of proofs were sent to his brothers, who did not return them ; others were lost in his transits from one lodging to another. One set remained, however, but Wilfrid was loath to send forth these articles again. If an editor had written him a personal letter containing a word of encouragement he might have——

A thought breaking into his memories of his past attempts to find employment brought him to his feet. He knew a little French, and there must be a newspaper whose staff was depleted by the war. And it was in this hope that he went forth every day to seek his fortune in the Strand and Fleet Street. Occasionally he was invited upstairs and allowed to plead with elderly men in armchairs, who gave him sometimes a few minutes of their attention, but before he arrived at the end of his patter he had begun to read in their eyes that he was not wanted. Some of the less important newspapers asked him if he had had any experience, and he answered them that he had edited the *East Anglian Advertiser* for some time, offering some of the articles that he contributed to that newspaper to be reprinted. Some, he said, I feel sure are as topical to-day as on the day they were written; and he offered to send these for the editor's consideration, but the editor said he would prefer to read something that had not yet been published. Wilfrid promised to send an article, and returned to his lodgings trying to think of a subject that would appeal to the editor, his thoughts reverting to the belief that Isolde must have been an Irish Princess, for the French chronicler had so written it, and there was no other evidence; so——

His thoughts were interrupted by the postman's knock, and, listening to receding footsteps and fainter knocks, he once again began to ask himself if his aunt's death was the cause of the delay. Should he write for news of her? Of what use? If she were dead, her daughter would have written. His aunt, who knew of his necessities, had never failed before, nor would she fail this time; all the same—— He pulled a sheet of paper towards him with the intention of writing to her, and in doing this he disturbed a heap of papers, bringing into view some numbers of the *Daily Courier*. It must have been the landlady who left these for me, he said, and began to read of a blackbird who could whistle a tune of six or eight notes. The publication of the tune had encouraged other readers to send examples of blackbird melody, and a correspondence was in progress regarding the origin of these tunes, some correspondents averring that the blackbirds had not invented but learnt them, other correspondents holding that, since the cuckoo produced two distinct notes, there was no reason to suppose that any other bird might not produce eight. It was not likely that all the blackbirds that whistled tunes had learnt them in a captivity from which the birds had escaped, and the point was made that the musical ear varied in different birds. At last a correspondent wrote that he had taught a blackbird who frequented his garden part of a well-known air. The bird whistled correctly till he came to a minor third, and then, conscious of his failure to catch the note, he broke into an angry : Chuck, chuck, chuck, in the shrubbery. Wilfrid remembered a bullfinch that whistled a once popular song, *Pretty Polly Perkins of Paddington Green*. The bird's cage hung in the kitchen, and the best way to persuade him out of his silence was to rattle the plates on the dresser. The sound of the plates inspired him, and he whistled the song in fragments, breaking off suddenly. Why not write about the bullfinch ? Wilfrid asked himself, and before he had made up his mind another thought came into his mind. It was to pick eight bars of tune from one of the many scores that met his eyes when he looked round his room, all of which were unknown.

Who, except myself, he asked, could whistle a single note from *Le Canard à Trois Becs* or from *Les Quenouilles de Verre* ? Or if I were to send one of my own tunes the publication might bring me the harmonist I have been waiting for so long. A moment after he remembered the notes that a blackbird used to sing in one of the shrubberies that surround Bushfield Park, the notes that had inspired—— His face lighted up for the first time since the day he left the museum in the midst of a twofold misfortune, and, catching up a pen, he wrote the notes.

I shall point out in a second letter that the phrase as
likely as not comes out of one of the many French operettes
composed in the 'seventies and 'eighties. The wiseacres
will sit surrounded with scores, reading, reading, and for
ever reading, and then the question will come : How did the
blackbird learn a tune unknown in England ? The editor
will send for me, and perhaps will give me a job.

DEAR SIR,—I have followed with interest the letters you
are publishing concerning the musical ear of the blackbird,
a little surprised, however, to learn that the bird that picked
up the well-known song mentioned by the correspondent
signing himself X. could not manage the minor third. The
bullfinch would catch the note, of a certainty, and I can but
think that the blackbird I once heard sing the first bars of
a waltz in the garden, or rather yard, enclosed by high walls
shadowed by tall elms, would speedily have conquered and
retained the minor third in his every subsequent rendering
of the song. He alighted on the branch under which I and a
friend were sitting at tea, and sang the tune twice over.
To hear the first bars of a French waltz (part of a French
operette I should guess it to be, but perhaps one of your
correspondents will be able to identify it) was not a little
bewildering. The friend with whom I was sitting at tea
is no relation of Mrs. Harris ; he exists in the flesh, and
will testify that the bird's song was noted by me on a scrap
of paper which he handed to me, that no interval was changed,
and that the time was waltz time. I am, Sincerely yours,

WILFRID HOLMES.

The letter was published in the *Daily Courier*, and the
conjecture that the little waltz was an extract from a French
operette aroused many minds out of the daily torpor of
existence, many deeming it to be a quatrain from one of
Lecoq's early and little-known works. Other writers de-
tected a Germanic flavour, and Offenbach was spoken of,
and then Suppé. Somebody thought that he remembered

a waltz very like the blackbird's in an opera by Serpett.
An almost forgotten composer, Wilfrid said to himself as
he sat eating his bread-and-margarine, who never caught
the public ear with an air. I should have thought that his
name was forgotten by everybody but myself; but there's
always somebody who remembers. Now what did he write?
An opera for the Variétés; but the name?

He sat searching his memory for a long time, and, giving
up the search for the moment, he said : Litoff's name doesn't
seem to have occurred to anybody. And, drawing a sheet
of paper towards him, he began a letter to the editor of the
Daily Courier asking to be allowed to write the musical
criticisms for the paper. He had not written many lines
when he was disturbed by his landlady coming to tell him
that a gentleman from the *Daily Courier* had called to see
him and was waiting in the passage.

Will you be kind enough to bring him upstairs, Mrs.
Douglas, or would you prefer that I went down to see him
in your parlour?

There are people in my parlour waiting to see me; I
think I had better bring him up to you, sir.

Yes, yes, bring him up; or shall I go down and speak
to him? Wilfrid answered, his lethargic nature quickening
to an intenser life than he had ever known before. And
while hesitating at the stairhead he heard Mrs. Douglas's
voice saying : Will you come this way, sir? As soon as
the footsteps reached the drawing-room floor he hurried
back to his room to receive his visitor, who, he doubted not,
was bringing him good news ; news he was bringing him for
certain, and any news was good news.

The editor of the *Daily Courier* has asked me to call and
thank you for the little tune and the interesting letter that
accompanied it. He would have written to you himself
if he had not been suddenly called away ; and the journalist
began to tell of a Cabinet crisis, Wilfrid giving him an attentive
ear, in the hope that his appreciation of his interlocutor's

narrative would influence the account of him the editor
would get from his colleague ; and he held his soul in patience
till the journalist came to a sudden break in his story.   The
rest, he said, is on the knees of the Gods—and he apologised
for having been so long-winded.   Wilfrid protested, and
the journalist revealed the object of his visit, which was
to ask Mr. Wilfrid Holmes if he knew the name of the composer of the waltz measure.   If the waltz be a French one,
as I believe yourself has suggested, the bird was most probably a French bird imported into England ; probably, I say,
not necessarily, for most waltzes, French and German, if
a waltz can be said to have any nationality, are known to——
I was writing, Wilfrid interrupted, a letter to the editor
of the *Daily Courier* dealing with that very question when
you called.   He picked up his half-finished letter from the
table and continued : My proposal to the editor was to tell
him the name of the waltz if in return for my doing so he
engaged me on the staff of the paper.   I can write English
and French correctly, and know enough music to write
criticisms, and my knowledge of light French music is as
complete as anybody's you 'd be likely to find in London.
For years I 've collected the least-known scores ;   many
of those you see are out of print, and to get a sight of them
you would have to cross over to France and investigate the
archives of most of the theatres in the boulevards.   *La Reine
de Navarre* is a very scarce score, *Les Quenouilles de Verre*
still scarcer, and for the score of *Héloïse et Abélard* you would
have to go to the Bibliothèque Nationale.   Your editor
may be able to procure the scores of *Le Roi l'a dit* and *La
Boite de Pandore* through Messrs. Chappell, but I doubt if
Messrs. Chappell would be able to supply *La Fiancée du Roi
de Garbe*, *Pont des Soupirs*, or *La Belle Poule*.   I run through
these on my flute when the house is empty (our lodgers are
more tolerant to the piano than to the flute), and in every
one of these operettes there are some pretty passages, better
than any to be found in better-known works.

Nobody but you knows these forgotten scores ? asked the journalist. I am sure that mine is the only copy in London of *La Fiancée du Roi de Garbe*. And if you did not run these scores over on your flute they would lie mute, replied the journalist. That thought has often come into my mind whilst standing by this window on a summer evening ; and the journalist, beguiled by pity or curiosity, he knew not which, began to ask Wilfrid if the flute played an important part in the score of *La Fiancée du Roi de Garbe*.

A good writer never forgets the flute, Wilfrid replied, for without the flute the orchestra would be inhuman. The journalist raised his eyes. The flute represents the human voice in the orchestra, Wilfrid continued, his face suddenly changing from gay to grave. He would have dearly loved to show his beautiful-keyed flute, a present from his aunt, to the journalist. It was in pawn, alas ! But remembering his piccolo suddenly, he opened a drawer, and, taking from it a sheet of manuscript music, he pinned it to the wall by the window and said he was going to play the great air from his opera, *The Mulberry Tree*. And upon a diminutive instrument, hardly larger than a toothbrush, Wilfrid whistled out a simple air that the journalist began to perceive to be the summary of the author's musical imagination, it never being far distant from all the subsequent pieces that were taken from the drawer.

But the top line, said the journalist, is but a small part of the music contained in a modern opera. Modern music can hardly be said to exist apart from the harmonies that sustain it. A modern air rises out of the harmony for a moment only, like a flag from the flagstaff. And then there 's the orchestration. The orchestration, Wilfrid answered, is mere colouring matter ; the harmony, I admit, is essential. And what you or the editor of the *Daily Courier* might do for me is to give me a letter to ——. Wilfrid mentioned a name famous in modern music, saying : A great musician, no doubt, but one who cannot write melody. Now I can, but in harmony I am deficient. What do you think ? But, said the journalist, taking a piece of music from the heap, I see that you have not only composed the airs sung by the soprano, the tenor, and the bass, you have also written some concerted pieces—here is a quintet. And without some knowledge of harmony, at least of counterpoint, I don't understand how you could have written it. I will play it to you, Wilfrid replied ; and when he had played the quintet to the journalist on his piccolo he explained that he had followed the form of the quintet in *La Fiancée du Roi de Garbe*, writing other tunes, of course. And now, if you will allow me, I will play the air that the *prima donna* sings out of the branches of the mulberry tree in the second act. From a safe hiding-place among the leaves she has heard all the plotting of her enemies, who have discovered that she is an heiress to an uninhabited island in which is hidden immense treasure. After listening to the air, the journalist sat looking into Wilfrid's large face, striving to read his history out of his little eyes. Of course, said Wilfrid, the air will sound much richer, completer, when it gets its accompaniment, for, as you say, in modern music the air rises out of the accompaniment ; it is dependent upon it, too dependent to my taste, but still it cannot be denied that harmony is more important to-day than it was when Bellini and Donizetti were writing operas. All the same, melody is what the public follows. Don't you think that the editor would give me a letter of introduction ? Or perhaps you think that Mr. X. can write melody ?

Your question, Mr. Holmes, can best be answered by another, the journalist replied. Before entering into a discussion as to whether Mr. X. can or cannot write melody, I would like to ask you if you think that Mr. X. is aware of his melodic deficiencies. Well, said Wilfrid, they should have become apparent to him by this time—at which the journalist laughed. But he stopped laughing suddenly, for Wilfrid's courage gave way before this last rebuke. I am afraid, he said, drawing his hand across his eyes, dashing aside some tears, that there is very little hope for me. And, walking up and down the room, he related the story of the delayed cheque, saying that for twenty years his aunt had never failed to send him his cheque. Only once before did it arrive late, and then only a day late. But now fifteen days have passed without my getting any tidings of her; she may be dead. It was three days before I noticed the delay, so absorbed was I in the legend of *Tristan and Isolde*, a work on which I have been engaged for the last twenty years.

At work on the legend of *Tristan and Isolde* for twenty years! said the journalist.

Yes, quite that, Wilfrid replied; and the journalist, anxious to help him, began to ask him what discoveries he had made. And Wilfrid, taking courage, tried to relate his conjectures, till overcome by a sudden weakness he said : I cannot go on talking. I have lived for the last ten days on bread-and-margarine. Yesterday I had to buy a packet of cocoa and some milk; the success of my letter in the *Daily Courier* tempted me to risk the extravagance, and I hoped for a post on the paper. I hoped that something would happen, but nothing has. The journalist asked Wilfrid why he did not write to his relations for the loan of enough money to carry him over till he received his allowance, and learnt that Wilfrid had broken with all his brothers and sisters. They are always quarrelling among themselves, he said, and I try to keep outside of the family strife, and the only way to do it is to avoid seeing them.

This little confession, so sincere and so artless, awakened the journalist's pity still further, and then, his pity quickening to a sort of literary interest, he began to speak of the family as the worst enemy of the individual, with a view to leading Wilfrid into confidences. The journalist had some literary pretensions, and, foreseeing literary material in Wilfrid, he listened, saying to himself: He is typical of many ;

in every boarding-house in London there is the lag-end of a
family, playing the piano in the evenings. We accuse these
waifs of idleness, but they were born idle and cannot be else
than idle, for they are without the needful instinct to pick
up a living, or have lost it, as wild birds do after being kept
in cages. This man's mother kept him in a cage long after
he should have been put out to work. And then, the journalist's thoughts turning from the general to the particular, he
began to consider if he might advise one of his editors to
take on Wilfrid as a musical critic—For with all his short-
comings he knows a little music, the keys, doubtless, whereas
the ordinary musical critic cannot tell one key from another.
But his copy would be unprintable. And certain that there
was nothing to be done for Wilfrid in journalism, he began
to think how he might take his leave. A knock came to the
door. A letter has just come for you, Mr. Holmes. And
from my aunt ! he cried, forgetful of the journalist and Mrs.
Douglas. She has been very unwell lately but is better now,
and she sends a cheque for two hundred pounds. Two
hundred pounds ! he said, and held the cheque out to the
journalist in trembling fingers. I feel as if I could buy
half London. So you do not care that I should recommend
you for the post of musical critic, if perchance I should
hear of a vacancy ?

I shall now be able, Wilfrid answered, to fill in the last
links of the chain of evidence which shows that——

The moment seemed favourable to the journalist to take
his leave, and it was not till he had left the house and was
half-way down the street that he remembered he had not
asked Wilfrid which illustrious composer was the author
of the waltz tune that the blackbird had learnt in France,
or from Wilfrid Holmes himself. Most likely the author of
the tune is Holmes himself, he said stopping, for that moment
the musical phrase that came from a top window seemed
to represent, and completely, the man he had left—one
of those weak, timid, harmless souls, come out of the mould

that Nature reserves for some great purpose known only to herself, mayhap the preservation of pity and compassion in the world. And, humming the little tune over to himself as he went towards the railway-station, he said : A humble aspiration, part of a chorus from *The Mulberry Tree*, no doubt.

Dan - cing a - round,   Dan-cing   a - round,

Dan - cing   a - round the   mul - berry tree.

PRISCILLA AND EMILY LOFFT

A BLACKBIRD whistled in the garden when Emily flung the drawing-room door open and gazed into the emptiness of the old faded room, her eyes falling straightway upon a portrait painted in clear tones of two children sitting on a green bank overshadowed by trees, turning the leaves of a picture book, twins, seemingly, so like were they one to the other, light-hearted girls, with brown ringlets showering about their faces. Emily had just returned from Priscilla's grave, and the portrait telling a sunny past so plainly, warned her that henceforth she would be alone—she knew not for how long ; and too terrified for tears, she began to ask herself if she could continue her life in this old house that she and Priscilla had grown up in from childhood to womanhood, everything in it associated with her sister, every room, every table and chair, dinner services and tea services, the books on the shelves and on the tables. All these things had belonged to Priscilla as much as they had to herself, and now they belonged only to her.

The old Victorian paper was still on the walls, hardly more stained or faded than it was on the first day they saw it ; and in spite of her desire to put all memories behind her, she remembered her delight and Priscilla's delight at the tapestry screens in rich wools, the faint water-colours on the walls, mills and ruins and mountain streams, the school exercises of their aunts. Aunt Clara and Aunt Margaret and Aunt Jane were dead; but their handiwork remained to tell of them. Priscilla and she had often talked of repapering the room, of replacing the squab sofa by a comfortable Chesterfield. It was only last week they were considering

these things, and that the red damask curtains needed
cleaning. The carpets would have had to come up. . . .
If Priscilla had lived another month, the house would have
been in the hands of the workmen ; had she lived another
two months, all would have been changed ; and Emily asked
herself if it would be harder for her to live in a new house,
a house repapered, repainted, and refurnished, a house that
would bear no memory of Priscilla, or to live in this old house
in which her sister's presence lingered like a ghost. Every
piece of furniture, every picture, reminded her of something
she had said to Priscilla or Priscilla had said to her. If
that bird would only cease, she muttered, and fell to thinking
that she had hated to hear him sing on the day that Priscilla
died. Yes, he had sung that day—she had heard him, and
to-day he was singing, the day of the funeral, forgetful of
Priscilla, who had never forgotten to scatter crumbs under
the great apple tree in which he sang, or to bring a dish of
water for him to drink from and to bathe in.

A blackbird was whistling in the apple boughs the evening
they had come up from Mayo to live with Aunt Clara at
number four, Smith's Buildings—two little children of ten,
dressed in black, for their father was dead. But neither of
them understood the meaning of death at that time, and
Priscilla had cried out and she had cried out to their aunt to
be allowed to go into the lovely garden. It wasn't a lovely
garden at all then, but a wilderness, though there were
many hawthorns overtopping the railings, a great ash by
the gate, and a little alley of lilac bushes ; and tired though
they were from the long railway journey, they would have
liked to run round the garden, to play perhaps a game of
hide-and-seek among the lilac bushes. So it was with much
sorrow that they heard their aunt tell that nobody in Smith's
Buildings cared to go into the garden ; it was taboo because
everybody living in the five houses could go into it, a reason
that their minds could not apprehend, for they did not know
then that a benefit extended to all appeals to none in

c

particular. And they had gone to bed asking themselves
why nobody went into the garden just because the people from
the other houses might go into it. And next day and the
next they cast longing eyes upon the rood of ground, filled
with apple trees and lilacs and hawthorns, and begged so
hard to go and play in it that Aunt Clara had perforce to
think of what arrangement might be come to with the agent
for the property. Her nieces were little heiresses, each
owning a property in the west of Ireland that produced
about three hundred a year. Out of this six hundred a year
we can easily afford to pay a gardener, Aunt Clara said, and
the agent was invited to call, the proposal made to him
being that Miss Lofft should have the exclusive possession
of the garden on condition that she paid for its upkeep, a
thing that the other tenants had refused to do. Why,
they asked, should they pay for the upkeep of a garden
that they never entered and did not wish to enter ? But
if I pay for the upkeep, and make a fine border of London
Pride, and fill the beds with snapdragons, Canterbury bells,
honesty, columbines, Madonna lilies, pansies, and put holly-
hocks along the wall, all the other tenants will benefit by
the scent and colour of the garden, Aunt Clara had said, an
argument that the agent accepted, asking, however, for
some rent ; four pounds a year was the price of their play-
ground, that was all, and they had enjoyed this rood of
ground all their lives, since they were ten to the present day.

She dropped her head into the cushion and lay shaken
with grief till she could weep no more, and when she raised
her face, swollen with tears, the blackbird, that had been
silent for long, broke into another rich lay, calling her thoughts
again to the distant but clear past of her childhood, and the
fine days under the apple tree with her sister, dressing dolls
or learning the lessons that they took to the convent school
at the corner of the Green. Priscilla was a little slow at her
lessons, and though she looked so demure in that picture,
almost dull, that was the fault of the artist ; for she was

not demure, at least she was not dull, and in the middle of
learning French verbs would pick up her hoop and trundle
it round the garden with so much joy that Emily had to
pick up her hoop and trundle it after her, though she would
have liked to master her lessons first. But Priscilla always
had her way with her, and her thoughts dropped into consideration of her love for her sister ; an almost mystical
attachment it had often seemed to her, going back to the time
when they had lain in the womb together. Priscilla had
never seemed another being to her, but her second self,
her shadow, her ghost, each akin to the other as the sound
and its echo. In appearance they were the same, and she
remembered how the Reverend Mother had once said :
You are as alike as two casts come out of the same mould.
She had said something more than that to the nun standing
by, but Emily had only heard half the sentence, something
about the master-hand having been over one, whereas—
the rest of the sentence she did not catch, but guessed it
to be a disparagement of Priscilla, whom the convent did
not appreciate, for Priscilla did not seem to them to be
shaping into a prize pupil. Prize pupils were all the convent
cared for, the superficial qualities with which educational
grants are earned.

They were indeed as alike as two casts come out of the
same mould, and this likeness was not a mere chance ; it
penetrated from the surface into the heart and brain. Aunt
Clara had realised the importance of their likeness one to the
other better than the Reverend Mother had, and dressed
them alike so that others might see it, and of all, that Emily
and Priscilla might be conscious of it always. So they
had grown up to look upon themselves not as two but as one,
and when it came for her to take Priscilla to the dressmaker,
after their aunt's death, she had never allowed any change
to be made. If Mrs. Symond said : I think you might
wear this ribbon with advantage, she always answered : I
think, Mrs. Symond, that we both like the ribbon you speak

of.   One day Mrs. Symond had asked them when they were
going to be presented at Court. Of course she did, for
two debutantes meant many dresses for her to make. And
to persuade them to do what she herself had always refrained from doing for Priscilla's sake, Mrs. Symond called
her assistant, and asked her to show off the dresses they
were making that year. The prettiest fashions that have
appeared for many a year, the dressmaker said. And they
were shown berthas, flounces, plumes, stomachers, lappets,
and veils. But we are not going to the Castle, are we ?
Priscilla had whispered, for you know, Emily, I never should
have the courage to dance with a man I didn't know. But
if he didn't know you, he wouldn't ask you, Emily answered.
I never could grasp that three-step, Emily. I should feel
such a fool. And as Emily could not go alone to the Castle,
she postponed their presentation at Court till next year.

Looking back on that day at Mrs. Symond's, Emily felt
that it was not because Priscilla was afraid of dancing with
men who had only just been introduced to her, or could
not dance the three-step (Priscilla danced very well—the
dancing-master had always said so), that she had shrunk,
frightened at the thought of the Castle, but because some
instinct warned her that they would meet their fate at the
Castle. Priscilla may well have had a premonition that at
the Castle a man would rob her of her sister. But we cannot
escape our fate ; and they might just as well have gone to
the Castle to meet different men, to dance with them, aye,
to marry them, for though marriage sunders, it is not as
irreparable as death. It might have been better if she had
married James Mease. But none can escape her fate.
Theirs was waiting for them in the Shelbourne Hotel, whither
they went to see the dresses of some friends who were going
to the Drawing-Room.

It was that evening she had met James Mease, a young
man who at first had not attracted her—almost repelled
her ; but she had come to like him, and during the Castle

season they saw a great deal of each other. She had lost
her head, thinking of nothing else for six weeks but James
Mease, who, though almost a stranger to her, had made
her think she was willing to leave Priscilla to go to live with
him ; Priscilla was willing that it should be so. And Emily
fell to thinking of Priscilla's kindness, never complaining,
never saying to her : If you marry this young man I shall
be left alone, but trying always to efface herself, unwilling
to come between her sister and her sister's happiness. A
sad happiness was that month of courtship, a great cloud
coming up in her blue sky at the end of the three weeks,
when James's father and mother came to Dublin to make
the acquaintance of their future daughter-in-law, saying :
Our son will have ten thousand pounds, but the woman he
marries must bring as much. Even when added together,
her share of the money from her aunt's fortune and her own
money did not amount to ten thousand pounds. Priscilla
had offered to give up her share, but she would have to
live somewhere, and James would not consent to live with
his sister-in-law. Priscilla was willing to sacrifice herself,
to give up her money and live in the same house as James
(whom she had never liked) for the sake of her sister's happiness. Emily, too, though she had begun to think of James
Mease differently, was willing to sacrifice herself for the
same reasons as moved Priscilla ; and she tried to persuade
him that Priscilla would never divide them, that they would
be happier together than separated, that he did not know
Priscilla, or understand her, but would learn to.

She remembered the long wrangle between herself and
James, up and down and along and across Stephen's Green,
through many streets, by the canal, and on its bridges while
the boats passed through the locks. Everything was said
that could be said, not once, but twenty, a hundred times.
She had done all she could to persuade him, and had failed,
saying often : But even if I wished to leave my sister, I
couldn't, for she is giving up her money to satisfy your father

and mother. She had clung to him till she almost hated him and was ashamed of herself. The wisest words she had uttered were on her own doorstep, when she said : I give you your liberty. He had taken her at her word, and the last news she had of him was the news of his marriage. That was her luck—that he had married and was out of her life for ever ; for if he had not married and had come back to her saying : Now that your sister is gone we can marry, she would have hated him. And he was the kind of man who would have done this, unfeeling, lacking in perception, unaware always that he had divided them for a time, and was seeking to divide them for ever. He had done that, for he was the cause of Priscilla's death. Once it was known that her engagement with James Mease was broken off, they had had to go away somewhere, and where could they go to live down the scandal better than to their own lodge in the glen under Croagh Patrick ? It was there, during the winter, that Priscilla caught the cold that preceded her cough. What is a cold and a cough ? Emily asked herself. Nothing in nine hundred and ninety-nine cases. But there was blood-spitting with Priscilla's cough, and this had brought them to Dublin, to their friend Sir Stanley Forbes, who advised them to winter in the south.

She had not the courage to think it all out again. Of what avail was this thinking ? If she could only hush her thoughts ! But the mind refuses to be hushed, and a new thought suddenly presented itself, that perhaps it was Priscilla's wish that she should remain in Smith's Buildings, lest the dead might be forgotten. The dead are never really dead, Emily said, until we cease to think of them. I should always be thinking of her, wherever I was. But if she wills it . . . And sitting on the little rep sofa, her eyes brimming with occasional tears, she bethought herself of the life that awaited her without Priscilla, alone in the world, without parents or relations. Aunt Clara was gone ; a few distant cousins there were, dispersed over the world ; a few neigh-

bours, a few friends, scattered through Dublin ; but nobody
whom she could love. Lonely evenings, she said, the words
provoked by the sight of the books in the bookcase, Scott,
Dickens, Thackeray, the Brontës, Anthony Trollope, Mrs.
Henry Wood, and Charlotte Yonge. All these she and
Priscilla had read together on either side of the fireplace.
They had been reading *Lord Oakburn's Daughters* and were
but half-way through the story ; it would remain unread
now, for she would not care to finish it since she could not
share it with Priscilla. And she began to think of that
strange death that none had foreseen. Sir Stanley was
disappointed that the winter in the south had not shown
a greater improvement in Priscilla's health ; she was thin,
and white like a magnolia, his very words. But he did not
anticipate that death was so near. I know he didn't, she
said, speaking aloud. I know he didn't, she repeated, rising
from the sofa, as if to give emphasis to her belief that the
doctor had not suspected death to be so near.

After wandering around the faded room aimlessly, the
doctor's study, by the spell of contrast, appeared to her,
and she saw the old man, with his short, clipped beard,
sitting in his Chippendale chair on the left of the carved
Italian fireplace, all the carved tops of the bookcases, the
infoliated mirrors with their perching birds, the inlaid tables,
the bronzes and the vases. Was the rest of her life to be
spent in collecting furniture and china ? she asked herself ;
and returning to the sofa she began to listen, in her imagination, to the doctor, hearing him tell her that he did not despair
of Priscilla's ultimate recovery if she avoided living within
doors as far as possible. Tuberculosis, he said, is contracted
in byres and houses, never in the open air ; and since you have
a garden where you can sleep in hammocks every night it is
not raining, I don't see that you can do any better than to
remain in Dublin. In the autumn you will go south again,
where you will spend, I hope, as much of your time as possible
in the open air. These were his very words. But despite

C

all her care, Priscilla's health did not improve, remaining about the same.

Emily's thoughts concentrated on a few yards beyond the gates of Smith's Buildings, for half-way between these gates and the doctor's house last Friday she had met Esther Nunan coming from number four. Your maid told me that you were out, Esther said, and when I asked if Priscilla was at home, I learnt she had just come in from the garden and had gone up to her room to lie down, feeling rather poorly. Emily remembered repeating the words : Feeling rather poorly, and then turning suddenly, she said : I think I 'll go for the doctor and bring him home with me. He spoke of a bad sore throat, and wrote a prescription for a gargle ; but Priscilla could not gargle, her throat being too swollen. She drank a little milk that evening, and during the night her breathing became more and more difficult.   And all next day she struggled, dying towards evening, Sir Stanley's opinion being that the consumption from which she was suffering had flown to her throat and choked her. An ulcera-tion of the larynx was the only explanation he could give of Priscilla's sudden death.

Emily buried her face in the cushions to shut out the sight of Priscilla's struggles for breath ; she could not endure the memory of them, and it was not until she had exhausted her tears that she remembered a fact forgotten till now, that Priscilla had died struggling for speech. She had died with something on her mind ; and Emily bethought herself of the paper and pencil that Priscilla had signed to her for. She had given her both, and waited anxiously, but Priscilla was not able to write ; her hand fell away, and Emily read in her eyes : I cannot speak, I cannot write. It now seemed to her that she had only read Priscilla's eyes superficially. In her remembrance of them they seemed to say : I would give all the world to tell you, but I cannot.

Now what could Priscilla have had to tell me ? she asked herself, forgetful of her grief for the moment. We had no secrets from each other, and yet Priscilla died with something upon her mind, something that she had not told me, something that she desired above all things to confide to me. What could it be ? They had never been separated ; only at Aix had they ever occupied different rooms. And her thoughts passing out of Dublin back to Aix-les-Bains, to the day they arrived there, to the moment when the carriage stopped in front of the boarding-house, Emily remembered saying : Vous avez une chambre à coucher ? But when it came to saying : Can we have a double-bedded room ? she began to stammer : Nous voulons un lit doublé, at which the proprietress's face changed expression. We haven't any double-bedded rooms, she answered, but you can have two small rooms for the same price on the same floor. The thought of different rooms had frightened her, and they were about to tell the porter to replace their luggage in the carriage, when the proprietress warned them that they would find it very hard to get a double-bedded room in any of the hotels. It being the height of the season, she said, you may not be able to get a room at all. And have to sleep in the streets, Emily whispered to Priscilla, forgetful that the proprietress spoke English. The nights are very cold, the proprietress answered, and the thought of the danger that a cold night might be to Priscilla compelled her to accept the two rooms, which, after all, were in the same corridor. I will come and unlace your dress for you, and call you in the morning, Priscilla, so after all it won't matter much. You won't be frightened, dear, and will not forget to lock your door ?

The proprietress had promised that as soon as a double-bedded room was vacant, they should have it, but nobody left for weeks, and the room that was offered to them at last didn't seem to please Priscilla. It wasn't a very good room, it is true, but she wouldn't have minded sharing it with Priscilla, and perhaps Priscilla wouldn't have minded sharing it with her, but—— It may have been only a fancy, but she fancied that Priscilla had come to like a room to

herself; or perhaps Priscilla thought that it would be safer
for them to occupy different rooms ; she might have heard
of the danger, or had an instinct of it. Be this as it may,
Priscilla never forgot to lock her door, except once, and she
was about to reprove Priscilla for her carelessness—the words
were on her lips, but were stayed by the sight of Priscilla's
embarrassment at the sudden intrusion. It had seemed
to her that something was thrust under the pillow ; she was
about to ask Priscilla what she was hiding, and she wished
now that she had asked her, for if she had things might have
turned out differently. But the fact that Priscilla should
hide anything from her had hurt her so deeply that she
asked no questions, and after unlacing Priscilla's dress left
the room abruptly.

This was the first and only misunderstanding that had
ever occurred between them ; and it must be something
relating to that evening, perhaps it was about the book or
letter, whatever she had thrust under the sofa pillow, that
Priscilla wished to tell her. But no ; for she had written
on a piece of paper : In the garden, or words that read like :
In the garden. What connection could the garden of Smith's
Buildings have with Aix-les-Bains ? It was sad, it was heart-
breaking, that Priscilla should have had a secret from her,
but it was worse that she should have died unable to tell it.
At the memory of Priscilla's hand dropping away from the
paper, unable to write, tears rose to Emily's eyes, and she
began to think it was her duty to start for Aix to enquire
the matter out at the hotel. But what could the proprietress
tell her ? The key to Priscilla's secret was not in Aix but
in the words she had written : In the garden. One word
more would have been enough, and that word was withheld
from her, and she stood thinking, wondering, not whether
she would ever be happy again, but if she would be less
unhappy than she was to-day.

Her friends were not unmindful ; all were anxious to
help, but their efforts to detach her thoughts from the gone

were unavailing. Emily acquiesced in their proposals for drives, but her thoughts were far away, and once when the friend sitting beside her asked what was the matter, she answered : The matter is that Priscilla is dead. And during the summer months, alone in Dublin, she indulged her grief till grief became a companion, a friend, which she clung to desperately, dreading its decline or death, feeling that her grief was all that remained to her now of Priscilla, asking herself often what she would be without it, answering that she would hate herself, all self-respect would be taken from her. But in grief, as in all human things, there is a grain of insincerity. Who can say for certain that he is sincere, who can say for certain that he believes ? In the midst of our deepest emotions we are acting a comedy with ourselves ; within us one self is always mocking another self. And it came to pass that Emily did not dare to recall Priscilla trying to write something on a piece of paper which she wished to communicate to her, for to recall that moment would be to seek tears, and sought tears are contemptible ; and Emily was ashamed and looked upon herself as a hypocrite.

But grief, like everything else, changes, and Emily very soon began to notice that her grief was no longer the same as it was when tears and sobs were frequent. Her grief became, as it were, more spiritual, and it often fell out that while she was working in the garden Priscilla returned to her, in her thought, of course, but it seemed to her that she often saw her sister passing across the sward from the potting shed, and so clearly that she could not do else than leave the bed she was weeding. But not many steps were taken before the dear phantom vanished ; and the pain that these visitations caused her was so like physical pain that she clasped her heart with her hand. In the evening, as she sat reading in the old faded room, she often saw her lost sister, not when she looked up, expecting to see her, but when her thoughts were away from her. It was then that Priscilla crossed the room, looking back as if to assure herself that her sister was there. If Emily called her sister's name, if she rose from her seat, the appearance vanished, but as long as she looked steadily she saw Priscilla, not wan and shadowy as a ghost, but plainly, as in the flesh.

At times it seemed to her that her sister returned to ask her help, but could not speak her wish. The Priscilla that she saw come out of the back drawing-room was the Priscilla who had tried to write on the piece of paper, but could write only three words : In the garden. Emily longed to help her sister, but she was powerless, and it was her powerlessness to help that detained her in Dublin, for she could never quell the thought that Priscilla's secret would be revealed to her one day. How and when, she knew not, so she had perforce to deny herself to her friends, who were leaving Dublin for the summer months. Mountain and river scenery were proposed to her in vain, and if her resolution to wait for a sign wavered, as it sometimes did, the words : In the garden, repeated themselves in her mind. And under their sway one day she left the house and descended the steps into the garden, and looked round, thinking that the secret was about to be revealed to her.

But she heard no voice and saw no phantom in the lilac alley, where she expected to meet one, and the days and the weeks and even years went by, till one day a sudden shower of rain drove her for shelter to the potting shed ; and while waiting there, amidst the dust and cobwebs, hearing the rain patter on the large, heart-shaped leaves of the lilac, she noticed that one of the few planks piled against the wall of the shed had fallen awry, and that behind it was something that looked like a book. She moved the plank a little to one side, and found a French book and a dictionary. Left here by Priscilla, she said to herself. At the same moment the words : In the garden, came into her mind, and she stood tremulous, thinking of Priscilla retiring in secret to the potting shed to read this book. But why were her last thoughts about it ? Emily asked herself, as she turned the book over, a thick one, closely printed. That the book contained something of importance to Priscilla and to herself she had no doubt, and the rain having ceased she went towards the house and began to read, continuing to read till supper time, the book dropping upon her knees from time to time. To think that it had come to pass that such a one as Priscilla had read this book, and with a dictionary ! For the subject of it was a woman who was unfaithful to her husband with two different men, written in a French that must have puzzled Priscilla, so elaborate and careful was it. It often sent Emily to the dictionary, and she knew more French than her sister (Priscilla had never been able to master the verbs at school, and at Aix she had never tried to improve herself by talking or reading, whereas Emily had grappled with French speech at the table d'hôte, and all the books she read were French). The name of the Aix bookseller was upon the dictionary, and during supper Emily thought of the purchase of the dictionary, saying to herself as she went upstairs to the drawing-room : It was the dictionary or the book that Priscilla hid under the sofa pillow the night she forgot to lock her door and I entered unexpectedly. On this remembrance she threw herself into an armchair and continued her reading of Priscilla's book, and it was not long before she came to a passage that caused it to drop upon her knees once again.

For in the chapter she had just read it was related how the heroine's bedchamber was in a distant wing of the house, only one other bedchamber being near it, and that as the heroine passed she knocked at the door of the spare room ; and while waiting for her lover, began her preparations for the night before a toilet table covered with cut-glass bottles. And before this table, the lady, garbed in the finest muslin, sat combing her hair with tortoiseshell combs and brushing it with ivory brushes for the admiration of her lover, who sat watching, flattered that his lady should deem him worthy of so much thought and expensive care.

Again Emily paused in her reading to ponder on the woman represented in the book, and to remember the words of a man she had heard discourse at the table d'hôte at Aix. The subject of his discourse was that men and women were made of the same stuff in all ages, the stuff coming into the world the same, to be immediately modified by circumstance ; and in proof of his theory, he told that France had produced in the sixteenth century the most beautiful poetry that the world had ever known, reciting some short poems which had seemed very beautiful to her so far as she could judge. Yet poetry, the man said, had left France like a migrating bird, not to return again for more than two hundred years. If men, he continued, were able to lose the poetic sense for two hundred years, might we not infer that they might lose their moral sense, to return to it later, and to lose it again ? And now, making application of what she had heard at Aix to the woman in the book, Emily sat thinking that though men and women might be immoral in France, they might be moral in Ireland. It seemed to her hard to believe that a woman had ever lived in Ireland so licentious as the woman in the book, even during the Protestant ascendancy. It was impossible to believe that Aunt Clara, for instance, or Aunt Margaret, or Aunt Jane, had ever conducted themselves as the woman in the book did, or would have found pleasure in reading this book that Priscilla had brought home from France.

Emily sat thinking, almost forgetful of the people in the fiction, admitting, however, to herself that the book was written in a style that beguiled the reader, one which she could appreciate. She would have liked to read on for the sake of the style, but Priscilla had never read for style. She was not interested in literature for its own sake, and the questions that Priscilla had put to her about married life, asking why James would not consent to live with them both, left no doubt in her mind that Priscilla was altogether ignorant of the relations between men and women. It was therefore extraordinary that such a book as this should have come into Priscilla's hands, and that she should have taken enough pleasure in the reading of it to buy a dictionary. She was dying, it is true, and knew that she was dying, and no doubt felt death to be near her, almost impending. Might she not therefore have availed herself of the chance that had put this book into her hands to learn before she died something of the world she was about to leave ? A morbid desire, no doubt, hardly legitimate, but comprehensible. She might have felt, Emily continued, that she had never looked on the true face of life, but on a mask, and that of the true face she could only catch a glimpse in a book. It would have been better, perhaps, if the book had not come into her hands, for what did it profit her to learn what the world was ? Better that she should have gone out of it thinking it pure, good, and kind—much better.

But how did the book come into Priscilla's hands ? Did a man give it to her ? But Priscilla was intimate with no man ; she hardly answered when spoken to at the table d'hôte. The mystery seemed to grow denser. The book must have been given to her, Emily continued, or she must have found it. But where could she find it ? In her bedroom —there was nowhere else. And then—— ?

Emily struggled to carry the story on, but she could not move it a step further, till one day there came a great rush of thought. Some previous occupant of Priscilla's room at Aix might have forgotten the book ; it might have been left in a wardrobe or chest of drawers. But the housemaids could not have overlooked it. Another rush of thought ! The book may have dropped behind the chest of drawers and was caught between it and the wall, and when Priscilla moved the chest of drawers the book fell. This conjecture seemed more in character with what she knew of Priscilla than any other. But much remained to be accounted for, and she could not think how it was that Priscilla had brought back to England a book that did not belong to her. Several days passed in vain conjectures, and she remembered at last that having found the book Priscilla could not take it downstairs to the office and say : A previous occupant left this book in my room. The proprietress would open it, and would at once suspect that Priscilla had read it ; nor could Priscilla leave the book where she had found it, for when the room was next turned out the story would begin to run that the quiet English girl, as demure as an image, read improper books in her bedroom. A moment after, Emily discovered another link. Priscilla could not burn the book, for there were no fires ; she was ashamed to confess to her sister that she had seen the book, and thinking that she could get rid of it in Ireland she had slipped it into her placket and travelled over with it, to her great inconvenience. Her thought might have been to bury it in the garden when she had finished reading it. But she had never finished it, and Emily was glad that Priscilla was spared the end. She had read enough, however, to know that the book was a disgrace.

And it was to burn this book that her spirit has kept me here, Emily said, raising her eyes to the clock, which was striking twelve, two hours after her usual bedtime. Yet she could not go to bed before she had accomplished some of her duty to Priscilla, and she sat up till one, tearing paper from the book and watching the text disappear into black ashes. But a book is not burnt quickly, and she had to take a large remnant of it to her room, for she did not dare leave it torn for the servants to look into, since they might suspect something, though it was in French. Nowhere would it be safe except under her pillow ; and if she were to die that night and be found dead with it under her pillow !

But death did not come to take her that night, and the next evening what remained of the book perished in the grate, and as the last page curled and blackened, she began to apprehend all that the burning of the book meant to her. Now that it was gone she was free to leave this dusty old house and the dusty conventions in which half her life had been spent. She was free to return to Aix and to live like other English spinsters on a small income, travelling whither she listed, from one boarding-house to another, seeking—— Does anybody do more than to seek and to find, mayhap, something ? Does any woman find even the shadow of her dream at thirty-five ? she asked. Her thoughts began to doze again, and whilst she dozed the day returned to the garden and the blackbird whistled again in the dusk. But would she be able to match that bird's song again ? Once, ah, once ; and between waking and dream she rose to her feet and went upstairs, forgetful of all things but her bed.

ALBERT NOBBS

When we went up to Dublin in the 'sixties, Alec, we always
put up at Morrison's Hotel, a big family hotel at the corner
of Dawson Street, one that was well patronised by the gentry
from all over Ireland, my father paying his bill every six
months when he was able, which wasn't very often, for what
with racing stables and elections following one after the other,
Moore Hall wasn't what you 'd call overflowing with money.
Now that I come to think of it, I can see Morrison's as clearly
almost as I do Moore Hall : the front door opening into a
short passage, with some half-dozen steps leading up into the
house, the glass doors of the coffee-room showing through
the dimness, and in front of the visitor a big staircase running
up to the second landing. I remember long passages on
the second landing, and half-way down these passages was
the well. I don't know if it 's right to speak of the well of
a staircase, but I used to think of it as a well. It was
always being drummed into me that I mustn't climb on to
the banisters, a thing I wished to do, but was afraid to
get astride of them, lest I should lose my head and fall all
the way down to the ground floor. There was nothing to
stop me from reaching it, if I lost my balance, except a few
gas lamps. I think that both the long passages led to minor
stairs, but I never followed either lest I should miss my way.
A very big building was Morrison's Hotel, with passages
running hither and thither, and little flights of stairs in all
kinds of odd corners by which the visitors climbed to their
apartments, and it needed all my attention to remember
the way to our rooms on the second floor. We were always
on the second floor in a big sitting-room overlooking College

Green, and I remember the pair of windows, their lace curtains and their rep curtains, better than the passages, and better than the windows I can remember myself looking through the pane interested in the coal carts going by, the bell hitched on to the horse's collar jangling all the way down the street, the coalman himself sitting with his legs hanging over the shafts, driving from the wrong side and looking up at the windows to see if he could spy out an order. Fine horses were in these coal carts, stepping out as well as those in our own carriage.

I 'm telling you these things for the pleasure of looking back and nothing else. I can see the sitting-room and myself as plainly as I can see the mountains beyond, in some ways plainer, and the waiter that used to attend on us, I can see him, though not as plainly as I see you, Alec ; but I 'm more knowledgeable of him, if you understand me rightly, and to this day I can recall the frights he gave me when he came behind me, awaking me from my dream of a coalman's life—what he said is forgotten, but his squeaky voice remains in my ears. He seemed to be always laughing at me, showing long, yellow teeth, and I used to be afraid to open the sitting-room door, for I 'd be sure to find him waiting on the landing, his napkin thrown over his right shoulder. I think I was afraid he 'd pick me up and kiss me. As the whole of my story is about him, perhaps I 'd better describe him more fully, and to do that I will tell you that he was a tall, scraggy fellow, with big hips sticking out, and a long, thin throat. It was his throat that frightened me as much as anything about him, unless it was his nose, which was a great high one, or his melancholy eyes, which were pale blue and very small, deep in the head. He was old, but how old I cannot say, for everybody except children seems old to children. He was the ugliest thing I 'd seen out of a fairy-book, and I 'd beg not to be left alone in the sitting-room ; and I 'm sure I often asked my father and mother to take another set of rooms, which they never did, for they liked Albert Nobbs. And the guests liked him, and the proprietress liked him, as well she might, for he was the most dependable servant in the hotel ; no running round to public-houses and coming back with the smell of whisky and tobacco upon him ; no rank pipe in his pocket ; and of all, no playing the fool with the maid-servants. Nobody had ever been heard to say he had seen Albert out with one of them—a queer, hobgoblin sort of fellow that they mightn't have cared to be seen with, but all the same it seemed to them funny that he should never propose to walk out with one of them. I 've heard the hall-porter say it was hard to understand a man living without taking pleasure in some-thing outside of his work. Holidays he never asked for, and when Mrs. Baker pressed him to go to the salt water for a week, he 'd try to rake up an excuse for not going away, asking if it wasn't true that the Blakes, the Joyces, and the Ruttledges were coming up to town, saying that he didn't like to be away, so used were they to him and he to them. A strange life his was, and mysterious, though every hour of it was before them, saving the hours he was asleep, which weren't many, for he was no great sleeper. From the time he got up in the morning till he went to bed at night he was before their eyes, running up and down the staircase, his napkin over his arm, taking orders with cheerfulness, as if an order were as good as a half-crown tip to him, always good-humoured, and making amends for his lack of interest in other people by his willingness to oblige. No one had ever heard him object to doing anything he was asked to do, or even put forward an excuse for not being able to do it. In fact, his willingness to oblige was so notorious in the hotel that Mrs. Baker (the proprietress of Morrison's Hotel at the time) could hardly believe she was listening to him when he began to stumble from one excuse to another for not sharing his bed with Hubert Page, and this after she had told him that his bed was Page's only chance of getting a stretch that night. All the other waiters were married men and went home to their wives. You see, Alec, it was Punchestown week, and beds are as scarce in Dublin that week as diamonds are on the slopes of Croagh Patrick.

But you haven't told me yet who Page was, Alec interjected, and I thought reprovingly. I 'm just coming to him, I answered. Hubert Page was a house-painter, well known and well liked by Mrs. Baker. He came over every season, and was always welcome at Morrison's Hotel, and so pleasant were his manners that one forgot the smell of his paint. It is hardly saying too much to say that when Hubert Page had finished his job everybody in the hotel, men and women alike, missed the pleasant sight of this young man going to and fro in his suit of hollands, the long coat buttoned loosely to his figure with large bone buttons, going to and fro about his work, up and down the passages, with a sort of lolling, idle gait that attracted and pleased the eye—a young man that would seem preferable to most men if a man had to choose a bed-fellow, yet seemingly the very one that Albert Nobbs couldn't abide lying down with, a dislike that Mrs. Baker could understand so little that she stood staring at her confused and embarrassed waiter, who was still seeking excuses for his dislike to share his bed with Hubert Page. I suppose you fully understand, she said, that Page is leaving for Belfast by the morning train, and has come over here to ask us for a bed, there not being one at the hotel in which he is working ? Albert answered that he understood well enough, but was thinking—— He began again to fumble with words. Now, what are you trying to say ? Mrs. Baker asked, and rather sharply. My bed is full of lumps, Albert answered. Your mattress full of lumps ! the proprietress rapped out ; why, your mattress was repicked and buttoned six months ago, and came back as good as any mattress in the hotel. What kind of story are you telling me ? So it was, ma'am, so it was, Albert mumbled, and it was some time before he got out his next excuse : he was a very light sleeper and had never slept with anybody before and was sure he wouldn't close his eyes ; not that that would matter

much, but his sleeplessness might keep Mr. Page awake.
Mr. Page would get a better stretch on one of the sofas in
the coffee-room than in my bed, I'm thinking, Mrs. Baker.
A better stretch on the sofa in the coffee-room ? Mrs. Baker
repeated angrily. I don't understand you, not a little bit ;
and she stood staring at the two men, so dissimilar. But,
ma'am, I wouldn't be putting Mr. Nobbs to the inconvenience
of my company, the house-painter began. The night is a
fine one ; I'll keep myself warm with a sharp walk, and the
train starts early. You'll do nothing of the kind, Page, she
answered ; and seeing that Mrs. Baker was now very angry
Albert thought it time to give in, and without more ado he
began to assure them both that he'd be glad of Mr. Page's
company in his bed. I should think so indeed ! interjected
Mrs. Baker. But I'm a light sleeper, he added. We've
heard that before, Albert ! Of course, if Mr. Page is pleased
to share my bed, Albert continued, I shall be very glad. If
Mr. Nobbs doesn't like my company I should—— Don't say
another word, Albert whispered, you'll only set her against
me. Come upstairs at once ; it'll be all right. Come along.

Good-night, ma'am, and I hope—— No inconvenience
whatever, Page, Mrs. Baker answered. This way, Mr. Page,
Albert cried ; and as soon as they were in the room he said :
I hope you aren't going to cut up rough at anything I've
said ; it isn't at all as Mrs. Baker put it. I'm glad enough
of your company, but you see, as I've never slept with anybody in my life, it may be that I shall be tossing about all
night, keeping you awake. Well, if it's to be like that,
Page answered, I might as well have a doze on the chair
until it's time to go, and not trouble you at all. You won't
be giving me any trouble ; what I'm afraid of is—but
enough has been said ; we have to lie down together, whether
we like it or whether we don't, for if Mrs. Baker heard that
we hadn't been in the same bed together all the fault would
lie with me. I'd be sent out of the hotel in double-quick time.
But how can she know ? Page cried. It's been settled one
way, so let us make no more fuss about it.

Albert began to undo his white neck-tie, saying he would try to lie quiet, and Page started pulling off his clothes, thinking he 'd be well pleased to be out of the job of lying down with Albert. But he was so dog-tired that he couldn't think any more about whom he was to sleep with, only of the long days of twelve and thirteen hours he had been doing, with a walk to and from his work ; only sleep mattered to him, and Albert saw him tumble into bed in the long shirt that he wore under his clothes, and lay himself down next to the wall. It would be better for him to lie on the outside, Albert said to himself, but he didn't like to say anything lest Page might get out of his bed in a fit of ill-humour ; but Page, as I 've said, was too tired to trouble himself which side of the bed he was to doss on. A moment after he was asleep, and Albert stood listening, his loosened tie dangling, till the heavy breathing from the bed told him that Page was sound asleep. To make full sure he approached the bed stealthily, and overlooking Page, said : Poor fellow, I 'm glad he 's in my bed, for he 'll get a good sleep there and he wants it ; and considering that things had fallen out better than he hoped for, he began to undress.

He must have fallen asleep at once, and soundly, for he awoke out of nothingness. Flea ! he muttered, and a strong one, too. It must have come from the house-painter along-side of me ; a flea will leave anyone to come to me. And turning round in bed he remembered the look of dismay that had appeared on the housemaids' faces yesterday on his telling them that no man would ever love their hides as much as a flea loved his, which was so true that he couldn't under-stand how it was that the same flea had taken so long to find him out. Fleas must be as partial to him, he said, as they are to me. There it is again, trying to make up for lost time ! and out went Albert's leg. I 'm afraid I 've awakened him, he said, but Hubert only turned over in the bed to sleep more soundly. It 's a mercy indeed that he is so tired, Albert

said, for if he wasn't very tired that last jump I gave would
have awakened him. A moment after Albert was nipped
again by another flea, or by the same one, he couldn't tell ;
he thought it must be a second one, so vigorous was the bite,
and he was hard put to it to keep his nails off the spots. I
shall only make them worse if I scratch, he said, and he strove
to lie quiet. But the torment was too great. I 've got to
get up, he muttered, and raising himself up quietly, he listened.
The striking of a match won't awaken him out of that sleep !
and remembering where he had put the match-box, his hand
was on it at once. The match flared up ; he lighted the
candle, and stood a while overlooking his bed-fellow. I 'm
safe, he said, and set himself to the task of catching the flea.
There he is on the tail of my shirt, hardly able to move with
all the blood he 's taken from me. Now for the soap ; and as
he was about to dab it upon the blood-filled insect the painter
awoke with a great yawn, and turning round, he said : Lord
amassy ! what is the meaning of this ? Why, you 're a woman !

If Albert had had the presence of mind to drop her shirt
over her shoulders and to answer : You 're dreaming, my
man, Page might have turned over and fallen asleep and in
the morning forgotten all about it, or thought he had been
dreaming. But Albert hadn't a word in her chops. At last
she began to blub. You won't tell on me, and ruin a poor
man, will you, Mr. Page ? That is all I ask of you, and on
my knees I beg it. Get up from your knees, my good woman,
said Hubert. My good woman ! Albert repeated, for she
had been about so long as a man that she only remembered
occasionally that she was a woman. My good woman,
Hubert repeated, get up from your knees and tell me how
long you have been playing this part. Ever since I was a
girl, Albert answered. You won't tell upon me, will you,
Mr. Page, and prevent a poor woman from getting her living ?
Not likely, I 've no thought of telling on you, but I 'd like to
hear how it all came about. How I went out as a youth to
get my living ? Yes ; tell me the story, Hubert answered,

for though I was very sleepy just now, the sleep has left
my eyes and I 'd like to hear it. But before you begin, tell
me what you were doing with your shirt off. A flea, Albert
answered. I suffer terribly from fleas, and you must have
brought some in with you, Mr. Page. I shall be covered in
blotches in the morning. I 'm sorry for that, Hubert said ;
but tell me how long ago it was that you became a man.
Before you came to Dublin, of course ? Oh, yes, long before.
It is very cold, she said, and shuddering, dropped her shirt
over her shoulders and pulled on her trousers.

II

It was in London, soon after the death of my old nurse, she
began. You know I 'm not Irish, Mr. Page. My parents
may have been, for all I know. The only one who knew who
they were was my old nurse, and she never told me. Never
told you ! interjected Hubert. No, she never told me, though
I often asked her, saying no good could come of holding it back
from me. She might have told me before she died, but she died
suddenly. Died suddenly, Hubert repeated, without telling
you who you were ! You 'd better begin at the beginning.
I don't know how I 'm to do that, for the story seems to
me to be without a beginning ; anyway I don't know the
beginning. I was a bastard, and no one but my old nurse,
who brought me up, knew who I was ; she said she 'd tell
me some day, and she hinted more than once that my people
were grand folk, and I know she had a big allowance from
them for my education. Whoever they were, a hundred a
year was paid to her for my keep and education, and all
went well with us so long as my parents lived, but when they
died the allowance was no longer paid, and my nurse and
myself had to go out to work. It was all very sudden : one
day the Reverend Mother (I got my education at a convent
school) told me that Mrs. Nobbs, my old nurse, had sent for
me, and the first news I had on coming home was that my
parents were dead and that we 'd have to get our own living

henceforth. There was no time for picking and choosing.
We hadn't what would keep us until the end of the month
in the house, so out we had to go in search of work ; and
the first job that came our way was looking after chambers
in the Temple. We had three gentlemen to look after, so
there was eighteen shillings a week between my old nurse
and myself ; the omnibus fares had to come out of these
wages, and to save sixpence a day we went to live in Temple
Lane. My old nurse didn't mind the lane ; she had been a
working woman all her life ; but with me it was different,
and the change was so great from the convent that I often
thought I would sooner die than continue to live amid rough
people. There was nothing wrong with them ; they were
honest enough ; but they were poor, and when you are very
poor you live like the animals, indecently, and life without
decency is hardly bearable, so I thought. I 've been through
a great deal since in different hotels, and have become used
to hard work, but even now I can't think of Temple Lane
without goose-flesh ; and when Mrs. Nobbs' brother lost his
berth (he 'd been a bandmaster, a bugler, or something to
do with music in the country), my old nurse was obliged to
give him sixpence a day, and the drop from eighteen shillings
to fourteen and sixpence is a big one. My old nurse worried
about the food, but it was the rough men I worried about ;
the bandsman wouldn't leave me alone, and many 's the time
I 've waited until the staircase was clear, afraid that if I
met him or another that I 'd be caught hold of and held and
pulled about. I was different then from what I am now, and
might have been tempted if one of them had been less rough
than the rest, and if I hadn't known I was a bastard ; it was
that, I think, that kept me straight more than anything else,
for I had just begun to feel what a great misfortune it is for
a poor girl to find herself in the family way ; no greater
misfortune can befall anyone in this world, but it would
have been worse in my case, for I should have known that I
was only bringing another bastard into the world.

I escaped being seduced in the lane, and in the chambers the barristers had their own mistresses; pleasant and considerate men they all were—pleasant to work for; and it wasn't until four o'clock came and our work was over for the day that my heart sank, for after four o'clock till we went to bed at night there was nothing for us to do but to listen to the screams of drunken women; I don't know which was the worser, the laughter or the curses.

One of the barristers we worked for was Mr. Congreve; he had chambers in Temple Gardens overlooking the river, and it was a pleasure to us to keep his pretty things clean, never breaking one of them; it was a pleasure for my old nurse as well as myself, myself more than for her, for though I wasn't very sure of myself at the time, looking back now I can see that I must have loved Mr. Congreve very dearly; and it couldn't be else, for I had come out of a convent of nuns where I had been given a good education, where all was good, quiet, refined and gentle, and Mr. Congreve seemed in many ways to remind me of the convent, for he never missed Church; as rare for him to miss a service as for parson. There was plenty of books in his chambers and he'd lend them to me, and talk to me over his newspaper when I took in his breakfast, and ask about the convent and what the nuns were like, and I'd stand in front of him, my eyes fixed on him, not feeling the time going by. I can see him now as plainly as if he were before me—very thin and elegant, with long white hands, and beautifully dressed. Even in the old clothes that he wore of a morning there wasn't much fault to find; he wore old clothes more elegantly than any man in the Temple wore his new clothes. I used to know all his suits, as well I might, for it was my job to look after them, to brush them; and I used to spend a great deal more time than was needed taking out spots with benzine, arranging his neck-ties—he had fifty or sixty, all kinds—and seven or eight greatcoats. A real toff—my word he was that, but not one of those haughty ones too proud to give one a nod. He always smiled and nodded if we met under the clock, he on his way to the library and I returning to Temple Lane. I used to look round after him saying : He 's got on the striped trousers and the embroidered waistcoat. Mr. Congreve was a compensation for Temple Lane ; he had promised to take me into his private service, and I was counting the days when I should leave Temple Lane, when one day I said to myself : Why, here 's a letter from a woman. You see, Mr. Congreve wasn't like the other young men in the Temple ; I never found a hairpin in his bed, and if I had I shouldn't have thought as much of him as I did. Nice is in France, I said, and thought no more about the matter until another letter arrived from Nice. Now what can she be writing to him about ? I asked, and thought no more about it until the third letter arrived. Yesterday is already more than half forgotten, but the morning I took in that last letter is always before me. And it was a few mornings afterwards that a box of flowers came for him. A parcel for you, sir, I said. He roused himself up in bed. For me ? he cried, putting out his hand, and the moment he saw the writing, he said : Put the flowers in water. He knows all about it, I said to myself, and so overcome was I as I picked them up out of the box that a sudden faintness came over me, and my old nurse said : What is the matter with thee ? She never guessed, and I couldn't have told her if I had wished to, for at the time it was no more than a feeling that so far as I was concerned all was over. Of course I never thought that Mr. Congreve would look at me, and I don't know that I wanted him to, but I didn't want another woman about the place, and I seemed to know from that moment what was going to happen. She isn't far away now, in the train maybe, I said, as I went about my work, and these rooms will be mine no longer. Of course they never were mine, but you know what I mean.

A week later he said to me : There 's a lady coming to luncheon here, and I remember the piercing that the words caused me ; I can feel them here still ; and Albert put her hand to her heart. Well, I had to serve the luncheon, working round the table and they not minding me at all, but sitting looking at each other lost in a sense of delight ; the luncheon was forgotten. They don't want me waiting about, I thought. I knew all this, and said to myself in the kitchen : It's disgraceful, it's wicked, to lead a man into sin—for all my anger went out against the woman, and not against Mr. Congreve ; in my eyes he seemed to be nothing more than a victim of a designing woman ; that is how I looked at it at the time, being but a youngster only just come from a convent school.

I don't think that anyone suffered more than I did in those days. It all seems very silly now when I look back upon it, but it was very real then. It does seem silly to tell that I used to lie awake all night thinking to myself that Mr. Congreve was an elegant gentleman and I but a poor serving girl that he'd never look twice at, thinking of her only as somebody to go to the cellar for coal or to the kitchen to fetch his breakfast. I don't think I ever hoped he'd fall in love with me. It wasn't as bad as that. It was the hopelessness of it that set the tears streaming down my cheeks over my pillow, and I used to stuff the sheet into my mouth to keep back the sobs lest my old nurse should hear me ; it wouldn't do to keep her awake, for she was very ill at that time; and soon afterwards she died, and then I was left alone, without a friend in the world. The only people I knew were the charwomen that lived in Temple Lane, and the bugler, who began to bully me, saying that I must continue to give him the same money he had had from my old nurse. He caught me on the stairs once and twisted my arm until I thought he'd broken it. The month after my old nurse's death till I went to earn my living as a waiter was the hardest time of all, and Mr. Congreve's kindness seemed to hurt me more than anything. If only he'd spared me his kind words, and not spoken about the extra money he was going to give me for my attendance on his lady, I shouldn't have felt so much that they had lain side by side in the bed that I was making. She brought a dressing-gown to the chambers and some slippers, and then more luggage came along ; and I think she must have guessed I was in love with Mr. Congreve, for I heard them quarrelling —my name was mentioned ; and I said : I can't put up with it any longer ; whatever the next life may be like, it can't be worse than this one for me at least ; and as I went to and fro between Temple Lane and the chambers in Temple Gardens I began to think how I might make away with myself. I don't know if you know London, Hubert ? Yes, he said ; I 'm a Londoner, but I come here to work every year. Then if you know the Temple, you know that the windows of Temple Gardens overlook the river. I used to stand at those windows watching the big brown river flowing through its bridges, thinking all the while of the sea into which it went, and that I must plunge into the river and be carried away down to the sea, or be picked up before I got there. I could only think about making an end to my trouble and of the Frenchwoman. Her suspicions that I cared for him made her harder on me than she need have been ; she was always coming the missis over me. Her airs and graces stiffened my back more than anything else, and I 'm sure if I hadn't met Bessie Lawrence I should have done away with myself. She was the woman who used to look after the chambers under Mr. Congreve's. We stopped talking outside the gateway by King's Bench Walk—if you know the Temple, you know where I mean. Bessie kept talking, but I wasn't listening, only catching a word here and there, not waking up from the dream how to make away with myself till I heard the words : If I had a figure like yours. As no one had ever spoken about my figure before, I said : Now what has my figure got to do with it ? You haven't been listening to me, she said, and I answered that I had only missed the last few words. Just missed the last few words, she said testily ; you didn't hear me telling you that there is a big dinner at the Freemason's Tavern to-night, and they 're short of waiters. But what has that got to do with my figure ? I asked. That shows, she rapped out, that you haven't been listening to me. Didn't I say that if it wasn't for my hips and bosom I'd very soon be into a suit of evening clothes and getting ten shillings for the job. But what has that got to do with my figure ? I repeated. Your figure is just the one for a waiter's. Oh, I'd never thought of that, says I, and we said no more. But the words : Your figure is just the one for a waiter's, kept on in my head till my eyes caught sight of a bundle of old clothes that Mr. Congreve had given me to sell. A suit of evening clothes was in it. You see, Mr. Congreve and myself were about the same height and build. The trousers will want a bit of shortening, I said to myself, and I set to work ; and at six o'clock I was in them and down at the Freemason's Tavern answering questions, saying that I had been accustomed to waiting at table. All the waiting I had done was bringing in Mr. Congreve's dinner from the kitchen to the sitting-room : a roast chicken or a chop, and in my fancy it seemed to me that the waiting at the Freemason's Tavern would be much the same. The head waiter looked me over a bit doubtfully and asked if I had had experience with public dinners. I thought he was going to turn me down, but they were short-handed, so I was taken on, and it was a mess that I made of it, getting in everybody's way ; but my awkwardness was taken in good part and I received ten shillings, which was good money for the sort of work I did that night. But what stood to me was not so much the ten shillings that I earned as the bit I had learned. It was only a bit, not much bigger than a threepenny bit ; but I had worked round a table at a big dinner, and feeling certain that I could learn what I didn't know, I asked for another job. I suppose the head waiter could see that there was the making of a waiter in me, for on coming out of the Freemason's Tavern he stopped me to ask if I was going back to private service as soon as I could get a place. The food I'd had and the excitement of the dinner, the guests, the lights, the talk, stood to me, and things seemed clearer than they had ever seemed before. My feet were of

the same mind, for they wouldn't walk towards the Temple,
and I answered the head waiter that I 'd be glad of another
job. Well, said he, you don't much know about the work,
but you 're an honest lad, I think, so I 'll see what I can do
for you ; and at the moment a thought struck him. Just take
this letter, said he, to the Holborn Restaurant. There 's a
dinner there and I 've had word that they 're short of a waiter
or two. Be off as fast as you can. And away I went as fast
as my legs could carry me, and they took me there in good
time, in front, by a few seconds, of two other fellows who were
after the job. I got it. Another job came along, and another
and another. Each of them jobs was worth ten shillings to
me, to say nothing of the learning of the trade ; and having,
as I 've said, the making of a waiter in me, it didn't take more
than about three months for me to be as quick and as smart
and as watchful as the best of them, and without them
qualities no one will succeed in waiting. I have worked round
the tables in the biggest places in London and all over
England in all the big towns, in Manchester, in Liverpool,
and Birmingham ; I am well known at the old Hen and
Chickens, at the Queen's, and the Plough and Harrow in
Birmingham. It was seven years ago that I came here, and
here it would seem that I 've come to be looked on as a fixture,
for the Bakers are good people to work for and I didn't like
to leave them when, three years ago, a good place was offered
to me, so kind were they to me in my illness. I suppose one
never remains always in the same place, but I may as well
be here as elsewhere.

Seven years working in Morrison's Hotel, Page said, and
on the second floor ? Yes, the second floor is the best in the
hotel ; the money is better than in the coffee-room, and
that is why the Bakers have put me here, Albert replied.
I wouldn't care to leave them ; they 've often said they
don't know what they 'd do without me. Seven years,
Hubert repeated, the same work up the stairs and down the
stairs, banging into the kitchen and out again. There 's

more variety in the work than you think for, Hubert, Albert
answered. Every family is different, and so you 're always
learning. Seven years, Page repeated, neither man nor
woman, just a perhapser. He spoke these words more to
himself than to Nobbs, but feeling he had expressed himself
incautiously he raised his eyes and read on Albert's face
that the words had gone home, and that this outcast from
both sexes felt her loneliness perhaps more keenly than before.
As Hubert was thinking what words he might use to con-
ciliate Albert with her lot, Albert repeated the words :
Neither man nor woman ; yet nobody ever suspected, she
muttered, and never would have suspected me till the day
of my death if it hadn't been for that flea that you brought
in with you. But what harm did the flea do ? I 'm bitten
all over, said Albert, scratching her thighs. Never mind the
bites, said Hubert; we wouldn't have had this talk if it hadn't
been for the flea, and I shouldn't have heard your story.

Tears trembled on Albert's eyelids ; she tried to keep
them back, but they overflowed the lids and were soon
running quickly down her cheeks. You 've heard my story,
she said. I thought nobody would ever hear it, and I thought
I should never cry again ; and Hubert watched the gaunt
woman shaking with sobs under a coarse nightshirt. It 's
all much sadder than I thought it was, and if I 'd known how
sad it was I shouldn't have been able to live through it. But
I 've jostled along somehow, she added, always merry and
bright, with never anyone to speak to, not really to speak
to, only to ask for plates and dishes, for knives and forks and
such like, tablecloths and napkins, cursing betimes the life
you 've been through ; for the feeling cannot help coming
over us, perhaps over the biggest as over the smallest, that
all our trouble is for nothing and can end in nothing. It
might have been better if I had taken the plunge. But why
am I thinking these things ? It 's you that has set me
thinking, Hubert. I 'm sorry if—— Oh, it 's no use being
sorry, and I 'm a great silly to cry like this. I thought that

E

regrets had passed away with the petticoats. But you 've awakened the woman in me. You 've brought it all up again. But I mustn't let on like this; it 's very foolish of an old perhapser like me, neither man nor woman! But I can't help it. She began to sob again, and in the midst of her grief the word loneliness was uttered, and when the paroxysm was over, Hubert said : Lonely, yes, I suppose it is lonely ; and he put his hand out towards Albert. You 're very good, Mr. Page, and I 'm sure you 'll keep my secret, though indeed I don't care very much whether you do or not. Now, don't let on like that again, Hubert said. Let us have a little chat and try to understand each other. I 'm sure it 's lonely for you to live without man or without woman, thinking like a man and feeling like a woman. You seem to know all about it, Hubert. I hadn't thought of it like that before myself, but when you speak the words I feel you have spoken the truth. I suppose I was wrong to put off my petticoats and step into those trousers. I wouldn't go so far as to say that, Hubert answered, and the words were so unexpected that Albert forgot her grief for a moment and said : Why do you say that, Hubert ? Well, because I was thinking, he replied, that you might marry. But I was never a success as a girl. Men didn't look at me then, so I 'm sure they wouldn't now I 'm a middle-aged woman. Marriage ! whom should I marry ? No, there 's no marriage for me in the world ; I must go on being a man. But you won't tell on me ? You 've promised, Hubert. Of course I won't tell, but I don't see why you shouldn't marry. What do you mean, Hubert ? You aren't putting a joke upon me, are you ? If you are it 's very unkind. A joke upon you ? no, Hubert answered. I didn't mean that you should marry a man, but you might marry a girl. Marry a girl ? Albert repeated, her eyes wide open and staring. A girl ? Well, anyway, that 's what I 've done, Hubert replied. But you 're a young man and a very handsome young man too. Any girl would like to have you, and I dare say they were all after you before

you met the right girl. I 'm not a young man, I 'm a woman,
Hubert replied. Now I know for certain, cried Albert,
you 're putting a joke upon me. A woman ! Yes, a woman ;
you can feel for yourself if you won't believe me. Put your
hand under my shirt; you 'll find nothing there. Albert
moved away instinctively, her modesty having been shocked.
You see I offered myself like that feeling you couldn't take
my word for it. It isn't a thing there can be any doubt
about. Oh, I believe you, Albert replied. And now that
that matter is settled, Hubert began, perhaps you 'd like to
hear my story ; and without waiting for an answer she related
the story of her unhappy marriage : her husband, a house-
painter, had changed towards her altogether after the birth
of her second child, leaving her without money for food and
selling up the home twice. At last I decided to have another
cut at it, Hubert went on, and catching sight of my husband's
working clothes one day I said to myself : He 's often made
me put these on and go out and help him with his job ; why
shouldn't I put them on for myself and go away for good ?
I didn't like leaving the children, but I couldn't remain with
him. But the marriage ? Albert asked. It was lonely going
home to an empty room ; I was as lonely as you, and one day,
meeting a girl as lonely as myself, I said : Come along, and
we arranged to live together, each paying our share. She
had her work and I had mine, and between us we made a
fair living ; and this I can say with truth, that we haven't
known an unhappy hour since we married. People began to
talk, so we had to. I 'd like you to see our home. I always
return to my home after a job is finished with a light heart
and leave it with a heavy one. But I don't understand,
Albert said. What don't you understand ? Hubert asked.
Whatever Albert's thoughts were, they faded from her, and
her eyelids dropped over her eyes. You 're falling asleep,
Hubert said, and I 'm doing the same. It must be three
o'clock in the morning and I 've to catch the five o'clock
train. I can't think now of what I was going to ask you,

Albert muttered, but you 'll tell me in the morning ; and
turning over, she made a place for Hubert.

III

What has become of him ? Albert said, rousing herself,
and then, remembering that Hubert's intention was to
catch the early train, she began to remember. His train,
she said, started from Amiens Street at—I must have slept
heavily for him—for her not to have awakened me, or she
must have stolen away very quietly. But, lord amassy,
what time is it ? And seeing she had overslept herself a full
hour, she began to dress herself, muttering all the while :
Such a thing never happened to me before. And the hotel
as full as it can hold. Why didn't they send for me ? The
missis had a thought of my bed-fellow, mayhap, and let me
sleep it out. I told her I shouldn't close an eye till she left
me. But I mustn't fall into the habit of sheing him. Lord,
if the missis knew everything ! But I 've overslept myself
a full hour, and if nobody has been up before somebody soon
will be. The greater haste the less speed. All the same,
despite the difficulty of finding her clothes, Albert was at
work on her landing some twenty minutes after, running up
and down the stairs, preparing for the different breakfasts
in the half-dozen sitting-rooms given to her charge, driving
everybody before her, saying : We 're late to-day, and the
house full of visitors. How is it that 54 isn't turned out ?
Has 35 rung his bell ? Lord, Albert, said a housemaid, I
wouldn't worry my fat because I was down late ; once in a
way don't hurt. And sitting up half the night talking to
Mr. Page, said another maid and then rounding on us.
Half the night talking, Albert repeated. My bed-fellow !
Where is Mr. Page ? I didn't hear him go away ; he may
have missed his train for aught I know. But do you be
getting on with your work, and let me be getting on with
mine. You 're very cross this morning, Albert, the maid-

servant muttered, and retired to chatter with two other maids
who were looking over the banisters at the time.

Well, Mr. Nobbs, the head porter began, when Albert
came running downstairs to see some visitors off, and to receive
her tips—well, Mr. Nobbs, how did you find your bed-fellow ?
Oh, he was all right, but I 'm not used to bed-fellows, and he
brought a flea with him, and it kept me awake ; and when I
did fall asleep, I slept so heavily that I was an hour late. I
hope he caught his train. But what is all this pother about
bed-fellows ? Albert asked herself, as she returned to her
landing. Page hasn't said anything, no, she 's said nothing,
for we are both in the same boat, and to tell on me would be to
tell on herself. I 'd never have believed if—Albert's modesty
prevented her from finishing the sentence. She 's a woman
right enough. But the cheek of it, to marry an innocent
girl ! Did she let the girl into the secret, or leave her to
find it out when—— The girl might have called in the police !
This was a question one might ponder on, and by luncheon
time Albert was inclined to believe that Hubert told his wife
before—— She couldn't have had the cheek to wed her,
Albert said, without warning her that things might not turn
out as she fancied. Mayhap, Albert continued, she didn't
tell her before they wedded and mayhap she did, and being
one of them like myself that isn't always hankering after
a man she was glad to live with Hubert for companionship.
Albert tried to remember the exact words that Hubert had
used. It seemed to her that Hubert had said that she lived
with a girl first and wedded her to put a stop to people's
scandal. Of course they could hardly live together except
as man and wife. She remembered Hubert saying that she
always returned home with a light heart and never left it
without a heavy one. So it would seem that this marriage
was as successful as any and a great deal more than most.

At that moment 35 rang his bell. Albert hurried to answer
it, and it was not till late in the evening, between nine and
ten o'clock, when the guests were away at the theatres and

concerts and nobody was about but two maids, that Albert,
with her napkin over her shoulder, dozed and meditated on
the advice that Hubert had given her. She should marry,
Hubert had said ; Hubert had married. Of course it wasn't
a real marriage, it couldn't be that, but a very happy one it
would seem. But the girl must have understood that she
was not marrying a man. Did Hubert tell her before wedding
her or after, and what were the words ? She would have
liked to know the words : For after all I 've worked hard,
she said, and her thoughts melted away into meditation of
what her life had been for the last five-and-twenty years, a
mere drifting, it seemed to her, from one hotel to another,
without friends ; meeting, it is true, sometimes men and
women who seemed willing to be friendly. But her secret
forced her to live apart from men as well as women ; the
clothes she wore smothered the woman in her ; she no longer
thought and felt as she used to when she wore petticoats,
and she didn't think and feel like a man though she wore
trousers. What was she ? Nothing, neither man nor woman,
so small wonder she was lonely. But Hubert had put off her
sex, so she said. . . . Albert turned over in her mind the
possibility that a joke had been put upon her, and fell to
thinking what Hubert's home might be like, and was vexed
with herself for not having asked if she had a clock and vases on
the chimney-piece. One of the maids called from the end of
the passage, and when Albert received 54's order and executed
it, she returned to her seat in the passage, her napkin over
her shoulder, and resumed her reverie. It seemed to her
that Hubert once said that her wife was a milliner ; Hubert
may not have spoken the word milliner ; but if she hadn't,
it was strange that the word should keep on coming up in her
mind. There was no reason why the wife shouldn't be a
milliner, and if that were so it was as likely as not that they
owned a house in some quiet, insignificant street, letting the
dining-room, back room and kitchen to a widow or to a pair
of widows. The drawing-room was the workroom and show-

room ; Page and his wife slept in the room above. On second thoughts it seemed to Albert that if the business were millinery it might be that Mrs. Page would prefer the ground floor for her showroom. A third and fourth distribution of the ' premises ' presented itself to Albert's imagination. On thinking the matter over again it seemed to her that Hubert did not speak of a millinery business but of a seamstress, and if that were so, a small dressmaker's business in a quiet street would be in keeping with all Hubert had said about the home. Albert was not sure, however, that if she found a girl willing to share her life with her, it would be a seamstress's business she would be on the look-out for. She thought that a sweet-meat shop, newspapers and tobacco, would be her choice.

Why shouldn't she make a fresh start ? Hubert had no difficulties. She had said—Albert could recall the very words —I didn't mean you should marry a man, but a girl. Albert had saved, oh ! how she had tried to save, for she didn't wish to end her days in the workhouse. She had saved up-wards of five hundred pounds, which was enough to purchase a little business, and her heart dilated as she thought of her two successful investments in house property. In six months' time she hoped to have six hundred pounds, and if it took her two years to find a partner and a business, she would have at least seventy or eighty pounds more, which would be a great help, for it would be a mistake to put one's money into a falling business. If she found a partner, she 'd have to do like Hubert ; for marriage would put a stop to all tittle-tattle ; she 'd be able to keep her place at Morrison's Hotel, or perhaps leave Morrison's and rely on jobs ; and with her connection it would be a case of picking and choosing the best : ten and sixpence a night, nothing under. She dreamed of a round. Belfast, Liverpool, Manchester, Bradford, rose up in her imagination, and after a month's absence, a couple of months maybe, she would return home, her heart anticipating a welcome—a real welcome, for though she would continue to be a man to the world, she would be a woman to the dear

one at home. With a real partner, one whose heart was in
the business, they might make as much as two hundred
pounds a year—four pounds a week! And with four pounds
a week their home would be as pretty and happy as any in
the city of Dublin. Two rooms and a kitchen were what she
foresaw. The furniture began to creep into her imagination
little by little. A large sofa by the fireplace covered with
a chintz! But chintz dirtied quickly in the city; a dark
velvet sofa might be more suitable. It would cost a great
deal of money, five or six pounds; and at that rate fifty
pounds wouldn't go very far, for they must have a fine
double-bed mattress; and if they were going to do things
in that style, the home would cost them eighty pounds.
With luck these eighty pounds could be earned within the
next two years at Morrison's Hotel.

Albert ran over in her mind the tips she had received. The
people in 34 were leaving to-morrow; they were always good
for half a sovereign, and she decided then and there that
to-morrow's half-sovereign must be put aside as a beginning
of a sum of money for the purchase of a clock to stand on a
marble chimney-piece or a mahogany chiffonier. A few
days after she got a sovereign from a departing guest, and
it revealed a pair of pretty candlesticks and a round mirror.
Here tips were no longer mere white and yellow metal
stamped with the effigy of a dead king or a living queen,
but symbols of the future that awaited her. An unexpected
crown set her pondering on the colour of the curtains in their
sitting-room, and Albert became suddenly conscious that a
change had come into her life: the show was the same—
carrying plates and dishes upstairs and downstairs, and taking
orders for drinks and cigars; but behind the show a new life
was springing up—a life strangely personal and associated
with the life without only in this much, that the life without
was now a vassal state paying tribute to the life within.
She wasn't as good a servant as heretofore. She knew it.
Certain absences of mind, that was all; and the servants

as they went by with their dusters began to wonder whatever Albert could be dreaming of.

It was about this time that the furnishing of the parlour at the back of the shop was completed, likewise that of the bedroom above the shop, and Albert had just entered on another dream—a dream of a shop with two counters, one at which cigars, tobacco, pipes and matches were sold, and at the other all kinds of sweetmeats, a shop with a door leading to her wife's parlour. A changing figure the wife was in Albert's imagination, turning from fair to dark, from plump to slender, but capturing her imagination equally in all her changes; sometimes she was accompanied by a child of three or four, a boy, the son of a dead man, for in one of her dreams Albert married a widow. In another and more frequent dream she married a woman who had transgressed the moral code and been deserted before the birth of her child. In this case it would be supposed that Albert had done the right thing, for after leading the girl astray he had made an honest woman of her. Albert would be the father in everybody's eyes except the mother's, and she hoped that the child's mother would outgrow all the memory of the accidental seed sown, as the saying runs, in a foolish five minutes. A child would be a pleasure to them both, and a girl in the family way appealed to her more than a widow; a girl that some soldier, the boot-boy, or the hotel porter, had gotten into trouble; and Albert kept her eyes and ears open, hoping to rescue from her precarious situation one of those unhappy girls that were always cropping up in Morrison's Hotel. Several had had to leave the hotel last year, but not one this year. But some revivalist meetings were going to be held in Dublin. Many of our girls attend them, and an unlucky girl will be in luck's way if we should run across one another. Her thoughts passed into a dream of the babe that would come into the world some three or four months after their marriage, her little soft hands and expressive eyes claiming their protection, asking for it. What matter whether she calls me father or mother ? They are but mere words that the lips speak, but love is in the heart and only love matters.

Now whatever can Albert be brooding ? an idle housemaid asked herself as she went by. Brooding a love-story ? Not likely. A marriage with some girl outside ? He isn't over-partial to any of us. That Albert was brooding something, that there was something on his mind, became the talk of the hotel, and soon after it came to be noticed that Albert was eager to avail himself of every excuse to absent himself from duty in the hotel. He had been seen in the smaller streets looking up at the houses. He had saved a good deal of money, and some of his savings were invested in house property, so it was possible that his presence in these streets might be explained by the supposition that he was investing new sums of money in house property, or, and it was the second suggestion that stimulated the imagination, that Albert was going to be married and was looking out for a house for his wife. He had been seen talking with Annie Watts ; but she was not in the family way after all, and despite her wistful eyes and gentle voice she was not chosen. Her heart is not in her work, Albert said ; she thinks only of when she can get out, and that isn't the sort for a shop, whereas Dorothy Keyes is a glutton for work; but Albert couldn't abide the tall, angular woman, built like a boy, with a neck like a swan's. Besides her unattractive appearance, her manner was abrupt. But Alice's small, neat figure and quick intelligence marked her out for the job. Alas ! Alice was hot-tempered. We should quarrel, Albert said, and picking up her napkin, which had slipped from her knee to the floor, she considered the maids on the floor above. A certain stateliness of figure and also of gait put the thought into her mind that Mary O'Brien would make an attractive shopwoman. But her second thoughts were that Mary O'Brien was a Papist, and the experience of Irish Protestants shows that Papists and Protestants don't mix.

She had just begun to consider the next housemaid, when a voice interrupted her musing. That lazy girl, Annie Watts, on the look-out for an excuse to chatter the time away instead of being about her work, were the words that crossed Albert's mind as she raised her eyes, and so unwelcoming were they that Annie in her nervousness began to hesitate and stammer, unable for the moment to find a subject, plunging at last, and rather awkwardly, into the news of the arrival of the new kitchen-maid, Helen Dawes, but never dreaming that the news could have any interest for Albert. To her surprise, Albert's eyes lighted up. Do you know her ? Annie asked. Know her ? Albert answered. No, I don't know her, but——— At that moment a bell rang. Oh, bother, Annie said, and while she moved away idling along the banisters, Albert hurried down the passage to enquire what No. 47 wanted, and to learn that he needed writing-paper and envelopes. He couldn't write with the pens the hotel furnished ; would Albert be so kind as to ask the page-boy to fetch some J's ? With pleasure, Albert said ; with pleasure. Would you like to have the writing-paper and envelopes before the boy returns with the pens, sir ? The visitor answered that the writing-paper and envelopes would be of no use to him till he had gotten the pens. With pleasure, sir ; with pleasure ; and whilst waiting for the page to return she passed through the swing doors and searched for a new face among the different young women passing to and fro between the white-aproned and white-capped chefs, bringing the dishes to the great zinc counter that divided the kitchen-maids and the scullions from the waiters. She must be here, she said, and returned again to the kitchen in the hope of meeting the new-comer, Helen Dawes, who, when she was found, proved to be very unlike the Helen Dawes of Albert's imagination. A thick-set, almost swarthy girl of three-and-twenty, rather under than above the medium height, with white, even teeth, but un-

fortunately protruding, giving her the appearance of a rabbit.
Her eyes seemed to be dark brown, but on looking into them
Albert discovered them to be grey-green, round eyes that
dilated and flashed wonderfully while she talked. Her face
lighted up ; and there was a vindictiveness in her voice that
appeared and disappeared ; Albert suspected her, and was
at once frightened and attracted. Vindictiveness in her
voice !   How could such a thing have come into my mind ?
she said a few days after. A more kindly girl it would be
difficult to find. How could I have been so stupid ? She
is one of those, Albert continued, that will be a success in
everything she undertakes ; and dreams began soon after
that the sweetstuff and tobacco shop could hardly fail to
prosper under her direction. Nobody could befool Helen, and
when I am away at work I shall feel certain that everything
will be all right at home. It 's a pity that she isn't in the
family way, for it would be pleasant to have a little one
running about the shop asking for lemon drops and to hear
him calling us father and mother. At that moment a strange
thought flitted across Albert's mind—after all, it wouldn't
matter much to her if Helen were to get into the family way
later ; of course, there would be the expense of the lying-in.
Her second thoughts were that women live happily enough
till a man comes between them, and that it would be safer
for her to forgo a child and choose an older woman. All the
same, she could not keep herself from asking Helen to walk
out with her, and the next time they met the words slipped
out of her mouth : I shall be off duty at three to-day, and if you
are not engaged—— I am off duty at three, Helen answered.
Are you engaged ? Albert asked. Helen hesitated, it being
the truth that she had been and was still walking out with
one of the scullions, and was not sure how he would look upon
her going out with another, even though that one was such
a harmless fellow as Albert Nobbs. Harmless in himself,
she thought, and with a very good smell of money rising out
of his pockets, very different from Joe, who seldom had a

train fare upon him. But she hankered after Joe, and wouldn't give Albert a promise until she had asked him. Wants to walk out with you ? Why, he has never been known to walk out with man, woman or child before. Well, that 's a good one ! I 'd like to know what he 's after, but I 'm not jealous ; you can go with him, there 's no harm in Albert. I 'm on duty : just go for a turn with him. Poke him up and see what he 's after, and take him into a sweetshop and bring back a box of chocolates. Do you like chocolates ? Helen asked, and her eyes flashing, she stood looking at Joe, who, thinking that her temper was rising, and wishing to quell it, asked hurriedly where she was going to meet him. At the corner, she answered. He is there already. Then be off, he said, and his tone grated. You wouldn't like me to keep him waiting ? Helen said. Oh, dear no, not for Joe, not for Joseph, if he knows it, the scullion replied, lilting the song.

Helen turned away hoping that none of the maids would peach upon her, and Albert's heart rejoiced at seeing her on the other side of the street waiting for the tram to go by before she crossed it. Were you afraid I wasn't coming ? she asked, and Albert, not being ready with words, answered shyly : Not very. A stupid answer this seemed to be to Helen, and it was in the hope of shuffling out of a tiresome silence that Albert asked her if she liked chocolates. Something under the tooth will help the time away, was the answer she got ; and they went in search of a sweetmeat shop, Albert thinking that a shilling or one and sixpence would see her through it. But in a moment Helen's eyes were all over the shop, and spying out some large pictured boxes, she asked Albert if she might have one, and it being their first day out, Albert answered : Yes ; but could not keep back the words : I 'm afraid they 'd cost a lot. For these words Albert got a contemptuous look, and Helen shook her shoulders so disdainfully that Albert pressed a second box on Helen—one to pass the time with, another to take home. To such a show of goodwill Helen felt she must respond, and her tongue rattled on pleasantly as she walked, crunching the chocolates, two between each lamp-post, Albert stinting herself to one, which she sucked slowly, hardly enjoying it at all, so worried was she by the loss of three and sixpence. As if Helen guessed the cause of Albert's disquiet, she called on her suitor to admire the damsel on the box, but Albert could not disengage her thoughts sufficiently from Helen's expensive tastes. If every walk were to cost three and sixpence there wouldn't be a lot left for the home in six months' time. And she fell to calculating how much it would cost her if they were to walk out once a week. Three fours are twelve and four sixpences are two shillings, fourteen shillings a month, twice that is twenty-eight; twenty-eight shillings a month, that is if Helen wanted two boxes a week. At this rate she'd be spending sixteen pounds sixteen shillings a year. Lord amassy! But perhaps Helen wouldn't want two boxes of chocolates every time they went out together—— If she didn't, she'd want other things, and catching sight of a jeweller's shop, Albert called Helen's attention to a cyclist that had only just managed to escape a tram car by a sudden wriggle. But Albert was always unlucky. Helen had been wishing this long while for a bicycle, and if she did not ask Albert to buy her one it was because another jeweller's came into view. She stopped to gaze, and for a moment Albert's heart seemed to stand still, but Helen continued her chocolates, secure in her belief that the time had not yet come for substantial presents.

At Sackville Street bridge she would have liked to turn back, having little taste for the meaner parts of the city, but Albert wished to show her the north side, and she began to wonder what he could find to interest him in these streets, and why he should stand in admiration before all the small newspaper and tobacco shops, till she remembered suddenly that he had invested his savings in house property. Could these be his houses? All his own? and, moved by this consideration, she gave a more attentive ear to Albert's account of the daily takings of these shops, calculating that he was a richer man than anybody believed him to be, but a mean one. The idea of his thinking twice about a box of chocolates ! I 'll show him ! and coming upon a big draper's shop in Sackville Street she asked him for a pair of six-button gloves. She needed a parasol and some shoes and stockings, and a silk kerchief would not be amiss, and at the end of the third month of their courtship it seemed to her that the time had come for her to speak of bangles, saying that for three pounds she could have a pretty one—one that would be a real pleasure to wear ; it would always remind her of him. Albert coughed up with humility, and Helen felt that she had ' got him,' as she put it to herself, and afterwards to Joe Mackins. So he parted easily, Joe remarked, and pushing Helen aside he began to whip up the *rémoulade*, that had begun to show signs of turning, saying he 'd have the chef after him. But I say, old girl, since he 's coughing up so easily you might bring me something back ; and a briar-wood pipe and a pound or two of tobacco seemed the least she might obtain for him. And Helen answered that to get these she would have to ask Albert for money. And why shouldn't you ? Joe returned. Ask him for a thin 'un, and mayhap he 'll give you a thick 'un. It 's the first quid that 's hard to get ; every time after it 's like shelling peas. Do you think he 's that far gone on me ? Helen asked. Well, don't you ? Why should he give you these things if he wasn't ? Joe answered. Joe asked her of what she was thinking, and she replied that it was hard to say : she had walked out with many a man before but never with one like Albert Nobbs. In what way is he different ? Joe asked. Helen was perplexed in her telling of Albert Nobbs' slackness. You mean that he doesn't pull you about, Joe rapped out ; and she answered that there was something of that in it. All the same, she continued, that isn't the whole of it. I 've been out before with men that didn't pull me about, but he seems to have something on his mind, and half the time he 's thinking. Well, what does it matter, Joe asked, so

long as there is coin in the pocket and so long as you have
a hand to pull it out ?   Helen didn't like this description of
Albert Nobbs' courtship, and the words rose to her lips to
tell Joseph that she didn't want to go out any more with
Albert, that she was tired of her job, but the words were
quelled on her lips by a remark from Joe. Next time you
go out with him work him up a bit and see what he is made
of ; just see if there 's a sting in him or if he is no better than
a capon. A capon ! and what is a capon ? she asked. A
capon is a cut fowl. He may be like one. You think that,
do you ? she answered, and resolved to get the truth of the
matter next time they went out together. It did seem odd
that Albert should be willing to buy presents and not want
to kiss her. In fact, it was more than odd. It might be as
Joe had said. I might as well go out with my mother.
Now what did it all mean ? Was it a blind ? Some other
girl that he—— Not being able to concoct a sufficiently
reasonable story, Helen relinquished the attempt, without,
however, regaining control of her temper, which had begun
to rise, and which continued to boil up in her and overflow
until her swarthy face was almost ugly. I 'm beginning to
feel ugly towards him, she said to herself. He is either in
love with me or he 's—— And trying to discover his purpose,
she descended the staircase, saying to herself : Now Albert
must know that I 'm partial to Joe Mackins. It can't be
that he doesn't suspect. Well, I 'm damned.

IV

But Helen's perplexity on leaving the hotel was no greater
than Albert's as she stood waiting by the kerb. She knew
that Helen carried on with Joe Mackins, and she also knew
that Joe Mackins had nothing to offer Helen but himself.
She even suspected that some of the money she had given
to Helen had gone to purchase pipes and tobacco for Joe :
a certain shrewdness is not inconsistent with innocence, and
it didn't trouble her much that Helen was perhaps having

her fling with Joe Mackins. She didn't want Helen to fall
into evil ways, but it was better for her to have her fling
before than after marriage. On the other hand, a woman
that had been bedded might be dissatisfied to settle down
with another woman, though the home offered her was
better than any she could get from a man. She might
hanker for children, which was only natural, and Albert
felt that she would like a child as well as another. A child
might be arranged for if Helen wanted one, but it would
never do to have the father hanging about the shop : he
would have to be got rid of as soon as Helen was in the family
way. But could he be got rid of ? Not very easily if Joe
Mackins was the father ; she foresaw trouble and would
prefer another father, almost any other. But why trouble
herself about the father of Helen's child before she knew
whether Helen would send Joe packing ? which she 'd have
to do clearly if they were to wed—she and Helen. Their
wedding was what she had to look to, whether she should
confide her sex to Helen to-night or wait. Why not to-night
as well as to-morrow night ? she asked herself. But how
would she tell it to Helen ? Blurt it out—I 've something
to tell you, Helen. I 'm not a man, but a woman like yourself.
No, that wouldn't do. How did Hubert tell her wife she was
a woman ? If she had only asked she 'd have been spared
all this trouble. After hearing Hubert's story she should
have said : I 've something to ask you ; but sleep was so
heavy on their eyelids that they couldn't think any more
and both of them were falling asleep, which wasn't to be
wondered at, for they had been talking for hours. It was
on her mind to ask how her wife found out. Did Hubert
tell her or did the wife—— Albert's modesty prevented
her from pursuing the subject ; and she turned on herself,
saying that she could not leave Helen to find out she was a
woman ; of that she was certain, and of that only. She 'd
have to tell Helen that. But should the confession come
before they were married, or should she reserve it for the

F

wedding night in the bridal chamber on the edge of the bed
afterwards ? If it were not for Helen's violent temper——
I in my nightshirt, she in her nightgown. On the other
hand, she might quieten down after an outburst and begin
to see that it might be very much to her advantage to accept
the situation, especially if a hope were held out to her of a
child by Joe Mackins in two years' time ; she 'd have to
agree to wait till then, and in two years Joe would probably
be after another girl. But if she were to cut up rough and
do me an injury ! Helen might call the neighbours in, or
the policeman, who 'd take them both to the station. She 'd
have to return to Liverpool or to Manchester. She didn't
know what the penalty would be for marrying one of her own
sex. And her thoughts wandered on to the morning boat.

One of the advantages of Dublin is that one can get out
of it as easily as any other city. Steamers were always
leaving, morning and evening ; she didn't know how many,
but a great many. On the other hand, if she took the straight
course and confided her sex to Helen before the marriage,
Helen might promise not to tell ; but she might break her
promise ; life in Morrison's Hotel would be unendurable, and
she 'd have to endure it. What a hue and cry ! But one
way was as bad as the other. If she had only asked Hubert
Page ! but she hadn't a thought at the time of going to do
likewise. What 's one man's meat is another man's poison,
and she began to regret Hubert's confession to her. If it
hadn't been for that flea she wouldn't be in this mess ; and
she was deep in it ! Three months' company isn't a day,
and everybody in Morrison's Hotel asking whether she or
Joe Mackins would be the winner, urging her to make haste
else Joe would come with a rush at the finish. A lot of
racing talk that she didn't understand—or only half. If
she could get out of this mess somehow—— But it was too
late. She must go through with it. But how ? A different
sort of girl altogether was needed, but she liked Helen.
Her way of standing on a doorstep, her legs a little apart,

jawing a tradesman, and she 'd stand up to Mrs. Baker and
to the chef himself.   She liked the way Helen's eyes lighted
up when a thought came into her mind ;   her cheery laugh
warmed Albert's heart as nothing else did.   Before she met
Helen she often feared her heart was growing cold.   She
might try the world over and not find one that would run the
shop she had in mind as well as Helen.   But the shop wouldn't
wait ;   the owners of the shop would withdraw their offer if
it was not accepted before next Monday.   And to-day is
Friday, Albert said to herself.   This evening or never.
To-morrow Helen 'll be on duty all day ;   on Sunday she 'll
contrive some excuse to get out to meet Joe Mackins.   After
all, why not this evening ?   for what must be had better be
faced bravely ;   and while the tram rattled down the long
street, Rathmines Avenue, past the small houses atop of
high steps, pretty boxes with ornamental trees in the garden,
some with lawns, with here and there a more substantial
house set in the middle of three or four fields at least, Albert
meditated, plan after plan rising up in her mind ;   and when
the car turned to the right and then to the left and proceeded
at a steady pace up the long incline, Rathgar Avenue, Albert's
courage was again at ebb.   All the subterfuges she had
woven—the long discussion in which she would maintain that
marriage should not be considered as a sexual adventure, but
a community of interests—seemed to have lost all significance ;
the points that had seemed so convincing in Rathmines
Avenue were forgotten in Rathgar Avenue, and at Terenure
she came to the conclusion that there was no use trying to
think the story out beforehand ;   she would have to adapt
her ideas to the chances that would arise as they talked
under the trees in the dusk in a comfortable hollow, where
they could lie at length out of hearing of the other lads and
lasses whom they would find along the banks, resting after
the labour of the day in dim contentment, vaguely conscious
of each other, satisfied with a vague remark, a kick or a push.

It was the hope that the river's bank would tempt him into

confidence that had suggested to Helen that they might spend the evening by the Dodder. Albert had welcomed the suggestion, feeling sure that if there was a place in the world that would make the telling of her secret easy it was the banks of the Dodder ; and she was certain she would be able to speak it in the hollow under the ilex-trees. But speech died from her lips, and the silence round them seemed sinister and foreboding. She seemed to dread the river flowing over its muddy bottom, without ripple or eddy ; and she started when Helen asked her of what she was thinking. Albert answered : Of you, dear ; and how pleasant it is to be sitting with you. On these words the silence fell again, and Albert tried to speak, but her tongue was too thick in her mouth ; she felt like choking, and the silence was not broken for some seconds, each seeming a minute. At last a lad's voice was heard : I 'll see if you have any lace on your drawers ; and the lass answered : You shan't. There 's a pair that 's enjoying themselves, Helen said, and she looked upon the remark as fortunate, and hoped it would give Albert the courage to pursue his courtship. Albert, too, looked upon the remark as fortunate, and she tried to ask if there was lace on all women's drawers ; and meditated a reply that would lead her into a confession of her sex. But the words : It 's so long since I 've worn any, died on her lips ; and instead of speaking these words she spoke of the Dodder, saying : What a pity it isn't nearer Morrison's. Where would you have it ? Helen replied—flowing down Sackville Street into the Liffey ? We should be lying there as thick as herrings, without room to move, or we should be unable to speak to each other without being overheard. I dare say you are right, Albert answered, and she was so frightened that she added : But we have to be back at eleven o'clock, and it takes an hour to get there. We can go back now if you like, Helen rapped out. Albert apologised, and hoping that something would happen to help her out of her difficulty, she began to represent Morrison's Hotel as being on the whole advantageous to servants. But Helen did not respond. She seems to be getting angrier and angrier, Albert said to herself, and she asked, almost in despair, if the Dodder was pretty all the way down to the sea. And remembering a walk with Joe, Helen answered : There are woods as far as Dartry—the Dartry Dye Works, don't you know them ? But I don't think there are any very pretty spots. You know Ring's End, don't you ? Albert said she had been there once ; and Helen spoke of a large three-masted vessel that she had seen some Sundays ago by the quays. You were there with Joe Mackins, weren't you ? Well, what if I was ? Only this, Albert answered, that I don't think it is usual for a girl to keep company with two chaps, and I thought—— Now, what did you think ? Helen said. That you didn't care for me well enough—— For what ? she asked. You know we 've been going out for three months, and it doesn't seem natural to keep talking always, never wanting to put your arm round a girl's waist. I suppose Joe isn't like me, then ? Albert asked ; and Helen laughed, a scornful little laugh. But, Albert went on, isn't the time for kissing when one is wedded ? This is the first time you 've said anything about marriage, Helen rapped out. But I thought there had always been an understanding between us, said Albert, and it 's only now I can tell you what I have to offer. The words were well chosen. Tell me about it, Helen said, her eyes and voice revealing her cupidity to Albert, who continued all the same to unfold her plans, losing herself in details that bored Helen, whose thoughts returned to the dilemma she was in—to refuse Albert's offer or to break with Joe ; and that she should be obliged to do either one or the other was a disappointment to her. All you say about the shop is right enough, but it isn't a very great compliment to a girl. What, to ask her to marry ? Albert interjected. Well, no, not if you haven't kissed her first. Don't speak so loud, Albert whispered ; I 'm sure that couple heard what you said, for they went away laughing. I don't care whether they laughed or cried, Helen answered. You don't want to kiss me, do you ? and I don't want to marry a man who isn't in love with me. But I do want to kiss you, and Albert bent down and kissed Helen on both cheeks. Now you can't say I haven't kissed you, can you ? You don't call that kissing, do you ? Helen asked. But how do you wish me to kiss you, Helen ? Well, you are an innocent ! she said, and she kissed Albert vindictively. Helen, leave go of me ; I 'm not used to such kisses. Because you 're not in love, Helen replied. In love ? Albert repeated. I loved my old nurse very much, but I never wished to kiss her like that. At this Helen exploded with laughter. So you put me in the same class with your old nurse ! Well, after that ! Come, she said, taking pity upon Albert for a moment, are you or are you not in love with me ? I love you deeply, Helen, Albert said. Love ? she repeated : the men who have walked out with me were in love with me—— In love, Albert repeated after her. I 'm sure I love you. I like men to be in love with me, she answered. But that 's like an animal, Helen. Whatever put all that muck in your head ? I 'm going home, she replied, and rose to her feet and started out on the path leading across the darkening fields. You 're not angry with me, Helen ? Angry ? No, I 'm not angry with you ; you 're a fool of a man, that 's all. But if you think me a fool of a man, why did you come out this evening to sit under those trees ? And why have we been keeping company for the last three months, Albert continued, going out together every week ? You didn't always think me a fool of a man, did you ? Yes, I did, she answered ; and Albert asked Helen for a reason for choosing her company. Oh, you bother me asking reasons for everything, Helen said. But why did you make me love you ? Albert asked. Well, if I did, what of it ? and as for walking out with you, you won't have to complain of that any more. You don't mean, Helen, that we are never going to walk out again ? Yes, I do, she said sullenly. You mean that for the future you 'll be walking out with Joe Mackins, Albert lamented. That 's my business, she answered. By this time they were by the stile at the end of the field, and in the next field there was a hedge to get through and a wood, and the little path they followed was full of such vivid remembrances that Albert could not believe that she was treading it with Helen for the last time, and besought Helen to take back the words that she would never walk out with her again.

The tram was nearly empty and they sat at the far end, close together, Albert beseeching Helen not to cast her off. If I 've been stupid to-day, Albert pleaded, it 's because I 'm tired of the work in the hotel ; I shall be different when we get to Lisdoonvarna : we both want a change of air ; there 's nothing like the salt water and the cliffs of Clare to put new spirits into a man. You will be different and I 'll be different ; everything will be different. Don't say no, Helen ; don't say no. I 've looked forward to this week in Lisdoonvarna, and Albert urged the expense of the lodgings she had already engaged. We shall have to pay for the lodgings ; and there 's the new suit of clothes that has just come back from the tailor's ; I 've looked forward to wearing it, walking with you in the strand, the waves crashing up into cliffs, with green fields among them, I 've been told ! We shall see the ships passing and wonder whither they are going. I 've bought three neck-ties and some new shirts, and what good will these be to me if you 'll not come to Lisdoonvarna with me ? The lodgings will have to be paid for, a great deal of money, for I said in my letter we shall want two bedrooms. But there need only be one bedroom ; but perhaps I shouldn't have spoken like that. Oh, don't talk to me about Lisdoonvarna, Helen answered. I 'm not going to Lisdoonvarna with you. But what is to become of the hat I have ordered for you ? Albert asked ; the hat with the big feather in it ; and I 've bought stockings and shoes for you. Tell me, what shall I do with these, and with the gloves ? Oh, the waste of money and the heart-breaking! What shall I do with the hat? Albert repeated. Helen didn't answer at once. Presently she said: You can leave the hat with me. And the stockings? Albert asked. Yes, you can leave the stockings. And the shoes? Yes, you can leave the shoes too. Yet you won't go to Lisdoonvarna with me? No, she said, I'll not go to Lisdoonvarna with you. But you'll take the presents? It was to please you I said I would take them, because I thought it would be some satisfaction to you to know that they wouldn't be wasted. Not wasted? Albert repeated. You'll wear them when you go out with Joe Mackins. Oh, well, keep your presents. And then the dispute took a different turn, and was continued until they stepped out of the tram at the top of Dawson Street. Albert continued to plead all the way down Dawson Street, and when they were within twenty yards of the hotel, and she saw Helen passing away from her for ever into the arms of Joe Mackins, she begged Helen not to leave her. We cannot part like this, she cried; let us walk up and down the street from Nassau Street to Clare Street, so that we may talk things over and do nothing foolish. You see, Albert began, I had set my heart on driving on an outside car to the Broadstone with you, and catching a train, and the train going into lovely country, arriving at a place we had never seen, with cliffs, and the sunset behind the cliffs. You've told all that before, Helen said, and, she rapped out, I'm not going to Lisdoonvarna with you. And if that is all you had to say to me we might have gone into the hotel. But there's much more, Helen. I haven't told you about the shop yet. Yes, you have told me all there is to tell about the shop; you've been talking about that shop for the last three months. But, Helen, it was only yesterday that I got a letter saying that they had had another offer for the shop, and that they could give me only till Monday morning to close with them; if the lease isn't signed by then we've lost the shop. But do you think, Helen asked, that the shop

will be a success ?   Many shops promise well in the beginning
and fade away till they don't get a customer a day.   Our
shop won't be like that, I know it won't ; and Albert began
an appraisement of the shop's situation and the custom it
commanded in the neighbourhood and the possibility of
developing that custom.   We shall be able to make a great
success of that shop, and people will be coming to see us, and
they will be having tea with us in the parlour, and they 'll
envy us, saying that never have two people had such luck
as we have had.   And our wedding will be—— Will be
what ?   Helen asked.   Will be a great wonder.   A great
wonder indeed, she replied, but I 'm not going to wed you,
Albert Nobbs, and now I see it 's beginning to rain.   I can't
remain out any longer.   You 're thinking of your hat ; I 'll
buy another.   We may as well say good-bye, she answered,
and Albert saw her going towards the doorway.   She 'll
see Joe Mackins before she goes to her bed, and lie dreaming
of him ; and I shall lie awake in my bed, my thoughts flying
to and fro the livelong night, zigzagging up and down like
bats.   And then remembering that if she went into the
hotel she might meet Helen and Joe Mackins, she rushed
on with a hope in her mind that after a long walk round
Dublin she might sleep.

At the corner of Clare Street she met two women strolling
after a fare—ten shillings or a sovereign, which ? she asked
herself—and terrified by the shipwreck of all her hopes, she
wished she were one of them.   For they at least are women,
whereas I am but a perhapser—— In the midst of her grief
a wish to speak to them took hold of her.   But if I speak to
them they 'll expect me to—— All the same her steps
quickened, and as she passed the two street-walkers she
looked round, and one woman, wishing to attract her attention, said : It was almost a love dream.   Almost a love
dream ? Albert repeated.   What are you two women talking
about ? and the woman next to Albert said : My friend here

was telling me of a dream she had last night. A dream, and what was her dream about ? Albert asked. Kitty was telling me that she was better than a love dream ; now do you think she is, sir ? I 'll ask Kitty herself, Albert replied, and Kitty answered him : A shade. Only a shade, Albert returned, and as they crossed the street a gallant attached himself to Kitty's companion. Albert and Kitty were left together, and Albert asked her companion to tell her name. My name is Kitty MacCan, the girl replied. It 's odd we 've never met before, Albert replied, hardly knowing what she was saying. We 're not often this way, was the answer. And where do you walk usually—of an evening ? Albert asked. In Grafton Street or down by College Green ; sometimes we cross the river. To walk in Sackville Street, Albert interjected ; and she tried to lead the woman into a story of her life. But you 're not one of them, she said, that think that we should wash clothes in a nunnery for nothing ? I 'm a waiter in Morrison's Hotel. As soon as the name of Morrison's Hotel passed Albert's lips she began to regret having spoken about herself. But what did it matter now ? and the woman didn't seem to have taken heed of the name of the hotel. Is the money good in your hotel ? Kitty asked ; I 've heard that you get as much as half-a-crown for carrying up a cup of tea ; and her story dribbled out in remarks, a simple story that Albert tried to listen to, but her attention wandered, and Kitty, who was not unintelligent, began to guess Albert to be in the middle of some great grief. It doesn't matter about me, Albert answered her, and Kitty being a kind girl said to herself : If I can get him to come home with me I 'll help him out of his sorrow, if only for a little while. So she continued to try to interest him in herself till they came to Fitzwilliam Place ; and it was not till then that Kitty remembered she had only three and sixpence left out of the last money she had received, and that her rent would be due on the morrow. She daren't return home without a gentleman ; her landlady would be

at her ; and the best time of the night was going by talking
to a man who seemed like one who would bid her a curt
good-night at the door of his hotel. Where did he say his
hotel was ? she asked herself ; and then, aloud, she said :
You 're a waiter, aren't you ? I 've forgotten which hotel
you said. Albert didn't answer, and, troubled by her companion's silence, Kitty continued : I 'm afraid I 'm taking you
out of your way. No, you aren't ; all ways are the same to
me. Well, they aren't to me, she replied. I must get some
money to-night. I 'll give you some money, Albert said.
But won't you come home with me ? the girl asked. Albert
hesitated, tempted by her company. But if they were to
go home together her sex would be discovered. But what did
it matter if it were discovered ? Albert asked herself, and the
temptation came again to go home with this woman, to lie
in her arms and tell the story that had been locked up so
many years. They could both have a good cry together,
and what matter would it be to the woman as long as she
got the money she desired. She didn't want a man ; it was
money she was after, money that meant bread and board
to her. She seems a kind, nice girl, Albert said, and she was
about to risk the adventure when a man came by whom
Kitty knew. Excuse me, he said, and Albert saw them walk
away together. I 'm sorry, said the woman, returning, but
I 've just met an old friend ; another evening, perhaps.
Albert would have liked to put her hand in her pocket and
pay the woman with some silver for her company, but she
was already half-way back to her friend, who stood waiting
for her by the lamp-post. The street-walkers have friends,
and when they meet them their troubles are over for the
night ; but my chances have gone by me ; and, checking
herself in the midst of the irrelevant question, whether it
were better to be casual, as they were, or to have a husband
that you could not get rid of, she plunged into her own grief,
and walked sobbing through street after street, taking no
heed of where she was going.

Why, lord, Mr. Nobbs, whatever has kept you out until this hour ? the hall-porter muttered. I 'm sorry, she answered, and while stumbling up the stairs she remembered that even a guest was not received very amiably by the hall-porter after two ; and for a servant to come in at that time ! Her thoughts broke off and she lay too tired to think any more of the hall-porter, of herself, of anything. If she got an hour's sleep it was the most she got that night, and when the time came for her to go to her work she rose indifferently. But her work saved her from thinking, and it was not until the middle of the afternoon, when the luncheon-tables had been cleared, that the desire to see and to speak to Helen could not be put aside ; but Helen's face wore an ugly, forbidding look, and Albert returned to the second floor without speaking to her. It was not long after that 34 rang his bell, and Albert hoped to get an order that would send her to the kitchen. Are you going to pass me by without speaking again, Helen ? We talked enough last night, Helen retorted ; there 's nothing more to say, and Joe, in such disorder of dress as behooves a scullion, giggled as he went past, carrying a huge pile of plates. I loved my old nurse, but I never thought of kissing her like that, he said, turning on his heel and so suddenly that some of the plates fell with a great clatter. The ill luck that had befallen him seemed well deserved, and Albert returned upstairs and sat in the passages waiting for the sitting-rooms to ring their bells ; and the housemaids, as they came about the head of the stairs with their dusters, wondered how it was that they could not get any intelligible conversation out of the love-stricken waiter. Albert's lovelorn appearance checked their mirth, pity entered their hearts, and they kept back the words : I loved my old nurse, etc. After all, he loves the girl, one said to the other, and a moment after they were joined by another housemaid, who, after listening for a while, went away, saying : There 's no torment like the love torment ; and the three housemaids, Mary, Alice, and Dorothy, offered Albert their sympathy, trying to lead her into little talks with a view to withdrawing her from the contemplation of her own grief, for women are always moved by a love story. Before long their temper turned against Helen, and they often went by asking themselves why she should have kept company with Albert all these months if she didn't mean to wed him. No wonder the poor man was disappointed. He is destroyed with his grief, said one ; look at him, without any more colour in his face than is in my duster. Another said : He doesn't swallow a bit of food. And the third said : I poured out a glass of wine for him that was left over, but he put it away. Isn't love awful ? But what can he see in her ? another asked, a stumpy, swarthy woman, a little blackthorn bush and as full of prickles ; and the three women fell to thinking that Albert would have done better to have chosen one of them. The shop entered into the discussion soon after, and everybody was of opinion that Helen would live to regret her cruelty. The word cruelty did not satisfy ; treachery was mentioned, and somebody said that Helen's face was full of treachery. Albert will never recover himself as long as she's here, another remarked. He'll just waste away unless Miss Right comes along. He put all his eggs into one basket, a man said ; you see he'd never been known to walk out with a girl before. And what age do you think he is ? I put him down at forty-five, and when love takes a man at that age it takes him badly. This is no calf love, the man said, looking into the women's faces, and you'll never be able to mend matters, any of you ; and they all declared they didn't wish to, and dispersed in different directions, flicking their dusters and asking themselves if Albert would ever look at another woman.

It was felt generally that he would not have the courage to try again, which was indeed the case, for when it was suggested to Albert that a faint heart never wins a fair lady she answered that her spirit was broken. I shall boil my pot and carry my can, but the spring is broken in me ; and it was these words that were remembered and pondered, whereas the joke—I loved my old nurse, etc.—raised no laugh ; and the sympathy that Albert felt to be gathering about her cheered her on her way. She was no longer friendless ; almost any one of the women in the hotel would have married Albert out of pity for her. But there was no heart in Albert for another adventure ; nor any thought in her for anything but her work. She rose every morning and went forth to her work, and was sorry when her work was done, for she had come to dread every interval, knowing that as soon as she sat down to rest the old torment would begin again. Once more she would begin to think that she had nothing more to look forward to ; that her life would be but a round of work ; a sort of treadmill. She would never see Lisdoonvarna, and the shop with two counters, one at which tobacco, cigarettes and matches were sold, and at the other counter all kinds of sweetstuffs. Like Lisdoonvarna, it had passed away, it had only existed in her mind—a thought, a dream. Yet it had possessed her completely ; and the parlour behind the shop that she had furnished and re-furnished, hanging a round mirror above the mantelpiece, papering the walls with a pretty colourful paper that she had seen in Wicklow Street and had asked the man to put aside for her. She had hung curtains about the windows in her imagination, and had set two armchairs on either side of the hearth, one in green and one in red velvet, for herself and Helen. The parlour too had passed away like Lisdoon-varna, like the shop, a thought, a dream, no more. There had never been anything in her life but a few dreams, and henceforth there would be not even dreams. It was strange that some people came into the world lucky, and others, for no reason, unlucky ; she had been unlucky from her birth ; she was a bastard ; her parents were grand people whose name she did not know, who paid her nurse a hundred a year to keep her, and who died without making any pro-vision for her. She and her old nurse had to go and live in Temple Lane, and to go out charing every morning ;

Mr. Congreve had a French mistress, and if it hadn't been for Bessie Lawrence she might have thrown herself in the Thames ; she was very near to it that night, and if she had drowned herself all this worry and torment would have been over. She was more resolute in those days than she was now, and would have faced the river, but she shrank from this Dublin river, perhaps because it was not her own river. If one wishes to drown oneself it had better be in one's own country. But why is it a mistake ? For a perhapser like herself, all countries were the same ; go or stay, it didn't matter. Yes, it did ; she stayed in Dublin in the hope that Hubert Page would return to the hotel. Only to Hubert could she confide the misfortune that had befallen her, and she 'd like to tell somebody. The three might set up together. A happy family they might make. Two women in men's clothes and one in petticoats. If Hubert were willing. Hubert's wife might not be willing. But she might be dead and Hubert on the look-out for another helpmate. He had never been away so long before ; he might return any day. And from the moment that she foresaw herself as Hubert's future wife her life began to expand itself more eagerly than ever in watching for tips, collecting half-crowns, crowns and half-sovereigns. She must at least replace the money that she had spent giving presents to Helen, and as the months went by and the years, she remembered, with increasing bitterness, that she had wasted nearly twenty pounds on Helen, a cruel, heartless girl that had come into her life for three months and had left her for Joe Mackins. She took to counting her money in her room at night. The half-crowns were folded up in brown-paper packets, the half-sovereigns in blue, the rare sovereigns were in pink paper, and all these little packets were hidden away in different corners ; some were put in the chimney, some under the carpet. She often thought that these hoards would be safer in the Post Office Bank, but she who has nothing else likes to have her money with her, and a sense of almost happiness

awoke in her when she discovered herself to be again as rich
as she was before she met Helen. Richer by twenty-five
pounds twelve and sixpence, she said, and her eyes roved
over the garret floor in search of a plank that might be lifted.
One behind the bed was chosen, and henceforth Albert slept
securely over her hoard, or lay awake thinking of Hubert,
who might return, and to whom she might confide the story
of her misadventure ; but as Hubert did not return her
wish to see him faded, and she began to think that it might
be just as well if he stayed away, for, who knows ? a wandering fellow like him might easily run out of his money and return
to Morrison's Hotel to borrow from her, and she wasn't going
to give her money to be spent for the benefit of another
woman. The other woman was Hubert's wife. If Hubert
came back he might threaten to publish her secret if she
didn't give him money to keep it. An ugly thought, of
which she was ashamed and which she tried to keep out of
her mind. But as time went on a dread of Hubert took possession of her. After all, Hubert knew her secret, and somehow it didn't occur to her that in betraying her secret Hubert
would be betraying his own. Albert didn't think as clearly
as she used to ; and one day she answered Mrs. Baker in
a manner that Mrs. Baker did not like. Whilst speaking
to Albert the thought crossed Mrs. Baker's mind that it was
a long while since they had seen the painter. I cannot
think, she said, what has become of Hubert Page ; we 've
not had news of him for a long time ; have you heard from
him, Albert ? Why should you think, ma'am, that I hear
from him ? I only asked, Mrs. Baker replied, and she heard
Albert mumbling something about a wandering fellow, and
the tone in which the words were spoken was disrespectful,
and Mrs. Baker began to consider Albert ; and though a
better servant now than he had ever been in some respects,
he had developed a fault which she didn't like, a way of
hanging round the visitor as he was preparing to leave the
hotel that almost amounted to persecution. Worse than

that, a rumour had reached her that Albert's service was measured according to the tip he expected to receive. She didn't believe it, but if it were true she would not hesitate to have him out of the hotel in spite of the many years he had spent with them. Another thing : Albert was liked, but not by everybody. The little red-headed boy on the second floor told me, Mrs. Baker said (her thoughts returning to last Sunday, when she had taken the child out to Bray), that he was afraid of Albert, and he confided to me that Albert had tried to pick him up and kiss him. Why can't he leave the child alone ? Can't he see the child doesn't like him ?

But the Bakers were kind-hearted proprietors, and could not keep sentiment out of their business, and Albert remained at Morrison's Hotel till she died.

An easy death I hope it was, your honour, for if any poor creature deserved an easy one it was Albert herself. You think so, Alec, meaning that the disappointed man suffers less at parting with this world than the happy one ? Maybe you 're right. That is as it may be, your honour, he answered, and I told him that Albert awoke one morning hardly able to breathe, and returned to bed and lay there almost speechless till the maid-servant came to make the bed. She ran off again to fetch a cup of tea, and after sipping it Albert said that she felt better. But she never roused completely, and the maid-servant who came up in the evening with a bowl of soup did not press her to try to eat it, for it was plain that Albert could not eat or drink, and it was almost plain that she was dying, but the maid-servant did not like to alarm the hotel and contented herself with saying : He 'd better see the doctor to-morrow. She was up betimes in the morning, and on going to Albert's room she found the waiter asleep, breathing heavily. An hour later Albert was dead, and everybody was asking how a man who was in good health on Tuesday could be a corpse on Thursday morning, as if such a thing had never happened before. However often it had happened, it did not seem natural, and it was whispered that

G

Albert might have made away with himself. Some spoke of apoplexy, but apoplexy in a long, thin man is not usual ; and when the doctor came down his report that Albert was a woman put all thought of the cause of death out of everybody's mind. Never before or since was Morrison's Hotel agog as it was that morning, everybody asking the other why Albert had chosen to pass herself off as a man, and how she had succeeded in doing this year after year without any one of them suspecting her. She would be getting better wages as a man than as a woman, somebody said, but nobody cared to discuss the wages question ; all knew that a man is better paid than a woman. But what Albert would have done with Helen if Helen hadn't gone off with Joe Mackins stirred everybody's imagination. What would have happened on the wedding night ? Nothing, of course ; but how would she have let on ? The men giggled over their glasses, and the women pondered over their cups of tea ; the men asked the women and the women asked the men, and the interest in the subject had not quite died down when Hubert Page returned to Morrison's Hotel, in the spring of the year, with her paint pots and brushes. How is Albert Nobbs.? was one of her first enquiries, and it fired the train. Albert Nobbs ! Don't you know ? How should I know ? Hubert Page replied. I 've only just come back to Dublin. What is there to know ? Don't you ever read the papers ? Read the papers ? Hubert repeated. Then you haven't heard that Albert Nobbs is dead ? No, I haven't heard of it. I 'm sorry for him, but after all, men die ; there 's nothing wonderful in that, is there ? No ; but if you had read the papers you 'd have learnt that Albert Nobbs wasn't a man at all. Albert Nobbs was a woman. Albert Nobbs a woman ! Hubert replied, putting as much surprise as she could into her voice. So you never heard ? And the story began to fall out from different sides, everybody striving to communicate bits to her, until at last she said : If you all speak together, I shall never understand it. Albert Nobbs a woman !

A woman as much as you 're a man, was the answer, and the story of her courtship of Helen, and Helen's preference for Joe Mackins, and Albert's grief at Helen's treatment of her trickled into a long relation. The biggest deception in the whole world, a scullion cried from his saucepans. Whatever would she have done with Helen if they had married ? But the question had been asked so often that it fell flat. So Helen went away with Joe Mackins ? Hubert said. Yes ; and they don't seem to get on over well together. Serve her right for her unkindness, cried a kitchen-maid. But after all, you wouldn't want her to marry a woman ? a scullion answered. Of course not ; of course not. The story was taken up by another voice, and the hundreds of pounds that Albert had left behind in many securities were multiplied ; nearly a hundred in ready money rolled up in paper, half-crowns, half-sovereigns and sovereigns in his bedroom ; his bedroom—her bedroom, I mean ; but we are so used to thinking of her as a him that we find it difficult to say her ; we 're always catching each other up. But what I 'm thinking of, said a waiter, is the waste of all that money. A great scoop it was for the Government, eight hundred pounds. The pair were to have bought a shop and lived together, Mr. Page, Annie Watts rapped out, and when the discussion was carried from the kitchen upstairs to the second floor : True for you, said Dorothy, now you mention it, I remember ; it 's you that should be knowing better than anybody else, Mr. Page, what Albert's sex was like. Didn't you sleep with her ? I fell asleep the moment my head was on the pillow, Page answered, for if you remember rightly I was that tired Mrs. Baker hadn't the heart to turn me out of the hotel. I 'd been working ten, twelve, fourteen hours a day, and when he took me up to his room I tore off my clothes and fell asleep, and went away in the morning before he was awake. Isn't it wonderful ? A woman, Hubert continued, and a minx in the bargain, and an artful minx if ever there was one in the world, and there have been a

good many. And now, ladies, I must be about my work.
I wonder what Annie Watts was thinking of when she stood
looking into my eyes ; does she suspect me ? Hubert asked
herself as she sat on her derrick. And what a piece of bad
luck that I shouldn't have found Albert alive when I returned
to Dublin.

You see, Alec, this is how it was. Polly, that was Hubert's
wife, died six months before Albert ; and Hubert had been
thinking ever since of going into partnership with Albert.
In fact Hubert had been thinking about a shop, like Albert,
saying to herself almost every day after the death of her wife :
Albert and I might set up together. But it was not until
she lay in bed that she fell to thinking the matter out, saying
to herself : One of us would have had to give up our job to
attend to it. The shop was Albert's idea more than mine,
so perhaps she 'd have given up waiting, which would not
have suited me, for I 'm tired of going up these ladders.
My head isn't altogether as steady as it used to be ; swinging
about on a derrick isn't suited to women. So perhaps it 's
as well that things have fallen out as they have. Hubert
turned herself over, but sleep was far from her, and she lay
a long time thinking of everything and of nothing in particular, as we all do in our beds, with this thought often
uppermost : I wonder what is going to be the end of my life.
What new chance do the years hold for me ?

And of what would Hubert be thinking, being a married
woman ? Of what else should she be thinking but of her
husband, who might now be a different man from the one she
left behind ? Fifteen years, she said, makes a great difference
in all of us, and perhaps it was the words, fifteen years, that
put the children she had left behind her back into her thought.
I wouldn't be saying that she hadn't been thinking of them,
off and on, in the years gone by, but the thought of them was
never such a piercing thought as it was that night. She 'd
have liked to have jumped out of her bed and run away to
them ; and perhaps she would have done if she only knew

where they were. But she didn't, so she had to keep to her bed ; and she lay for an hour or more thinking of them as little children, and wondering what they were like now. Lily was five when she left home. She 's a young woman now. Agnes was only two. She is now seventeen, still a girl, Hubert said to herself ; but Lily's looking round, thinking of young men, and the other won't be delaying much longer, for young women are much more wide-awake than they used to be in the old days. The rest of my life belongs to them. Their father could have looked after them till now ; but now they are thinking of young men he won't be able to cope with them, and maybe he 's wanting me too. Bill is forty, and at forty we begin to think of them as we knew them long ago. He must have often thought of me, perhaps oftener than I thought of him ; and she was surprised to find that she had forgotten all Bill's ill-usage, and remembered only the good time she had had with him. The rest of my life belongs to him, she said, and to the girls. But how am I to get back to him ? how, indeed ? . . . Bill may be dead ; the children too. But that isn't likely. I must get news of them somehow. The house is there ; and lying in the darkness she recalled the pictures on the wall, the chairs that she had sat in, the coverlets on the beds, everything. Bill isn't a wanderer, she said ; I 'll find him in the same house if he isn't dead. And the children ? Did they know anything about her ? Had Bill spoken ill of her to them ? She didn't think he would do that. But did they want to see her ? Well, she could never find that out except by going to see. But how was she going to return home ? Pack up her things and go dressed as a man to the house and, meeting Bill on the threshold, say : Don't you know me, Bill ? and are you glad to see your mother back, children ? No ; that wouldn't do. She must return home as a woman, and none of them must know the life she had been living. But what story would she tell him ? It would be difficult to tell the story of fifteen years, for fifteen years is a long

time, and sooner or later they 'd find out she was lying, for
they would keep asking her questions.

But sure, said Alec, 'tis an easy story to tell. Well, Alec,
what story should she tell them ?   In these parts, Alec said,
a woman who left her husband and returned to him after
fifteen years would say she was taken away by the fairies
whilst wandering in a wood.   Do you think she 'd be believed ?
Why shouldn't she, your honour ?   A woman that marries
another woman, and lives happily with her, isn't a natural
woman ; there must be something of the fairy in her.   But
I could see it all happening as you told it, the maid-servants
and the serving-men going their own roads, and the only
fault I 've to find with the story is that you left out some of
the best parts.   I 'd have liked to know what the husband
said when she went back to him, and they separated all the
years.   If he liked her better than he did before, or less.
And there is a fine story in the way the mother would be
vexed by the two daughters and the husband, and they at
her all the time with questions, and she hard set to find
answers for them.   But mayhap the best bit of all is when
Albert began to think that it wouldn't do to have Joe Mackins
hanging round, making their home his own, eating and
drinking of the best, and when there was a quarrel he 'd
have a fine threat over them, as good as the Murrigan herself
when she makes off of a night to the fair, whirling herself
over the people's heads, stirring them up agin each other,
making cakes of their skulls.   I 'm bet, fairly bet, crowed
down by the Ballinrobe cock.   And now, your honour, you
heard the Angelus ringing, and my dinner is on the hob,
and I 'll be telling you what I think of the story when I come
back ; but I 'm thinking already 'tis the finest that ever
came out of Ballinrobe, I am so.

It happened that Etta's carriage stopped within a few yards of where her brother was standing, and she went to him, saying : I thought the train journey would never end. The train is not late, he answered. If you had been in it, Harold, you would have thought it was ; and now it seems that we shall never get away. A bad crossing ? Harold interjected. My head is still full of it. We were packed like sardines, and a great tinful we should have been for the fishes if we had gone down. But shall we ever get away ? Look at the luggage and see how it accumulates !

A barrier was formed, and trunks of all shapes and kinds began to appear, round leather trunks, bound with straps, testifying to trousers, coats, greatcoats, boots, perchance a dressing gown on top ; great basket trunks went by, bespeaking dinner dresses, bodices, skirts, blouses, underlinen, shoes, everything except hats. A porter passed staggering under the weight of a long, shallow trunk, built to withstand the racket of travel to India and back, and he was followed by another porter carrying a suitcase and a Gladstone bag ; leather hat-boxes were rare, men preferring to take them into the carriages with them, fearing the crush in the vans. Oh, the multitudinous hills of luggage ! cried Etta. The boxes and the bags ! It will take hours to examine them all. We shall miss the connection and not get to Sutton until midnight. What is the matter, Etta ? Harold asked. Only nerves, she replied, but I'm making every effort to control myself. I will tell you about the boat train presently. Do you think we shall catch a train to Sutton this evening ? You've been overworking, Etta, I'm certain of that. The

train that comes up from Dover is one of our best trains.
Now here is the Customs House officer. But will he let my
trunks through, or shall I have to open them ? If you talk
like that in his hearing, he 'll ask you to open them all.
Answer his questions calmly, indifferently, and he may let
your trunks through without an examination.

Harold was right, for the Customs House officer, after
overlooking Etta carefully, and judging her not to be a
smuggler, marked her trunks with a piece of chalk. A porter
put them on a barrow, and half an hour later they were
in a slow train for Sutton. You 've been overworking,
Harold said, looking into his sister's face with a view to descry-
ing any change that may have befallen her during the months
she had passed in Paris, and she answered that she had
spent a great many hours every day in the studio and had
come home on account of the heat. Harold asked her why
she had not come home before, and she repeated that the
heat was unbearable, the sun pouring through the skylight
like a flame in July, driving the students out of Paris into
the country to paint landscapes. A week before she left
there was a great exodus, Renouf going away to Honfleur,
his native town, to paint fishermen, Doucet leaving for his
honeymoon (he was marrying an American girl who had
been courting him flagrantly all through the session), and
Jamain was on his way to Rome, having won the prize.
Only a few unworthy ones, she said, remained to continue
their grimy drawings. I really couldn't watch them blacken-
ing paper any longer, and feeling worn out I came back.
I wonder you didn't come back before, Harold said, and
inwardly he congratulated himself that Etta had not brought
back with her Renouf, Doucet or Jamain. He was always
a little nervous as to the class of man Fate would give him
for a brother-in-law.

Cissy Clive and Elsie Lawrence have gone to Fontainebleau with their young men to paint birches and oaks, Etta
said, and at the words : gone with their young men, Harold's

face deepened a little, for he remembered these girls as very middle-class; and despite Etta's admiration for Ralph Hoskin's talent, he still bore a grudge against the painter for the advice he had given Etta. If one wants to learn painting, he had said to her, one must go where painting is being done, and it's being done in Paris. And Harold's old aversions against Etta's National Gallery acquaintances returned to him on the journey to Sutton. Gone to Fontainebleau with their young men to paint birches and oaks, did not harmonise with his view of the acquaintances that Etta should choose for herself. But since she had decided to go to Paris, it was better that she went with Cissy Clive and Elsie Lawrence than alone. If he had been able to procure a chaperon for her, she would have flaunted his choice, so to some extent he was indebted to both of these girls, and would have to ask them to the Manor House when they returned to England. Gone to Fontainebleau with their young men, might only be Etta's way of talking, and as it seemed to him useless to express any disapproval of her friends, he began to ask her questions about her life in Paris, the hotel she and her friends lived in, and the eating-house they frequented. She had mentioned Duval in one of her letters, and he confused Duval with Durand, to Etta's great amusement. Durand, she said, is a great restaurant in Paris; the Duvals are eating-houses. But is it reasonable to expect me to know the names of the restaurants and the eating-houses in a city that I have never visited? And now that she had explained to him what the Duval really was, he began to wonder why his sister had chosen to live in such discomfort; for his sister, as far as he knew her, was more averse from squalor than another. He had always thought her one who preferred to look up rather than down, and it was on his lips to put some enquiries to her; but seeing that she was weary and tired, on the verge of a nervous breakdown, he thought it would be safer to ask her about her journey.

Whereupon she broke forth into a pleasant garrulousness, telling him that she had enjoyed watching the French country as it passed through a long stretch of fens, pools, meres, linking one into the other so closely that she never was sure that the train was not following the course of a marshy, sluggish river ; on one of these pools was an abandoned boat. But why do you think the boat was abandoned, Etta ? It is probably used daily. I hope it isn't, she answered ; it would be out of keeping with the landscape if it were. He asked if she had made a sketch of the boat, and learnt from her that lunch had helped the time away till the train passed into a landscape from which the sea never seemed to be far distant, sand-hills and pines ; and travelling on and on they caught sight of the sea at intervals, losing it again and again, till at last it appeared before them, calm as a lake, speckled with ships. We embarked, Harold, and voyaged under a pale mauve sky till the white cliffs came into view. You have no idea how fine they are, despite the fact that they have been called the parapets of an island of blowing woodland. Although Etta knew that the slightest memory of his business would wipe from his mind the most beautiful description of sea and sky ever penned, she returned to the sunset to plague him, and when she had exhausted her vocabulary in description of the trains she described how she had, during the whole of the crossing, walked to and fro, getting into her lungs as much sea breeze as she could, which they wanted sadly.

He will understand that, she said to herself, and was rewarded by some commendatory remarks from Harold as to her wisdom in remaining on deck, and of all, in returning home, remarks that provoked her out of her facetiousness, and becoming terribly serious she asked him if she was looking a fright. He answered that she was looking tired, and she replied that she was all right till she reached Dover. I 've never been in a train that crawled into Chatham up a long incline like a beldam, she said. At Chatham we

saw the sea again, which was a great discouragement, for
I thought we had left the sea a hundred miles behind us.
You know how in a dream we try to escape from something
and can't ? It was like that, and about an hour ago I seemed
to lose control of myself. Yes, you seemed very nervous
when you jumped out of the train at Charing Cross. I
don't know how it was, but the Dover train got upon my
nerves, she answered. The ten miles between London
and Sutton are passing pleasantly enough now. And the
Manor House, if I remember rightly, is near the station.
How far is it, Harold ? Now, Etta, I 'm not going to tell
you how far the Manor House is from the station. As if
you had forgotten !

Harold's density, or rather his lack of humour, his slow,
methodical mind, had always been an amusement to his
mother and sister, who looked upon him as a very pure
Marr in mind and in body ; and recalling her mother's words :
Never did a mind and body come together so harmoniously,
Etta applied them to Harold, thinking with amusement,
but not unkindly, that his mind was inevitable in a thin,
well-proportioned man, who walked with his shoulders set
well back, and caressed a long, golden moustache with a
short, crabbed hand. She acknowledged his nose to be
better shapen than her own ; but what she lost on the nose
she gained on the eyes—his wore the same brown stare
always, and she fell in with her mother's judgment that
whosoever saw Harold would recognise him to be the type
of the South-Saxon, commonplace and steadfast. And then
her thoughts passing from Harold to her mother, she remembered the pain that his mother's failings used to cause
Harold during the last years of her life ; for there was no
denying that her mother often drank more wine than was
good for her, and when that happened her tongue was
unrestrained—she talked with her butler during dinner
about the cedars of Lebanon ; and though Harold admired
his mother's contributions to the *Saturday Review*, he could

not bring himself to accept them as sufficient atonement for her social transgressions. Indeed, he would have preferred that she ceased to contribute to the *Saturday Review* and other papers, and in unguarded moments he was wont to produce his opinion that the people of the Manor House should refrain from playing the piano in public, and from suburban acquaintances.

Etta threw back to her mother in many little ways, for a true Marr would not have picked up acquaintances in the National Gallery—an Orme (Mrs. Marr was an Orme) might. Etta, too, recognised her kin in the Orme rather than in the Marr. The readiness with which she reproduced her musical memories on the piano came to her from her mother ; likewise her taste for art. Mrs. Marr had brought back copies of Andrea del Sarto and Luini from Italy, and visitors were expected to accept them as originals and Etta's water-colours as prodigies, which they were able to do without suffering in their consciences ; artists didn't come in those days to the Manor House. And Etta's thought on returning home was of her mother, who, with all her faults, would have rendered homage to the drawings she was bringing, some comprehension, some interest at least. Harold would, of course, ask to see her drawings, and the thought of showing drawings to Harold, who was a real Marr, more Marr than ever, more like himself, awoke the spirit of comedy in Etta ; and remembering that a man proclaims his inner entity in his choice of meats, she asked him what he had ordered for dinner.

Well, Etta, I 'm afraid that at this moment I can't recall the whole of the bill of fare, but I 'm sure there 's some salmon. That 's English enough, she answered slyly, detecting a better opening for her wit when Harold happened to mention jugged hare. Isn't that rather a sudden leap ? she enquired. Leap where ? Into England's most characteristic dish, she replied, her amusement suddenly checked by his answer that if jugged hare was not to her liking, the cook would be able to find something that was in the larder. It isn't a question of my liking it, Harold, she interrupted, fearing that she had offended him, a thing she did not wish to do. A year of hard work has made me nervous, and I 'm trying to forget myself in a joke, that is all, only you won't let me. I am so tired and weary that whether there was jugged hare or boiled chicken or grilled salmon—— Again you 're making fun of England, Etta. Oh no, Harold, I 'm not. I am too tired to eat, that 's all. He asked if she would come down to dinner. No, Harold ; let me have a cup of weak tea and a biscuit. You 'll forgive me for not sitting through the jugged hare with you, for I 'm very, very tired, and you 'll not expect me at breakfast and will go away as usual by the nine o'clock train ? His anxiety to catch the nine o'clock train to London was a family joke, and Harold was about to say that he was weary of the joke and that it was time a new one were invented ; but the train was running into Sutton, and he said instead : The carriage will be waiting for us, and don't ask me how far we are from the station. She welcomed this tardy appreciation of her joke, and a few minutes afterwards they passed through the lodge gates, and a footman came forth to take down Etta's luggage. You are sure, Etta, that you will not take even a little soup before going to bed ? No, Harold ; I couldn't eat anything, not even soup. And he watched her ascending step by step wearily, indulging in the hope that there was nothing radically wrong with her, and that she would be well again after a good night's rest.

It doesn't seem to me as if I shall ever be able to think of eating again. I am too tired even to sleep, she sighed as she laid her head on the pillow ; but the many restless hours she saw before her did not come to pass. I must have fallen asleep at once, she said, stretching herself voluptuously. The day is broad and bright, and how pleasant the room is. For how long have I slept ? What time is it ? Ten, eleven, or maybe twelve o'clock. Not so bad as that, she added, catching sight of the clock, only half-past ten. So she turned over and lay in a happy, lucid idleness among the pillows for another hour, thinking of her bathroom and the comfort of it, remembering that in the hotel in the Quartier Latin there was no bathroom, and that she and Cissy and Elsie had had to go to some public baths, a thing that she disliked to do. Bathing, she had said, where all the bodies in the town have been, a remark that provoked them to chide her. For fastidiousness, she said; and for coarseness on another occasion, when she had answered Elsie, who came into her room to borrow one of her dresses : With pleasure, Elsie, if you promise not to return it to me. I cannot abide anybody's sweat but my own.

Etta turned over and over, thinking how pleasant it was to go straight from one's bedroom to one's bath ; and re-turning from her bath in a white wrapper, she stood before the glass saying : What a fright I am looking ! I ought to be looking better after my long sleep. We are in for a hot day, she added, and began to consider what she should wear. One doesn't know what to wear in such weather as this, she continued, as she settled the ribbons in her white dress and looked once more into the glass to see if the soft, fluffy hair which the least breath disturbed was disarranged. She smoothed it with her short, white hand. There was a wistful expression in her brown eyes, a little, pathetic, won't-you-care-for-me expression which she culti-vated, knowing its charm in her somewhat short, rather broad face, ending in a pointed chin. The nose was slightly tip-tilted ; her teeth were white, but too large ; she was short, somewhat stocky, yet she seemed almost stately as she passed with measured and demure steps along the passages and down the high staircase, stopping in the break-fast-room in front of a ham and a tongue with a gesture, though nobody was there to admire it. Eggs, bacon, kidneys,

she said, lifting the covers of the dishes, and she crossed
to another table, to be tempted by a melon. Only a water
melon, but a good one, she said; and her thoughts went
to the great Canteloupe melons of France, rough-skinned
and wide-furrowed, just as if Nature had foreseen the silver
knives slicing them into portions, red inside, filled with
seeds. *De quoi manger et boire*, she muttered, airing her
French gaily, for her thoughts were still in France. Now
if Harold were to hear me criticising his melons, how angry
he 'd be !

The coffee, however, in Sutton was plentiful and good,
and having refreshed herself according to her appetite,
she strolled to the windows and walked through them on
to a flagged pathway, over which her father and mother
had built a veranda on their return from one of their Italian
journeys, forgetful that a veranda, as its name implies, is
not English, and that a sloping roof, a portico, connected
with a sturdily-built low house in grey stone, is an incongruous
adjunct. The house would have been better without it,
Etta reflected, though on a day like this, almost oriental,
a veranda is something more than a piece of unnatural
picturesqueness. We have been having the same weather
here for some time, miss, said the butler, to whom Mrs. Marr
used to address most of her conversation during dinner,
and all the fields about are opening in great cracks. It 's
just the same in France, Collar, Etta replied, and looking
at a stretch of country shelving down towards a shallow
valley, spreading gently into woods and fields, all dry as
tinder, that a match would set fire to, she thought of the
melancholy of summer-time, when the season is at pause
and the sap no longer rises and the leaves are withering.
They will be gone earlier this year than last, she said to
herself, and her reverie ending, she began to think if she
would walk across the parched fields to the point of view,
her thoughts turning to the prospect which she knew so
well, for long ago, when they were children, they went

thither for picnics, and heard a tale of their grandfather, John Marr, the founder of the family, whose wont it was to sit there dreaming of the purchase he would make of acres if his whisky continued to sell well. He owned but a few hundred acres, and coveted the thousands that reached up to the horizon, confiding to his son, Richard, that when he had bought Chown's farm on the horizon, he would be able to bring his friends to see the view, and to say—(For none will know that the piece lying in between does not belong to us): Our lands extend as far as the eye can see, to the horizon.

II

The rooms within the great stone walls of the Manor House at Sutton were large but somewhat low, the house being a low, three-storeyed house; and everywhere there were pictures, in the passages, in the drawing-rooms, in the dining-rooms, two generations having set themselves to form collections, and very disparate were the tastes of John and Richard Marr. John Marr, never having been to Italy, bought out of the Royal Academy, and in his share of the collection were pictures by Wilkie, Egg, Webster, and many brown glens by Linnell, his money not having come to him soon enough for the purchase of Turners.

Our grandfather seems to have liked Westhall and Stoddart, Etta said. If one likes one, it's only natural to like the other. And don't you like either? Harold asked. In a way, but English painting seems more or less amateurish. England never seems able to learn to draw. What, interjected Harold, not Wilkie? The Dutchman did all that he did, and better. But he seems to have been able to grasp the construction of a head better than the others, better than Hilton. Our grandfather's eyebrows, Etta added, after a pause, are very well done, and it is difficult to draw an eyebrow. Harold asked how this was, and a moment after they had forgotten the portrait they were looking at and were talking of the man himself, the founder of the family, whose instinct for business filled Harold with an admiration that he never was able wholly to conceal, even when talking to strangers, and Etta with a slight contempt, which she was never able wholly to conceal when Harold began to tell of his grandfather's admirable foresight when he lent a friend some money to pay a debt of honour, the security being a large number of shares in a distillery. She had heard the story many times in fragments, and foreseeing that she would have to hear it all again, she permitted herself to impugn her grandfather's conduct, asking Harold if it were true that, on being elected Chairman for his business instincts, he had allowed the trade of the distillery to die away till the shareholders were glad to get rid of their shares. The story ran that the shareholders had held on too long, and that their grandfather was afraid the reforms he had in mind would never enable him to recapture the trade he had let go.

I cannot understand how it is, Etta, that you take pleasure in trying to pick holes in those upon whose industry and foresight you are living. I admire my grandfather as much as you do, Harold, only I admire him for different reasons. I was anxious this morning to go to the point of view. If grandfather had not died when he did, he would have bought those five thousand acres, and would have been made a Baronet, perhaps a Lord. Brewers and distillers have never been raised to the Peerage, Etta. Oh yes, they have, Etta answered. Not in the 'forties, said Harold; don't forget that grandfather died in 'forty-five. We must give him credit for his good intentions, which father might have realised, and which you might realise, Harold, if you cared. But do you care so much, Etta ? I thought that you only cared for painting.

Their talk passed from their grandfather to their father, whom Sir Francis Grant had painted amid Italian mountain scenery, and Mrs. Marr in the midst of old masters, lost in admiration of a Guido Reni. On the walls were many copies, Andrea del Sarto being a favourite with both Mr. and Mrs. Marr. One of Mrs. Marr's *obiter dicta* was well known in Sutton and much admired ; she had said : If you have not money to buy Raphaels and Michael Angelos, the next best thing is to buy copies. Mother seems to have liked Salvator Rosa, Etta continued, but I think it was his name that exalted his landscapes in her eyes. You remember, Harold, mother always used to roll it out : Salvator Rosa. She never missed putting a great deal of R into Rosa, did she, and even went to the trouble of playing some of his music, for he composed songs, which she sang, do you remember, at the concerts ? Harold remembered his mother's follies and also her failings, but he was sensitive on the subject and did not wish them alluded to. Malice was, however, instinctive in Etta, and accepting his dark face for a reproof, she said : I have as much right to admire father and mother as you have, Harold. We don't admire them for the same things, that is all. Our father and mother had a house in Berkeley Square and received all London, and were received by all London. I have heard you say yourself that at the dinner father gave after winning the Lincoln-shire Handicap there was only one untitled person in the room—Aunt Mary.

The races that preceded and that followed the Lincoln-shire Handicap nearly cost us our business. Father and mother could not understand that the source of our fortune was not inexhaustible, and went on spending. At the end of her life mother couldn't see anything without wanting to buy it, and father never went to the office. I think they were both ashamed of it, as I think you are, Etta. A business that we are ashamed of hits back very quickly—— If father and mother had lived, Etta interjected—— Let us not think of that, Harold replied, and Etta asked him if the business, since he took it in hand, was reviving. The question untied Harold's tongue and he talked for a long time, wearying

Etta with details, for what interested her was how much
they would have to spend and how soon it would be before
Harold could afford to give her a house in Park Lane. But
I thought, Etta, that your idea was to live in the Quartier
Latin with students. You have no ambition, Harold, Etta
answered, to which he replied that every man has ambitions,
projects, call them what you will, and that his thought was
to realise his grandfather's idea—the purchase of a great
landed estate. And answering a look of perplexity which
had come into her brother's face, she said : When I am
in Paris I think of nothing but painting, for painting is being
done all round me. But if I had a house in Berkeley Square
I should think of other things besides painting. One likes
to know and to be known, and if one has not a title one
has to do something, to write a book or paint a picture.
But what I don't understand are people with titles bothering
themselves about books or pictures. Why aren't they
satisfied with their titles ?

I am glad to hear you speak like that, Etta, for I thought
you were going to spend your life in Paris. Not my life ;
but I am going back, although I don't feel sure that painting
is as deep in me as I thought for. A look of doubt, amount-
ing to sorrow, came into her face, and to cheer her Harold
reminded her that a certain staleness comes often after a
long year's work. Yes, she answered, a year of eight hours
a day is a long year. Yet you tell me that you think painting
is not so deep in you as you believed it to be. Is it the
weariness that comes after a year's work, or did you hear
anybody say so—Cissy, Elsie, or the Professor ? I shouldn't
pay any attention to what Cissy and Elsie said ; that would
be jealousy. The Professor, I assure you, thought a great
deal of my drawing. Lefebre went round the studio cor-
recting one Tuesday morning, and before leaving he said :
Miss Marr's drawing is the best in the studio, and I do not
except even Doucet's. And Doucet was his private pupil,
who worked in his studio. Of course I don't think that at

the end of the week my drawing was as good as Doucet's ;
I cannot carry out a thing to the rounded end as well as
he. But they mustn't expect too much from me. I am
only four-and-twenty, and at that age one isn't an Ingres,
not altogether, not even a Lefebre or a Bouguereau.

Her face lit up and pleasant laughter flowed from her
lips, for she was aware of her own vanity ; it amused her,
and she knew how to make good her retreat from it with
laughter. Harold, who had been brought up to admire
his sister, was caught by her delicious comedy and begged
that she would send upstairs for her portfolios ; and she,
nothing loath, asked him to ring for her maid. And her
drawings and sketches were overlooked till Harold had
exhausted his vocabulary and admitted pathetically : To
think you should have done all these drawings, Etta, and
that I should not be able to understand them, or very little.
I am afraid that I understand only whisky. And now about
the whisky. A nightcap would guarantee you a long night's
rest, I am sure, for you 're looking very tired, and I have
no hesitation in saying that it would be well if you remained
in bed for a few days. A rest cure is what you need.

III

As soon as she was able to leave her room, she was ordered
to the sea-side, and after a fortnight at Brighton she went
to stay with some friends in London, returning to the Manor
House for Christmas to entertain a large party of Harold's
friends, business men, several of whom looked upon themselves as patrons of the art of painting because they collected
bad pictures, which they bought right off the easel, a favourite
phrase when telling each other of their purchases. Sometimes it dropped into their conversations with Etta, provoking an ironical answer, a quick stab, reaching to the
very heart of their vanity ; and then she would sit listening
to them without even a look of weariness upon her face.

As soon as the holidays were over and she had bidden the last of Harold's friends good-bye, her thoughts turned to the room in which she used to paint before she went to Paris, and to a subject which she had had to abandon for lack of skill to carry it out. Having no song of their own, bullfinches can learn tunes more easily than other birds— two tunes, but not more; if they are taught a third, they forget the first, and if they are taught a fourth, they forget the second, their musical memory being limited to two, and these are imparted to them by means of a bird organ. She had never seen one of these bird organs, but imagined it to be set in motion by the turning of a handle, a sort of miniature hurdy-gurdy, the purpose of which would be difficult to make plain in a painting. Not difficult, but impossible, she said to herself, and her thoughts turned to a flute, and afterwards to a flageolet. And having come to a definite conception of her picture, she engaged a model, and had nearly finished before it struck her that girls do not play a pastoral instrument of a sort once associated with shepherds and of late with gate-keepers. A boy is more patient, she said; a girl would not sit hour after hour playing the same tune. And from that moment she lost interest in the chubby, blue-eyed, flaxen-haired girl, who held the flageolet in her lips, sucking the mouthpiece as she might a sugar stick, but with less interest. I ought to have had a boy, but it is too late to change now; and she continued in the hope that nobody would notice the discrepancy. After all, she said, if the painting be good—— But the bitter thought that her model should have been a boy filtered into the painting, poisoning it, and at the end of a week there was no more room for hope. She had spoilt her picture, and having spoilt it she might as well scrape it out and begin again, this time from a boy. The flaxen-haired girl might have a brother! She had, but the brother reminded Etta of his sister, and she preferred to make a fresh start, meeting with a child in Sutton who was the very model she had had

in her mind from the first. The child's mother brought him
next day to the Manor House, and whilst making a drawing
preparatory to painting, her thoughts often turned to Ralph
Hoskin, whom she had met in the National Gallery in the
very beginning of her career, before she knew anything
of her craft. Ralph could help her. But will he come to
Sutton if I write to him ?

She fell to thinking whether they were enemies or friends,
and to discover which she began to recall the story of their
friendship, how he had stopped before her easel and com-
plimented her on her work, one of Gainsborough's landscapes.
He was much admired among the copyists in the National
Gallery, for he was not an ordinary copyist. He had a
studio of his own, exhibited at the Royal Academy, and
only came to the National occasionally, in exceptional circumstances, to make a copy for himself or for a patron whom
he wished to oblige. Nobody's copies were so free as his,
for his object always was to catch the spirit of the original
rather than the special handicraft of the artist. She remembered how flattered she was by his notice of her picture,
and how she had asked him to criticise, saying : I am only
a beginner, and you can be of such help. You have got
the background wrong, he said ; if you will let me have
your palette I will mix you a tone. She handed him the
palette and stood by, full of anxiety, while he took off a
muddy-grey with the knife. There, it's better now, he
said, surveying the picture, his head on one side. And
they had walked through the galleries talking of Turner
and Claude, Ralph saying that he liked Claude, for he was
nearer to Nature ; there was less fake. Turner's fake
was good fake, but—he had to exclude the burnt-sienna
foregrounds.

She didn't think he liked her, not at first ; he didn't
seem even to see her. He stood staring, thinking, and
anxious to help him out she began to argue with him, saying
that the Turner he admired was merely a strip of sea with

some fishing boats. I have seen it myself a hundred times, she said, at Brighton, at Westgate, just like that, only not quite so dark. Turner didn't copy, he transposed, Ralph answered. I am afraid I don't express myself very well, but what I mean is that the more realistic you are the better, as long as you transpose ; but there must always be a transposition of tone. Look at the Jew merchant ; he rises up grand and mysterious as a pyramid. You can't say where the picture begins or ends ; the Jew rises out of the darkness like a vision. Look at his robe ; a few folds, that is all, and yet he is completely dressed. And his hand, how large, how beautiful ! Don't you see, don't you understand ? Ralph spoke with a low, gentle voice ; it was pleasant to think of his voice. She had never heard anybody talk so winningly before ; and feeling that she must not allow him to pass out of her reach, she said that she hoped he would come to her easel on the next students' day. For now that I have had your help, I don't think I shall ever be able to do without it.

She had always liked Ralph, and now in the great difficulty of the modelling of the boy's blowing cheeks, she began to consider how she might get him back again. But would he be satisfied with her friendship ? Ah, that was it ! And after telling the boy, her model, to continue blowing the flageolet till she told him to stop, she took note of the light and shade ; and having assimilated him as she thought he should be portrayed on the canvas, she began to paint, thinking at intervals of a delightful morning that she and Ralph had spent in the Green Park. It was whilst watching the ducks balancing themselves like little boats on the waves that he had told her his mother once kept a paper shop in Brixton, and that he used to draw behind the counter on every scrap of paper, till one day a man connected with one of the great newspapers took some two or three of his drawings to show to the editor, who was much struck by them. If a boy can draw like that, he said, without being

taught, what will he be able to do when he gets some instruction ? Everybody, Ralph said, as they stood on the
bridge looking into the water, believes in instruction, not
that he can be instructed himself, but that he can instruct
somebody else. It's either in you or it isn't. If a duck
had any more than : Quack, quack, in his bill, he would
speak it.

Her model asked Etta if he might leave off blowing the
flageolet, and she answered : Of course, my dear boy, you
can ; I had forgotten all about it ; and you can rest yourself. The boy rose with some difficulty from his chair,
crying : Oh, Lord ! pins and needles ! And whilst he
walked about the studio, Etta remembered the reasons
that had decided her to go to Paris with Elsie Lawrence
and Cissy Clive. It had seemed unkind to her to leave
Ralph, but if she wasn't going to marry him it would be
better for her to go away for a time, for in no other way
could she free herself from him. He had asked her to marry
him, and as she did not feel that she could marry him, she
had gone to Paris to learn painting. Had he not said it was
the only place where painting could be learnt ? So it was
his fault, to some extent, that she had left London. She
had written to him from Paris, and, she was prepared to
admit, more affectionately than she would have done in
pleasanter circumstances ; for she was not happy in France,
nor very well, and in one letter she wrote about her great
loneliness and of the joy it would be were he suddenly to
draw aside the curtain and seek her out among the students.
He had taken her at her word and come over, and she remembered how startled she was when one of the monitors
handed her Ralph's card, saying she would find him in the
ante-room. She had written to him out of the impulse of
the moment ; his arrival was provoking, but there was no
escape from him now. And they had gone downstairs
together, and after walking about the streets in the neighbourhood of the Place de la Bourse, she proposed a café

to him ; and once out of the heat and noise of the street, some of her old liking for him had returned, though indeed she was annoyed with herself for having written the letter, and with him for having taken her at her word so easily.

As she painted, she could see herself in her thought laying out her drawings on the café table, and Ralph taking them up one after the other, criticising them perfunctorily, for, as she soon perceived, he had not come to Paris to teach her drawing, but to ask her to marry him. She took pleasure in recalling his words : I have read your letters a thousand times, till at last I felt that I couldn't go on reading them without seeing you, till I began to be afraid that you would find somebody here to fall in love with, somebody whom you would prefer to me. Have you ? She remembered her very words : I don't know that I have. But unabashed by them, he had asked her to marry him. You mean now, in Paris ? Why not, Etta ? If you haven't met anybody you like better, you know. And give up my painting just at the time I 'm beginning to get on ! I 'd give anything to draw like Doucet. You don't know him—a student of the Beaux Arts. Ralph did not think that even if she could draw like Doucet, she would be any nearer painting a picture. A man in love hardly knows what he is saying, and they had left the café, Ralph pleading, saying that he would wait if she would only promise. And it was in the rue Vivienne, by the Café Vivienne (Davau was there, drinking coffee), that Ralph began to plead so earnestly that she had to make an end of it. She remembered her words : I really must send you away now. That was all. So you won't promise to marry me ? No, I cannot marry you. His face darkened. I cannot live without you, he said, and frightened at the thought of his suicide, she had tried to dissuade him, saying : You have your art to live for. You 're no longer a sentimental boy. You 've got your man's life to lead. You must think of it. But the words had barely passed her lips when it occurred to her that his was perhaps one of those narrow, gentle natures that cannot outlive a disappointment. He had never loved a woman before—all he knew of women was one of his models.

The sound of the flageolet recalled Etta from the memories of her unkindness to Ralph in Paris, for she admitted to herself that she had been unkind. Would you mind, miss, if I was to say something to you about the bird ? You tell me that you 're going to paint a bullfinch into this cage, and that he is learning a tune off me. Now, I could play the flageolet much better if there was a real bullfinch, and I knows where you can get one for one-and-six ; and then it would be a real picture, painted from me learning the bull- finch a tune on the flageolet. What do you say to paying one-and-six for the bird, miss ? You see, he 'll be listening, and will stay quiet on his perch for you. You are a clever little boy, Etta answered ; you can bring the bullfinch with you to-morrow.

IV

But in spite of the work that she did upon it, the picture did not progress ; instead of going forwards, it seemed to go backwards. She was in trouble in turn with the back- ground, the bird cage, and then the bird. She could not get the action of the cheeks blowing, nor the movement of the fingers on the flageolet, and after repeated efforts the picture began to show signs of weariness, becoming like woolly cotton in the whites, and in the blacks dim and lustreless. She lay awake thinking about her picture, and every morning before she finished dressing the canvas was wheeled into the light in the hope that yesterday's judgment of it was at fault. Sometimes she thought one thing and sometimes another, and all the time her heart misgave her. I shall never get it right, she said to herself, not without help. I want criticism. And her thoughts going back to the studio, she began to wonder what the Professor would say if she could summon him to her aid. Any one of the leading students could criticise her picture from a painter's point of view, and what would she not give to get it! But in England she knew nobody who could tell her whether she should scrape it down or start afresh on a new canvas, nobody but Ralph, and she was not certain that he would come down if she wrote to ask him, for Cissy and Elsie held that she had treated Ralph cruelly; he no doubt thought so himself, but that was several months ago, and she had never known a man who did not respond if she held up her little finger. And it was in this conviction that she went up to London one morning, telling her brother she must copy a certain picture in the National Gallery. He asked her why she felt obliged to copy it, and she answered petulantly that she could not explain. Only a painter would understand, she said, and fell to thinking that she would not walk round the students asking for news of Ralph Hoskin; being well known in the Gallery, if she began to copy somebody would come to speak to her, Ralph's name would crop up in the course of conversation, and she would get news of him without asking for it.

Nobody, however, came to talk to her. All her old acquaintances were away. But Etta was as patient as she was resolute in her flirtations, and she continued copying the Greuze till one day an acquaintance, an occasional copyist in the Gallery, caught sight of her; and she learnt from Miss Brand that Ralph had not been seen in the Gallery for more than a year. You know that he has been ill? asked Miss Brand. No; I was in France and have been ill myself and am only just recovering. But Ralph, I hope, is not seriously ill? Lung trouble, Miss Brand answered. That is always serious, Etta replied, and when her friend had left her she sat staring at her Greuze, till unable to endure its silly sentimentality any longer, she locked up her paint-box and left the gallery, walking without seeing or hearing,

even to the danger of getting herself run over, asking herself
if her refusal to marry him had anything to do with his
illness. She hoped it had not, admitting at the end of a
little sensuous meditation on the bridge in St. James's
Park that she might have led him to expect she would
marry him sooner or later. But she couldn't have made
him happy ; she was not sure that she could make any
man happy.

As she crossed the open space in front of Buckingham
Palace, the desire to see him laid hold of her, and hailing
a hansom she drove to his studio. The door was opened
by a young woman who looked like a servant, but Etta,
not deceived by her appearance, guessed her to be one of
his models. I 've come, she said, from the National Gallery,
where I heard that Mr. Hoskin is ill. Can I see him ? He
has just dozed off, the young woman answered. I dare
not awake him, but I 'll give him a message. Give him my
card and say I would like to see him. Stay, I 'll write a
word upon it. And whilst Etta wrote on the card the girl
watched her—her face full of suspicion, and when she read
the name an indiscreet Oh escaped from her, and Etta knew
that Ralph had spoken of her. His mistress, no doubt, she
thought ; she wouldn't be here nursing him if she wasn't.
And lowering her eyes she murmured : Thank you, reaching
the end of the street humiliated and angry, humiliated that
the girl should have seen through her so easily, angry that
Ralph should have spoken about her to his mistress ; for
she was sure that the woman was, or had been, his mistress.
She regretted having asked to see Ralph, but she had asked
for an appointment—she could hardly get out of it now.
. . . She would have to meet that woman again ; but she
wanted to see Ralph. Ralph, I suppose, told her the truth,
she thought. A moment's reflection convinced her that he
probably had, and reassured she went to bed, wondering
when she would get a letter. She might get one in the
morning.

The first letter she opened read :

MADAM,—Mr. Hoskin begs me to thank you for your kind
enquiry. He is feeling a little stronger and will be glad to
see you. His best time is in the afternoon, about three
o'clock. Could you make it convenient to call about that
time ? I think it right to warn you that it would be well
not to speak of anything likely to excite him, for the doctor
says that all hope of his recovery depends upon his being
kept quiet.—I am, madam, Yours truly,

ELLEN GIBBS.

Ellen Gibbs ; so that is her name, thought Etta. There
was a note of authority in the letter which did not escape
her. She did not like meeting this woman, but she wanted
to see Ralph ; and an expression of vindictiveness came
into her cunning eyes. If she dares to try to oppose me,
she 'll soon find out her mistake. She has been his mistress ;
I have not, and shall get the better of her easily. To-morrow !
This letter was written last night, so I have to go to see
him to-day, this afternoon, at three o'clock. I shall have
to go up after luncheon by the two o'clock train. That will
get me there by three. Now I wonder if he is really dying ?
If I were to go to see him and he were to recover, it would
mean beginning it over again. But would it ? And why
do base thoughts and calculations enter my head ? I don't
know, for I do not call them, nor do their promptings affect
me. I am going to see him because I was once very fond
of him, because I caused him, through no fault of mine, a
great deal of suffering. I know he 'd like to see me before
he dies, that 's why I 'm going, and yet horrid thoughts
will come into my head. To hear me thinking, anybody
would imagine that it was only on account of my own vanity
that I wanted to see him, whereas it 's quite the contrary.
As a rule, I hate sick people, and I 'm sure it is most
disagreeable to me to meet that woman.

The two o'clock train took her to town, a hansom from

Victoria to Chelsea, and she walked up the street thinking
of the woman who would open the door to her. There was
something about her she didn't like. But it didn't matter ;
she would be shown in at once, and of course left alone with
Ralph. . . . Supposing the woman were to sit there all the
while ! But it was too late now ; she had knocked. I 've
come to see Mr. Hoskin. Feeling that her speech was too
abrupt, she added : I hope he is better to-day. Ellen
answered that Mr. Hoskin seemed a little better and was
in the studio. Etta expected to find him dawdling from
easel to easel, and was shocked to catch sight of him in a
small iron bed, hardly more than a foot from the floor, his
large features wasted by illness. His eyes glowed, and Ellen
placed a chair by his bedside, saying that she was going out,
but would not be away for more than half an hour. As soon
as the door closed, Etta took the thin hand extended to her.

Oh, Ralph, I 'm so sorry to find you ill. But you 're
better to-day, aren't you ?

Yes, I feel a little better to-day. It was good of you
to come.

I came at once, Ralph.

How did you hear I was ill ? We 've not written to each
other for a long while.

I heard it in the National. Miss Brand told me.

You know her ? I remember, she wrote about the new
pictures for an American paper.

Yes ; how familiar it sounds ; those dear days in the
National. Ralph's eyes were fixed upon her. She could
not bear their wistfulness, and she lowered hers, saying :
She told me you were ill.

But when did you return from France ? Tell me.

About six weeks ago. I fell ill the moment I got back.

What was the matter ?

I had overdone it. I had overworked myself. I had
let myself get run down. The doctor said that I didn't eat
enough meat ; you know, I never did care for meat.

I remember.

When I got better I was ordered to the sea-side; then I went on a visit to some friends and didn't get back to Sutton till Christmas. We had a lot of stupid people staying with us. I couldn't do any work while they were in the house. When they left I began a picture, but I tried too difficult a subject and got into trouble with my drawing. You said I'd never succeed. I often thought of what you said. Well, then I went to the National. Ethel Brand told me you were ill, that you had been ill for some time, at least a month. A thin smile curled Ralph's red lips, and his eyes seemed to grow more wistful. I've been ill for more than a month, he said. But no matter. Ethel Brand told you, and——?

Of course I couldn't stay at the National. I felt I must see you, and my feet turned towards St. James's Park, to the little bridge where we used to stand talking of painting and each other. She looked at him sideways, so that her bright brown eyes might have all their charm. His pale eyes, wistful and dying, were fixed upon her, not intently as a few moments before, but vaguely, and the thought stirred in her mind that he might die before her eyes. In that event, what was she to do? Are you listening? she said. Oh yes, I'm listening, he answered. His smile was reassuring, and she continued: Suddenly I felt that—that I must see you. I felt I must know what was the matter, so I took a cab and came straight here. Your servant——

You mean Ellen.

I thought she was your servant. She said that you were lying down and couldn't be disturbed. She didn't seem to wish me to see you or to know what was the matter.

I was asleep when you called yesterday, but when I heard of your visit I told her to write the letter which you received this morning. It was kind of you to come.

Kind of me to come! You must think badly of me if you think I could have stayed away. But now tell me,

Ralph, what does the doctor say ? Have you had the best medical advice ? Are you in want of anything ? Can I do anything ? Pray don't hesitate. You know that I was, that I am, very fond of you, that I would do anything. You have been ill a long while now—what is the matter ?

Thank you, dear. Things must take their course. What that course is it is impossible to say. I 've had excellent medical advice, and Ellen takes care of me.

But what is your illness ? Ethel Brand told me that you caught a bad cold about a month ago. Perhaps a specialist——

Yes, I had a bad attack of influenza about a month or six weeks ago, and I hadn't strength, the doctor said, to recover from it. I have been in bad health for some time. I 've been disappointed. My painting hasn't gone very well lately That was a disappointment; and disappointment, I think, is as often the cause of a man's death as anything else. The doctors give it a name : influenza, paralysis of the brain, or failure of the heart's action ; but these are the superficial causes of death. There is oftener a deeper reason, one which medical science is unable to take into account.

Oh, Ralph, you mean me ! Don't say that I am the cause. It was not my fault. If I broke my engagement, it was because I knew I could not have made you happy. There's no reason to be jealous, it wasn't for any other man. I was really very fond of you. It wasn't my fault.

No, dear, it wasn't your fault. It wasn't anybody's fault. We were not in luck's way, that 's all.

Etta longed for tears, but her eyes remained dry, and rising from the chair Ellen Gibbs had given her, she wandered round the studio, examining the various canvases. In one, a woman who had just left her bath passed her arms into the sleeves of a long, white wrapper, and Etta admired its naturalness. But she was more interested in the fact that the picture was painted from the woman who had opened the door to her. She sits for the figure and attends on him when he is ill ! She must be his mistress ; since when, I wonder.

How do you like it, Etta ?

Very much. It is beautifully drawn, so natural and so original. How did you think of that movement ? How did you think of it ?

I don't know. She took the pose. I think the movement is all right.

Yes ; it is a movement that happens every morning, yet no one thought of it before. How did you think of it ?

I don't know ; I asked her to take some poses, and it came like that. I think it is good. I 'm glad you like it.

It is very different from the stupid things we draw in the studio.

I told you that you 'd do no good by going to France.

I learnt a good deal there. Everybody cannot learn by themselves, as you did. Only genius can do that.

Genius ! A few little pictures. . . . I think I might have done something if I 'd had the chance. I should have liked to finish that picture. It is a good beginning. I never did better.

Dearest, you will live to paint your picture. I want you to finish it. I want you to live for my sake. I will buy that picture.

There 's only one thing I should care to live for.

And that you shall have.

Then I 'll try to live. He raised himself a little in bed. His eyes were fixed on her and he tried hard to believe. I 'm afraid, he said, it 's too late now. She watched him with the eyes she knew he loved, and though ashamed of the question, she could not put it back : Would you sooner live for me than for that picture ?

One never knows what one would choose, he said. Such speculations are always vain, and never were they vainer than now. . . . But I 'm glad you like the movement; It

ı

doesn't matter even if I never finish it. I don't think it looks bad in its present state, does it ?

It is a sketch, one of those things that could not be finished. I recognised the model. *She* sat for it, didn't she ?

Yes.

And you never told me ! Oh, Ralph, while you were telling me you loved me, you were living with this woman !

It happened so. Things don't come out as straight or as nice as we 'd like them to ; that 's the way things come out in life—a bit crooked, tangled, cracked. I couldn't have done otherwise. That 's the way things happened to come out. There 's no other explanation.

And if I 'd consented to marry you, you 'd have put her away.

Etta, don't scold me. Things happened that way.

Etta did not answer, and Ralph continued : What are you thinking of ?

Of the cruelty, of the wretchedness of it all.

Why look at that side of it. If I did wrong, I 've been punished. She knows all. She has forgiven me. You can do as much. Forgive me ; kiss me. I 've never kissed you.

I cannot kiss you now. I hear her coming. Wipe those tears away. The doctor said that you were to be kept quiet.

Shall I see you again ?

I don't think I can come again. She 'll be here.

Etta ! What difference can it make ?

We shall see. . . .

The door opened. Ellen came in, and Etta got up to go. I hope you 've enjoyed your walk, Miss Gibbs ?

Yes, thank you. I haven't been out for some days.

Nursing is very fatiguing. . . . Good-bye, Mr. Hoskin. I hope I shall soon hear that you 're better. Perhaps Miss Gibbs will write.

Yes, I 'll write ; but I 'm afraid Mr. Hoskin has been talking too much. Let me open the door for you.

V

Two days afterwards she received a letter from Ellen Gibbs :

MADAM,—It is my sad duty to inform you that Mr. Ralph Hoskin died this afternoon at two o'clock. He begged me to write and thank you for the violets you sent him. The funeral will take place on Monday. If you come here to-morrow, you will see him before he is put into his coffin.—I am, Yours truly, ELLEN GIBBS.

The desire to see her dead lover was an instinct, and the journey from Sutton to Chelsea was unperceived by her ; and she did not recover from the febrile obedience her desire imposed until Ellen opened the studio door. I received a letter from you—Etta began. Yes, I know ; come in. Etta hated the plain, middle-class appearance and dress of this girl. She hated the tone of her voice, and walked without answering into the studio, drawing back affrighted, so different is death from life. But catching sight of the violets, she recovered herself, and overcome, she stood watching the dead man, forgetful whether Ellen knew or was ignorant of what her relations might have been, remembering only that he was dead. And the desire to say a prayer falling upon her, she knelt by the bedside.

Don't let me disturb you, said Ellen. When you have finished——

Will you not say a prayer with me ?

I have said my prayers. Our prayers would not mingle.

What does she mean ? thought Etta. Our prayers would not mingle ! Why ? Because I 'm a pure woman and she isn't ? I wonder if she meant that. I hope she does not intend any violence. Her heart throbbed with fear, her knees weakened, she thought she would faint. And resolved to faint on the slightest provocation, she rose from her knees and stood facing the other woman, who stood between her and the door. Etta tried to speak, but words stuck fast in her throat, and it was some time before her terror allowed her to see that the expression on Ellen's face was not one of anger, but of resignation. She was safe ! She has pretty eyes, thought Etta, a weak, nervous creature ; I can do with her what I like. If she thinks that she can get the better of me, I 'll very soon show her that she is mistaken. Of course, if it came to violence I could do nothing but scream, for I 'm not very strong.

Well, Ellen said, I hope you 're satisfied. He died thinking of you. I hope you 're satisfied.

Mr. Hoskin and I were intimate friends. It is only natural that he should think of me.

We were happy until you came. You 've made dust and ashes of my life. Why did you take the trouble to do this ? You were not in love with him, and I did you no injury.

I didn't know of your existence till the other day. I heard that——

That I was his mistress ? Well, so I was. It appears that you were not. But I should like to know which of us two is the most virtuous, which has done the least harm. I made him happy ; you killed him.

This is madness.

No, it is not madness. I know all about you. Ralph told me everything.

It surprises me very much that he should have spoken about me. It was not like him. I hope that he didn't tell you that—he didn't suggest that there were any improper relations between us.

I dare say that you were virtuous, more or less, as far as your own body is concerned.

I cannot discuss such questions with you, Etta said timidly, and swinging her parasol vaguely, she tried to pass Ellen by. But it was difficult to get by. The picture she had admired the other day blocked the way.

Yes, said Ellen, in her sad, doleful voice, you can look at it. I sat for it. I'm not ashamed; and perhaps I did more good by sitting than you'll do with your painting. . . . But look at him—there he lies. He might have been a great artist if he hadn't met you, and I should have been a happy woman. Now I've nothing to live for. . . . You said that you didn't know of my existence till the other day. But you knew that in making that man love you, you were robbing another woman.

That is very subtle.

You knew that you did not love him, and that it could end only in unhappiness. It has ended in death.

Etta looked at the cold face, so clay-like, and the horror of the situation creeping over her, she lost strength to go, and listened meekly to Ellen : He smiled a little—it was a little, sad smile—when he told me that I was to write saying that he would be glad if you would come to see him when he was dead. I think I know what was passing in his mind —he hoped that his death might be a warning to you. Not many men die of broken hearts, but one never knows ; one did ; look at him and take your lesson.

I assure you that we were merely friends. He liked me, I know—he loved me, if you will ; I could not help that. Etta drew on the floor of the studio with her parasol. I am very sorry ; it is most unfortunate. I did nothing wrong. I'm sure he never suggested——

How that one idea does run in your head ! I wonder if your thoughts are equally chaste. I read you in the first glance. One glance was enough. Your eyes tell a mean little soul ; you try to resist sometimes, but your nature turns naturally to evil. There are people like that.

If I had done what you seem to think I ought to have done, he would have abandoned you. And Etta looked at her rival triumphantly.

That would have been better than what has happened. Then there would have been only one heart broken.

Etta hated the woman for the humiliation she was imposing upon her, and at the same time she could not but feel admiration for such single-heartedness. And noticing on Etta's face the change of expression, but misinterpreting it, Ellen said : I can read you through and through. You have wrecked two lives. Oh, that anybody should be so wicked, that anybody should delight in wickedness ! I cannot understand it.

You are accusing me wrongly. But let me go. It is not likely that we shall arrive at any understanding.

Go, then.

Ellen threw herself on a chair by the bedside, and Etta whisked her black crape dress out of the studio.

VI

She began new pictures, attributing every failure to the death of Ralph, saying to herself or to Ethel Brand (if she happened to be a visitor at the Manor House, which she frequently was during the winter) : Ralph was the only painter in England, at least the only one I knew, who could help me, who could criticise my work from a painter's point of view. You know what I mean ? Ethel Brand, whose thoughts went into music rather than into painting, answered that her desire to compose ceased practically with Rubenstein's death. She had often held out against his emendations, which seemed to her alien from her idea, but she generally gave in, accepting them in the end. But are there not many musicians who can correct grammatical mistakes, though they can do nothing else ? Etta asked, and Ethel agreed that there were, but she felt that her life as a composer was ended. One never knows, she added, and there are times when I feel that I have not said all I have to say in music. For the moment, however, I am not writing music, but about music in the newspapers—it pays better, and to musical criticisms I have added art criticisms ; having lived a great deal with artists, I know how to do it. You could help me, Etta. Etta said that she would be delighted to do so, and in their walks round the galleries the women began to take pleasure in each other's company, and the intervals that divided them began to seem longer and longer, till at length a flat in Paris was spoken of. Ethel said that there were some nice apartments in the rue Hauteville, off the boulevard Montmartre. Which would not be far, dear, from your studio. I once thought of taking a flat in that street myself, but the flats were too large for one person.

Etta smiled upon her friend's project, but the idea was not ripe in her yet, and without knowing why, she lingered on in Sutton till the spring. It was not till the early spring that the nostalgia of the boulevards began to take possession of her, and then it was she who pressed Ethel to come away at once, saying that the Manor House and Harold had again become wearisome to her, and the whole neighbourhood oppressive. There isn't a room in the house in which I can paint, she argued when Harold tried to persuade her. Moreover, I cannot live in Sutton. If you will take a house in London. . . . I must live where painting is being done. I cannot afford two houses, he answered, and a month later Etta and Ethel were furnishing a flat in the rue Hauteville, a burden that Ethel took upon her own shoulders so that Etta should be free to attend to her work in the studio, whither she went every morning at eight, more intent upon painting than ever, or maybe more intent upon the studio, which in the person of its proprietor, M. Davau, attracted Etta. She was always talking of him, asking him to dinner at the flat, buying boxes for the theatre, hiring a carriage to take them, and detaining him in the café afterwards for as long as he consented to remain. She never seemed to weary of him. A strange choice indeed Davau seemed to Ethel, and she often wondered if Etta loved the great, black-bearded Southerner with conviction.

Very often after he had left them, speaking out of their
meditations, one would admit to the other that for some
reason which escaped them his beard and his belly were
forgotten in the charm of his personality. But in what did
this personality consist ? He was not a great artist ; as
an artist he was a failure. What then ? Ethel asked, and
Etta answered : He seems to know his own mind ; he is
true to himself, a sensualist, I think, unfortunately, but he
has himself well in hand. I don't like fat men, nor hairy
hands, but——

The sentence was left unfinished, and both women fell
to thinking of the pleasant stories that Davau told of the
days when he was a shepherd boy and afterwards a great
wrestler in the South. In wrestling he and his cousin over-
threw all competitors, and when he was not wrestling he
was drawing. And by spending the money he gained in
the circus, he had educated himself enough to come to Paris
and to make a success in the Salon des Refusés. Alfred
de Musset's poem supplied him with a subject—the moment
when Rolla leaves his mistress's bed to shoot himself, having
spent his last louis on the supper they had enjoyed before
returning home, the girl innocent of her lover's intention
to take his life at daybreak. Davau's picture represented
Rolla at the window pointing to the sunrise. His mistress
still slept, and it was the girl's carefully painted petticoat,
thrown over a chair, that caused the scandal and the success.
Davau told Etta and Ethel how a critic had said *que Rolla
montrait le soleil pendant qu'elle montrait la lune* ; and to explain
what he meant he asked for a piece of paper and made a
sketch of his picture, making them both laugh. But a
success like Davau's Rolla does not give a painter an income,
and Davau, reduced like Rolla to his last hundred francs,
bethought himself of an exhibition of wrestling. A circus
was built on a waste plot in the centre of the town, and
all the friends of Davau's youth came to Paris to initiate
the Parisians in *la lutte Romaine*. *Coeur de Lion* and *Bras*

de Fer were minor attractions, Davau relying on *L'Homme
Masqué* to fill his booth. He entered to wrestle with the
victor in all the contests and had never been overthrown,
and it became the brag of Paris to discover his name. His
cabriolet was overtaken miles away in the country, but
there was nobody in it ; and attempts were made to bribe
the wrestlers to drag the mask from his face, but the heralds
intervened. And then it began to be noticed, Davau said,
that I disappeared from the auditorium when *L'Homme
Masqué* was in the arena, and to show that I was not *L'Homme
Masqué* I took a seat in full view of the public ; and on
that very night it so happened that *L'Homme Masqué* only
just escaped defeat. The man who was nearly overthrown
was your cousin, Etta interjected. You were *L'Homme
Masqué* in turns. Davau did not answer, and he enter-
tained the ladies in the rue Hauteville till nearly midnight
with tales of *Coeur de Lion*, *Bras de Fer*, and *Poitrine de
Taureau*.

Etta was not satisfied with Davau's visits to the rue Hauteville ; she wished to show in the studio that she held him
in tether, and her attempts to exhibit her power were her
undoing. From the very first day that she ran across the
studio and took him by the sleeve, saying : Now, you must
come and look at my drawing, the crafty Southerner determined to put her aside. Her invitations to dinner were
refused ; he never accompanied her again to the theatre ;
he was polite, but distant always, and Etta confessed her
perplexities to Ethel, who could not dissuade her. The
difficulty and danger of this wooing whetted her appetite
for victory, and she might have pursued her quest with
ridiculous attentions if it had not been dropped in conversation with some of the other women in the studio during the
lunch hour that Mlle. Berge was Davau's mistress.

At first Etta could not believe that she had been deceived,
but once put on the track of the truth, she remembered
a hundred things that had passed unnoticed at the time,

words and incidents.   And these rousing in her a passion of
hatred, she began to vent her hatred of Mlle. Berge, making
insulting remarks in her hearing and relating conversations
she had had with Mlle. Berge, who had been foolish enough
once to tell her that she had prettier thighs than any of
the models.   An excellent subject for caricature this was,
which Etta availed herself of, sketching upon Mlle. Berge's
drawings.   Her hatred of Davau was as unmeasured ;   she
told stories about him, relating that she had been obliged
to refuse to see him in the rue Hauteville, that he used to
dine with them there, but his conduct was so extraordinary
one night that she could not receive him any more.   Davau
heard all these stories without making any protest, and
Etta rejoiced, unsuspicious that when she came to renew
her subscription to the studio, he would tell her that he was
sorry but he could not accept it, for he wished to reduce
the number of lady pupils.

VII

Expulsion from the studio made shipwreck of her life in
Paris ;   she took lessons in French, began a novel, and paid
many visits to the Louvre in search of a picture that would
interest her to copy, and meeting there a student from
Davau's she learnt from him that a subscription was being
promoted by the pupils to present Davau with a testimonial.
A subscription entitled a subscriber to a place at the banquet,
and at the banquet Davau could not do else than say to
Etta :   I think this is an occasion on which old differences
should be forgotten.   If you care to return to my studio,
you will find it open to you.   And to show that he wished
to let bygones be bygones, he often came to help her with
her drawing, whereat she rejoiced, thinking that during
Mlle. Berge's absence, she would be able to turn defeat
into victory.   But why had Mlle. Berge left the studio ?
A very bitter hatred rose up in her heart when she learnt

that Davau was living in a handsome flat with Mlle. Berge, his mistress and helpmate, whom he was soon to wed. Harsh words rose up in Etta's mind, but remembering the price her former indiscretions had cost her, she began a letter of congratulation, and would have written it probably if Ethel Brand's mother had not come to Paris to fetch her daughter home.

Ethel had fallen out of health, and her departure gave Etta an excuse for leaving the flat in the rue Hauteville. She could say that it was too large, too expensive, and too lonely. She hated the flat, for it was associated in her mind with Davau, and to forget him she went to live in a boarding-house on the other side of the water, where Cissy was staying. But at the end of the first quarter Etta thought the neighbourhood did not suit her, and she wandered from boarding-house to boarding-house, from hotel to hotel, to take at last another flat, one in which there was a studio, and to spend a good deal of money on models, frames, and costumes. But nothing she did satisfied her, and convinced that she must improve her drawing she joined a drawing-class—one run on the same lines as the studio in the Passage des Panoramas, and for three months she bore the strain of the long working hours, till one morning, near the middle of the fourth month, she paused in her dressing and sank into a chair, unable to summon enough strength to draw on her stockings. In this hour of mental and physical weakness life seemed hopeless. She did not doubt her own genius, but she could not do else than doubt her own strength. There it was. She was without strength to rise at seven in the morning, to arrive at the studio at eight and to draw there till five, like Doucet, and after all, hundreds had drawn better than Doucet. With Doucet's skill, she thought she could do something better than Doucet. But there, she had neither his skill nor his strength, not even strength to pull on her stockings, only just enough to pull them off and roll herself into bed again and rest, which she did, lying between sleeping and waking till the maid knocked at her door and handed her a letter from Elsie.

DEAR ETTA,—Here we are again in Barbizon, painting in the day and dancing in the evening, and there are a nice lot of fellows here, one or two very clever ones. I have already picked up a lot of hints. How we did waste our time in that studio. Square brush work, drawing by the masses—what rot! I suppose you have abandoned it all long ago. Cissy is here; she has thrown over Hopwood Blunt for good and all, and is at present interested in a division-of-the-tones man. A clever fellow, but not nearly so good-looking as mine. The inn stands in a large garden, and we dine and walk after dinner under the trees, and watch the stars come out. There's a fellow here who might interest you; his painting would, even if he failed to respond to the gentle platonism of your flirtations. The forest, too, would interest you. It is an immense joy. I'm sure you want change of air. Life here is very cheap, only five francs, room and meals—breakfast and dinner, everything included except coffee.

The letter dropped upon her knees, and a wonderful rejoicement began in her heart, so surprising and so spontaneous that she stopped in her packing to ask herself if it were true that she had been pursuing things long after they had ceased to interest her—dead things, she said. But is my interest in painting, once so vital, gone? But was it ever very vital? she asked herself, and unable to find an answer to the question, she put it aside, it seeming to her that all search for reasons might check the joy rising, bubbling, effervescing in her heart. Why ask myself questions, for am I not going to Barbizon to get away from questions, from ideas? But what is Barbizon but painting, tones, relations, composition? And stopping in her picking and choosing of hats and gowns, she fell to thinking that she would like to escape into some other world in which

there were no pictures, or only good ones, it being against
the law to paint bad ones, and as nobody could paint good
ones any longer men and women would be devoted to other
things. But to what ? She did not know, nor care, for
she was going to Barbizon, to a life in which there would
be no painting, at least none for her. Again the prospect
of an escape from Paris into the open air possessed her,
and she said : Though they are painters in Barbizon, they
are but landscape painters. Barbizon is without studios ;
the forest is the studio. And her face darkening quickly,
she added : And there is no Davau. A moment after her
eyes returned to Elsie's letter, and she read that she was
not to go to Fontainebleau, but to Melun, where she would
find an omnibus waiting that would take her to Barbizon ;
or, if she did not mind the expense, she could take a fly,
which would be pleasanter and quicker. But be sure not to
miss the five o'clock express, the letter said, and she felt
that Elsie's letter had restored her to health and strength.
Soon after she was out of the house in the street, making
purchases, returning with them, enjoying every minute :
the packing of her clothes, the drive through Paris to the
Gare de Lyons, the train journey, and the long plains that
Millet had painted.

VIII

So a formal avenue of trees leads out of the town of Melun,
she said, and the plain is girdled with a dark green belt
of distant forest   At the cross roads she noticed a still more
formal avenue, trees planted in a single line, curving like
a regiment of soldiers marching across a plain that seemed
to be incompletely cleared of forest. She missed the familiar
hedgerows which make England like a garden, and when
the carriage entered, half an hour later, a gaunt, white village,
Etta was glad to learn that it was not Barbizon. The driver
mentioned the name, but she did not catch it, for she was
thinking of certain Surrey villages where honeysuckle,

wistaria or clematis, clamber about the porches, and sun-
flowers raise gaudy heads over pretty palings. Barbizon,
she learnt from a somewhat persistent driver, was still a mile
away ; it lay at the end of the plain, and when the carriage
entered the long street it rocked over huge stones so violently
that she was nearly thrown into the roadway and had to
call to the driver to go slower ; but he smiled, just as if he
had not understood her, and pointing with his whip, said
that the hotel mademoiselle wanted was at the end of the
village, on the verge of the forest.

A few moments after, the carriage drew up before an
iron gateway, and Etta saw a small house at the bottom of
a garden, where a numerous company was dining beneath
the branches of a cedar. Elsie and Cissy ran to meet their
friend ; and all through dinner her impression was of English
girls dressed in cheap linen dresses and men in rough suits
and flowing neck-ties. She was given some soup, and when
the plate of veal was handed round and Elsie and Cissy had
exhausted their first store of questions, she was introduced
to Morton Mitchell, who leaned back in his chair till he
broke it. Another was given to him, and Etta liked his
brusque, but withal well-bred manner, and was sorry to leave
the table when dinner was over, but could not do else than
follow Elsie and Cissy, who wanted to talk to her. And the
three marched across the grass plot, their arms about each
other's waists, and whilst questioning Etta about herself
and telling her about themselves, they frequently looked
where their lovers sat smoking, Etta's attention drawn to a
girl who hung over Morton, desirous that he should listen
only to her. Elsie and Cissy whispered Rose Turner's story,
and Etta thought : What a fool. . . .

And when the attractions of *mazagans* and *les petits
verres* were over and the young men joined the ladies, Cissy
and Elsie forgot Etta, who had turned into the house to
view, so she said, the walls painted with landscapes, still
life, nude figures, rustic and elegiac subjects ; and she

remained looking at the pictures in the hope that Morton Mitchell would catch her admiring his. But he did not return, and she was beginning to wonder if he were still listening to Rose Turner, when she heard somebody say : Do you like being alone ? I am used to being alone, she answered, with a smile of welcome, for she recognised the voice as Morton's.

Use is a second nature ; I will not interrupt your solitude.

But sometimes one gets tired of solitude.

Would you like to share your solitude ? You can have half of mine.

I 'm sure it 's very kind of you, but—— It was on Etta's tongue to ask him what he had done with Rose Turner, but she said instead : Where does your solitude hang out ?

Chiefly in the forest.

I don't know where the others have gone.

We shall find them in the forest ; we walk there every evening. We shall meet them.

How far is the forest ?

At our door. We 're in the forest, he said ; and answering his questions, Etta followed Morton through great rocks filled with weird shadows, to where pines stood round the hill-top, with a round, yellow moon looking through them. Does it shock you, she asked, that I should prefer to work from the naked model among men ?

No ; nothing shocks me.

In the studio a woman puts off her sex. There 's no sex in art.

I quite agree with you. There 's no sex in art, and a woman would be very foolish to let anything stand between her and her art.

I 'm glad you think that. I 've made great sacrifices for painting.

What sacrifices ?

I 'll tell you one of these days when I know you better.

Will you ?

The conversation paused a moment, and Etta said : How wonderful it is here ! One hears the silence ; it enters into one's very bones. It is a pity one cannot paint silence.

Millet painted silence. The Angelus trembles with silence and sunset.

But the silence of the moonlight is more awful. It really is very awful ; I 'm afraid.

Afraid of what ? There 's nothing to be afraid of. You asked me if I believed in Davau's. I didn't like to say ; I had only just been introduced to you ; but it seems to me that I know you better now. Davau's is a curse. It is the sterilisation of art. You must give up Davau's and come to work here.

I 'm afraid it would make no difference. Elsie and Cissy have spent years here, and what they do does not amount to much. They wander from method to method, abandoning each in turn. I am utterly discouraged, and have made up my mind to give up painting.

What are you going to do ?

I don't know. One of these days I shall find out my true vocation.

You 're young, you are beautiful——

No, I 'm not beautiful, but there are times when I look nice. The others do not seem to be coming back. We had better return.

They moved out of the shadows of the pines and stood looking down the sandy pathway. I never saw anything like this before, Etta continued. This is primeval. I used to walk a good deal with a friend of mine in St. James's Park.

The park where the ducks are and a little bridge. Your friend was not an artist ?

Oh yes, he was, and a very clever artist, too.

Then he admired the park because you were with him.

Perhaps that had something to do with it. But the park is very beautiful.

I don't think I care much about cultivated Nature.

Don't you like a garden ?

Yes, a disordered garden, a garden that has been let run wild.

They walked down the sandy pathway and came unexpectedly upon Elsie, and asked where the others were. Elsie did not know. But at that moment voices were heard, and Cissy cried from the bottom of the glade : So there you are. We 've been looking for you. Looking for us ! said Etta. Yes ; we are going to dance. Rose will play when Etta is dancing, and when Rose is dancing Etta will play. Nobody can play waltzes better than Etta. Strauss himself would listen to her playing of the Blue Danube. I 'm not so sure of that, Etta answered, but I 'll do my best to help Rose to whirl away her evening, and she 'll do her best to help me to whirl away mine. And the evening whirled through music and moonlight till the painters began to think of the motives that awaited them in the morning.

IX

Etta was the first down. She wore a pretty, flowered dress, and her straw hat was trimmed with tremulous grasses and cornflowers. A faint sunshine floated in the wet garden. Well, you have got yourself up ! cried Elsie. We don't run to anything like that here. You 're going out flirting ; it 's easy to see that. My flirtations don't amount to much, Elsie. Kisses don't thrill me as they do you. I 'm afraid I 've never been what you call in love. You seem on the way there if I 'm to judge by last night, Elsie answered tartly. You know, Etta, I don't believe all you say, not quite all. An almost triumphant expression came upon Etta's face, and she said : Perhaps I shall meet a man one of these days who will inspire passion in me.

I hope so. It would be a relief to all of us. I wouldn't mind subscribing to present that man with a testimonial.

K

I often wonder what will become of me. I 've changed a good deal in the last two years. I 've had a great deal of trouble.

I 'm sorry you 're so depressed. But we all are. The art to which we give ourselves deceives us as you deceive your lovers.

But, Elsie, you haven't been deceived. You had a picture in the Salon, and Cissy had one too.

That doesn't mean much.

But do you think that I shall ever do as much ? Elsie did not think so, and the doubt caused her to hesitate. Etta perceived the hesitation, and said : Oh, there 's no necessity for you to lie. I know the truth well enough. I have resolved to give up painting. I have given it up.

You 've given up painting ! Do you really mean it ?

Yes ; I feel that I must. I 'm not very strong, and the long hours in the studio wear me out. What a relief your letter was—what a relief to be here !

Well, you see, something has happened. Barbizon has happened, Morton has happened.

I wonder if anything will come of it. He 's a nice fellow. I like him.

You 're not the first. All the women are crazy about him. He was the lover of Mérac, the actress of the Français, and it is said that she could only play Phèdre when he was in the stage-box. He always produced that effect upon her. Then he was the lover of the Marquise de la—de la Per—I can't remember the name.

Morton was talking to Rose, but Etta soon got his attention. You 're going to paint in the forest, she said. I wonder what your picture is like ; you haven't shown it to me.

It 's all packed up. But if you 're not painting with Miss Lawrence and Miss Clive you might come with me. And you 'd better take your painting materials ; you 'll find the time hang heavily if you don't.

The very thought of painting bores me.

Well, then, if you 're ready we might make a start; mine is a midday effect. I hope you 're a good walker. But you 'll never be able to get along in those shoes, and the dress you 've on is no dress for the forest. You 're dressed as for a garden-party.

It is only a little flowered muslin, there 's nothing to spoil; and as for my shoes, you 'll see, I shall get along all right, unless it is very far.

It is more than a mile. I shall have to take you down to the local cobbler and get you measured. I never saw such feet!

He was oddly matter of fact, and his almost childishness amused and interested Etta. With whom, she said, do you go out painting when I 'm not here? Every Jack seems to have his own Jill in Barbizon.

And don't they everywhere else? It would be damned dull without.

Do you think it would? Have you always got a Jill?

I 've been down on my luck lately.

Which of the women here has the most talent?

Perhaps Miss Lawrence. But Miss Clive does a nice thing occasionally.

What do you think of Miss Turner's work?

It 's pretty good. She has talent. She had two pictures in the Salon last year.

Have you ever been out with her?

Yes; but why do you ask?

Because I think she likes you. She looked very miserable when she heard that we were going out together. Just as if she were going to cry. If I thought I was making another person unhappy I would sooner give up the pleasure of going out with you.

And what about me? Don't I count for anything?

I must not do a direct wrong to another. Each of us has a path to walk in, and if we deviate from our path we bring unhappiness upon ourselves and upon others. Morton stopped and looked at her; his stolid stare made her laugh and it made her like him. I wonder if I am selfish, Etta continued reflectively. Sometimes I think I am, sometimes I think I am not. I 've suffered so much; my life has been all suffering. There 's no heart left in me for anything. I wonder what will become of me. I often think I shall commit suicide. Or I might go into a convent.

You 'd much better commit suicide than go into a convent. Those poor devils of nuns!

You 're not going to ask me to climb those rocks! said Etta. Mile after mile of rocks! What a scene, like a landscape by Salvator Rosa.

Climb that hill? You couldn't! I 'll wait until our cobbler has made you a pair of boots. Bah! Isn't that desolate region of blasted oaks and sundered rocks wonderful? And they had walked but a very little way when he stopped and said: Don't you call that beautiful? And leaning against the same tree, Morton and Etta looked into the summer wood, where the trunks of the young elms rose straight, and through the pale leafage the sunlight quivered, full of the impulse of the morning. Something ran through the grass, paused, and then ran again.

What is that? Etta asked.

A squirrel, I think. Yes; he 's going up that tree.

How pretty he is, his paws set against the bark.

Come this way and we shall see him better. But they caught no further sight of the squirrel, and Morton asked Etta the time. A quarter-past ten, she said, glancing at the tiny watch that she wore in a bracelet. Then we must be moving on, he answered. I ought to be at work by half-past. One can't work more than a couple of hours in this light. Etta opened her parasol, and they passed out of the wood and crossed an open space where rough grass grew in patches. You asked me just now if I ever went to England, she said, and that 's my difficulty. So long as I was painting,

there was a reason for my remaining in France, but now that
I 've given it up——

But you 've not given it up !

Yes, I have ; and if I don't find something else to do,
I suppose I must go back. That 's what I dread. We live
in Sutton. But that conveys no idea to your mind. Sutton
is a little town in Surrey. It was very nice once, but now
it is little better than a London suburb. My brother is a
distiller. He goes to town every day by the nine o'clock,
and he returns by the six o'clock. I 've heard of nothing
but those two trains all my life. We have many acres of
ground—gardens, greenhouses, and a number of servants.
Then there 's the cart—I go out for drives in the cart. We
have tennis parties—the neighbours, you know. And I
shall have to choose whether I look after my brother's house,
or marry and look after my husband's.

It must be very lonely in Sutton.

Yes, it is very lonely. There are a number of people
about, but I 've no friends I care for.

A moment after they passed out of the sunlight into the
green shade of some beech trees. Etta closed her parasol,
and swaying it to and fro amid the ferns she continued
telling in a low, laughing voice of a friend of hers who read
Comte, and the influence that this lady had exercised upon
her. Her words floated along in a current of quiet humour,
cadenced by the gentle swaying of her parasol and brought
into relief by a certain intentness of manner which was
peculiar to her, and which was not without charm for Morton,
who became more and more conscious of her. The charm
of her voice stole upon him, and once he lingered, allowing
her to get a few yards in front, so that he might notice the
quiet figure, a little demure and intensely itself in a yellow
gown. When he first saw her, she had seemed to him a
little sedate, even a little dowdy ; he had feared a bore,
but this she at least was not, and her determination to paint
no more announced an excellent sense of the realities of

things in which the other women—the Elsies and the Cissys —seemed to him deficient. Here is my subject, he said, and when he had set up his easel, he spread the rug for her in a shady place. But for the present she preferred to stand behind him, her parasol slanted slightly, talking, he thought very well, of the art of the great men who had made Barbizon rememberable. He was sorry when she said the sun was getting too hot for her, and she went and lay on the rug he had spread for her in the shade of the oak. She had brought a book to read, but she only read a line here and there. Her thoughts wandered from the page to the man sitting easily on his camp-stool, his long legs wide apart. His small head, his big hat, the line of his bent back, amused and interested her ; she liked his abrupt speech, and wondered if she could love him. A couple of peasant women came by, bent under the weight of the faggots they had picked, and Etta could see that Morton was watching the movements of these women, and she thought how well they would come into the picture he was painting. Soon after he rose from his easel and walked towards her. Have you finished ? she asked.

No, not quite, but the light has changed. I cannot go on any more to-day. One can't work in the sunlight above an hour.

You 've been working longer than that.

But haven't touched the effect. I 've been painting in some figures, two peasant women picking sticks. Come and look.

X

Morton had finished his picture, and now lunch was over and they lay on the rug under the oak tree talking eagerly. Corot never married, Morton remarked. He doesn't seem to have ever cared for any woman. They say he never had a mistress.

I hear that you have not followed his example.

Not more than I could help.

His candour amused her so that she laughed outright ; and she watched the stolid, childish stare that she liked, until a longing to take him in her arms and kiss him came upon her, and she asked him if he had ever been in love.

Yes, I think I was.

How long did it last ?

About five years.

And then ?

A lot of rot about scruples of conscience. I said : I give you a week to think it over, and if I don't hear from you in that time I 'm off to Italy.

Did she write ?

Not until I had left Paris. Then she spent five-and-twenty pounds in telegrams trying to get me back.

But you wouldn't go back ?

Not I ; with me, when an affair of that sort is over, it is really over. Don't you think I 'm right ?

Perhaps so. . . . But I 'm afraid we 've learnt love in different schools.

Then the sooner you relearn it in my school the better.

At that moment a light breeze came up the sandy path, carrying some dust on to the picture. Morton stamped and swore. For three minutes it was : Damn ! damn ! damn ! Do you always swear like that in the presence of ladies ? she asked. Well, what 's a fellow to do when a blasted wind comes up smothering his picture in sand ?

Etta could only laugh at him, and while he packed up his canvases, paint-box and easel, she thought that she understood him, and fancied that she would be able to manage him. And convinced of her power she said aloud, as they plunged into the forest : I always think it is a pity that it is considered vulgar to walk arm-in-arm. I like to take an arm. I suppose we can do what we like in the forest of Fontainebleau. But you 're too heavily laden——

No, not a bit. I should like it.

She took his arm with a caressing movement and walked by his side, and they talked until they reached the motive of his second picture.

What I've got on the canvas isn't very much like the view in front of you, is it ?

No, not much. I don't like it as well as the other picture.

I began it late one evening. I've never been able to get the same effect again. Now it looks like a Puvis de Chavannes—not my picture, but that hillside, that large space of blue sky and the woodmen.

It does a little. Are you going on with it ?

Why ?

Because there is no shade for me to sit in. I shall be roasted if we remain here.

What shall we do ? Lie down in some shady place ?

We might do that. . . . I know what I should like.

What ?

A long drive in the forest.

We can do that. We shall meet somebody going to Barbizon and we'll ask them to send us a fly.

And they wandered on through a pine wood where the heat was stifling, the dry trees like firewood, scorched and ready to break into flame ; their feet dragged through the loose sand till they came to a place where the trees had all been felled, and a green undergrowth of pines, two or three feet high, had sprung up. It was difficult to force their way through ; the prickly branches were disagreeable to touch, and underneath the ground was spongy with layers of fallen needles hardly covered with coarse grass. Morton missed the way, and his paint-box and canvases had begun to weigh heavily when they came upon the road they were seeking. But where they came upon it there was only a little burnt grass, and Morton proposed that they should toil on until they came to a pleasanter place. The road ascended along the verge of a steep hill, at the top of which they met a bicyclist, who promised to deliver Morton's note. It was pleasant to rest—they were tired, and it was pleasant to listen, for the forest murmured like a shell. But absorbed though they were by this vast Nature, each was thinking intensely of the other. Etta knew she was near the moment when Morton would take her hand and tell her that he loved her. She wondered what he would say. She did not think he would say he loved her ; he would say : You 're a damned pretty woman. She could see he was thinking of something, and suspected him of thinking out a phrase or an oath appropriate to the occasion. And she was nearly right. Morton was thinking how he should act. Etta was not the common Barbizon art student whose one idea is to become the mistress of a painter so that she may learn to paint. She had encouraged him, but she had kept her little dignity. Moreover, he did not feel sure of her. So the minutes went by in awkward expectancy, and Morton had not kissed her before the carriage arrived. But the kiss would come ; she was sure of that, and lay back in the fly smiling, Morton thought, superciliously. It seemed to him stupid to put his arm round her waist and try to kiss her. But, sooner or later, he would have to do this. Once this Rubicon was past, he would know where he was. As he debated, the trunks rose branchless for thirty or forty feet, and he asked her if the tall, thin, almost branchless beeches were not like lances bent in the shock of the encounter.

The forest now extended like a great temple, hushed in the ritual of the sunset. The light that suffused the green leaves overhead glossed the brown leaves underfoot, marking the smooth ground as with a pattern. Like chapels every dell seemed in the tranquil light, and Etta's eyes wandered from the colonnades to the underwoods, and were raised to the scraps of blue that appeared through the thick leafage, till she longed for a break in the trees, a vista, and at the end of it a plain or a pine-plumed hill-top. We are nearly there now, Morton said ; and leaving the carriage, which was to wait for them, Etta followed him through rocks and furze bushes, taking his arm, and once accidentally, or nearly accidentally, she sprang from a rock into his arms. She was surprised that he did not take advantage of the occasion to kiss her. Standing on this flat rock we 're like figures in a landscape by Wilson, she said. So we are, replied Morton, who was struck by the truth of the comparison. But there is too much colour in the scene for Wilson—he would have reduced it all to a beautiful blue, with only a yellow flush to tell where the sun had gone.

It would be very nice if you would make me a sketch of the lake. I 'll lend you a lead pencil; the back of an envelope will do.

I 've a water-colour box in my pocket and a block. Sit down there and I 'll do you a sketch.

And while you are accomplishing a work of genius, I 'll supply the levity; and don't you think I 'm just the sort of person to supply the necessary leaven of lightness? Look at my frock and my sunshade. Morton laughed, and she continued: What did you think of me the first time you saw me? What impression did I produce on you?

Do you want me to tell you, to tell you exactly?

Yes, indeed I do.

I don't think I can.

What was it? Etta asked in a low, murmurous tone, and when she leaned towards him the movement was intimate, affectionate, and false.

Well—you struck me as being a little dowdy.

Dowdy! I had a nice new frock on. I don't think I could have looked dowdy, and among the dreadful old rags that the girls wear here.

It had nothing to do with the clothes you wore. It is the quiet, sedate air that you wear sometimes.

I wasn't in good spirits when I came down here.

No, you weren't. I thought you might be a bore.

But I haven't been that, have I ?

No, I'm damned if you're that.

But what a charming sketch you're making. You take that ordinary common grey from the palette, and it becomes beautiful. If I were to take the very same tint and put it on the paper, it would be mud. Morton placed his sketch against a rock and surveyed it from a little distance, saying : I don't call it bad, do you ? I think I've got the sensation of the lonely lake. But the effect changes so rapidly. Those clouds are quite different from what they were just now. I never saw a finer sky ; it is wonderful ; it is splendid as a battle.

Write underneath it : That night the sky was like a battle.

Morton did not answer, and Etta continued : You think the suggestion would overpower the reality ? But it is a charming sketch and will remind me of a charming day, of a very happy day. She raised her eyes. The moment had come. He threw one arm round her, and raised her face with the other hand. She gave her lips easily, and during the drive home she lay upon his shoulder, allowing his arm to lie round her.

Elsie said you'd get round me.

What did she mean ?

Well, said Etta, nestling a little closer and laughing low, haven't you got round me ? Her playfulness enchanted her lover, but her tenderness in speaking of Ralph quickened his jealousy.

My violets lay under his hand ; he must have died thinking of me.

But the woman who wrote to you, his mistress, she must have known all about his love for you. What did she say ?

She said very little. She was very nice to me. She could see that I was a good woman.

But that made no difference so far as she was concerned. You took her lover away from her.

She knew that I hadn't done anything wrong, that we were merely friends. The conversation paused a moment, then Morton said : It seems to have been a mysterious kind of death. What did he die of ?

Ah, no one ever knew. The doctors could make nothing of his case. He had been complaining a long time. They spoke of overwork, but——

But what ?

I believe he died of slow poisoning.

Slow poisoning ! Who could have poisoned him ?

Ellen Gibbs.

What an awful thing to say. . . . I suppose you have some reason for suspecting her ?

His death was very mysterious. The doctors could not account for it. There ought to have been a post-mortem examination. In the silence that fell upon this avowal Etta remembered that Ralph had held socialistic theories and was a member of a sect of socialists, and she continued : Ralph was a member of a secret society. . . . He was an anarchist—no one suspected it ; but he told me everything, and it was I who persuaded him to leave the Brotherhood.

I do not see what that has to do with his death by slow poisoning.

Those who retire from these societies usually die.

But why Ellen Gibbs ?

She was a member of the same society ; it was she who got him to join. When he resigned, it was her duty to——

Kill him ! What a terrible story. I wonder if you 're right.

I know I 'm right. At the end of the pause Morton said : I wonder if you like me as much as you liked Ralph.

It is quite different. He was very good to me.

And do you think that I shall not be good to you ?

Yes, I think you will, she said, looking up and taking the hand which pressed against her waist.

You say he was a very clever artist. Do you like his work better than mine ?

It was as different as you yourselves are.

I wonder if I should like it.

He would have liked that ; and she pointed with her parasol towards an oak glade, golden-hearted and hushed.

A sort of Diaz, then ?

No, not in the least like that. No ; his wasn't the Rousseau palette.

How the motive could be treated except as Rousseau or Diaz would have treated it, I cannot imagine. And it does not matter. What matters now is that I can kiss you. If you loved me you would not kiss me dryly.

I don't know how to kiss otherwise. This is the first time we have been out together. I have never been out so late with a man before. It is almost night under these trees. You cannot love me. The other day you saw me for the first time.

But I am going to love you. Let me kiss you ; there is no other way.

I 'd like a man to love me before I kiss him.

Then you will never be loved, for it is through the lips that love steals into the blood, and you keep them closed.

But can I complete the conquest with my lips ?

Not with the lips alone.

And for how long shall I have to wait for your love, sir ?

It is a poor compliment to a woman to love her at first sight, or at second or third. In six months a man's love is at height. Is it not the same with you ?

I know nothing of love, but I can see that you have made love a great deal.

How can you tell that ?

Etta did not answer, and Morton, fearing his question to be a stupid one, began to struggle with her. I will kiss you, Morton, but you must take your hand from my knee. I do not like to be kissed like that and will not go out driving

with you again. I see that I cannot trust you. Morton
pleaded, but it was a long time before he could woo her
out of a silence that seemed to him sullen. At last she said,
as if she had come to a sudden resolve : No, I will not do
what you ask me. But I 'll marry you.

Let it be so, then. But marriage is far away. You will
have to go to England, and——

If you loved me you could wait a little. We have known
each other only a few days. In a month I may be a different
woman in your eyes. I beg of you to desist, else I shall not
be able to keep my promise to you. A month, two, three,
is not long to wait and during that time respect your be-
trothed. You will not regret the waiting. Love has come
to you in the past too easily. A change is good for us all.

XI

Every day a carriage came from Melun or Fontainebleau,
and Morton and Etta drove away from Lunions through
Barbizon, to the general admiration of the village, returning
at evening with recommendations of the inns they had
visited and the routes they had passed through, everybody
thinking how much more interesting a narrative would be
of what they said and did rather than what their eyes saw.
In the forest, among its rocks and glades, when the painters
visited each other's easels, Etta as a protagonist of unamiable
virtue was much discussed, different views being held regarding Morton's chances of success, some holding that
Etta held him fawning in a leash of hope, whilst others,
speaking out of the pride of sex, shook their heads, saying
that such a leash could not hold a man from his art ; only
the leash of the flesh could do that, they averred, without,
however, much conviction.

In September Elsie and Cissy were painting on a steep
hillside overlooking the high road, Elsie's subject almost
a sinister one ; rocks with great clefts—a den a passer-by

might think it to be of some wild animal, wolf or boar. And
feeling that it would not be wise to touch again the over-
hanging branches, having gotten as much effect as her
means allowed, and not certain whether she could persuade
Cissy to come up the hillside to criticise the lair on the easel,
Elsie descended the hillside with the picture in her hand
and set it before Cissy. Cissy liked it, but did not think
that rocks made so interesting a subject as three yellowing
birch trees bending across a lustral autumn sky. It is
strange, Elsie said, how people always disagree about pictures.
Etta thought mine the better subject, and the only fault
she found was that I hadn't introduced a wild boar. My
rocks, she said, were suitable for a sow to have her litter
among. Sow isn't the word she used; what did she say ?
Une laie ! She liked your rocks, Elsie, so that she might
bring that word into her talk. No doubt she had just learnt
it from the Comte de Malmédy. What a copycat she is ;
none was ever slyer. How she has turned Morton to her
purpose. It was he who introduced her to the Comte.
And the girls began to talk about the beautiful Renaissance
house that Henri quatre had built for *la belle Gabrielle*.
Who was *la belle Gabrielle* ? Cissy asked, and Elsie answered
that she thought *la belle Gabrielle* was the mistress of Henry
the fourth—she was sure her lover was one of the Henrys.
Cissy asked if the King had wearied of her and put her
in prison, or if he had ordered her head to be struck off,
as Henry the eighth treated his wives on more than one
occasion. Elsie could not call to mind that any great disaster
had befallen *la belle Gabrielle*, for whom Henry the fourth
had built a palace in view of the Seine, a palace now
held on lease from the State by the Comte, who, they heard
at Lunions that night, had been appointed to the Governor-
ship of Algeria, an appointment that might oblige him to
ask the State to relieve him of the lease, for, although he
was a rich man, it was hardly possible that he could bear
the expense of the Government House in Algiers and a

palace at Fontainebleau. It was not thought, however, that the State would relieve him of his lease, and in that case the Comte might decline to accept the appointment, great an honour as it was, for few men care to ruin themselves for a vanity, though the vanity be a beautiful one, as the house in view of the Seine was certainly.

The words : in view of the Seine, called forth the story of the great injustice that had been committed by the railway company, who had built an embankment thirty feet high (over which twenty or twenty-five trains passed daily) between the house and the river. The only concession the railway company had made was the building of a bridge, an archway through which the Comte could find his way to his yacht. He had offeréd the company five hundred thousand francs to bore a tunnel under the hill, but they would not accept this offer, and the Comte had gone to law ; and the Court had only allowed him sixty thousand francs for damages done to his grounds. That is how things are managed in France ! somebody said, and the remark provoked an answer : that it was by disregarding the aesthetic value of gardens and points of view that France possessed the advantage of cheap railways. In England railway companies had had to pay ten times the value of the grounds they appropriated, and that was why the cost of living was higher in England than in France, despite the advantages of free trade. Whereupon a tedious discussion began, free trade versus tariffs, which set Cissy and Elsie whispering together. If the Comtesse cannot accompany her husband to Algiers, Elsie said, I am afraid Etta will be cut out of her visit. You think, asked Cissy, that she was not lying when she told us that the Comtesse had invited her to the Government House at Algiers ? She would hardly dare to tell us that if it were not true, Elsie answered. Besides, there's nothing unlikely in it. She is now one of the house party. And maybe Morton will be asked too. I wonder ! said Cissy, looking up, for the talk showed signs of returning

from economics to the Comte and his household. But somebody intervened with a new argument in favour of tariffs,
and the girls listened wearily till it was mooted that the
Comte de Malmédy might let the palace. But to whom ?
France could not supply a tenant, that was certain, and it
was difficult to suppose that an Englishman or an American
would pay a large rent for a house, a historic monument,
that would have to be preserved intact by the tenant, no
additions or alterations being allowed.

It was said, and with truth, that it was difficult to find
in these modern times anybody rich enough to live in a palace ;
only a few soap boilers and sugar refiners could afford palaces,
and to live in *la maison de la belle Gabrielle* under three
hundred thousand francs a year was impossible. The Comte
spent at least five hundred thousand ; his expenditure could
not be less, so it was related. The hunting cost him a great
deal, and the scale upon which he lived was almost princely
—retinues of servants, huntsmen, coachmen, grooms, kennel
folk of all kinds and sorts. Five hundred thousand francs,
it was said, would not clear the Comte, who was spending
at least a million francs a year at Fontainebleau, and as
Governor of Algeria the pittance he would receive from
the Government would not make up the deficit. His ex-
penses at Fontainebleau would have to be reduced, and
maybe the hunt that would encircle Barbizon on the morrow
would be the last. On hearing that the hounds would
be laid on to the slot of a boar and not a deer, Elsie and
Cissy hoped the boar would not choose their hillside for a
line of retreat. We have no wish to be ripped up by tusks,
the girls said, and they thought of remaining at home, but
were assured that a hunted boar had other things to think
of than to attack stray painters. And so in their courage
they went forth on the morrow to their hillside to put the
finishing hand to their rocks and birches, and it was whilst
engaged in cleaning up some odd corners that their attention was drawn from their work by the sound of wheels,

L

and going to an opening in the trees they spied a carriage. Madame de Malmédy's carriage, Elsie whispered. Etta and Morton are in it. Morton sits opposite and settles the rugs across the ladies' knees. I wonder what the meaning of all this is, said Cissy, Morton selling his pictures to the Comte, and Etta becoming the Comtesse's friend. Suspicious, isn't it ? She has dined with them once, Elsie. Where Etta dines once, she dines again. One dinner doesn't make a mistress, Elsie replied. The girls hearkened to the horns in the forest. The carriage moved on, and all the afternoon they gave occasional ear to the hunting, sometimes hearing it from afar, sometimes the chase passing close by. Once three huntsmen came crashing through the brushwood, wound the long horns they wore about their shoulders, and dashed on again. Once a strayed hound came very near, so near that Elsie threw the dog a piece of bread ; but he did not see it, and trotted away in search of the pack. I think that hound must have followed a deer by himself until he lost him, said Elsie. I hear it 's very hard to keep hounds on the scent of a boar ; they don't like it. It 's almost as disagreeable to them as the scent of an otter, which they cannot abide ; whereas we like the smell. Wherever did you learn all that from, Elsie ? Were you ever in love with a huntsman. The girls screamed. Did you see the boar, Elsie ? Elsie didn't think that anything like a boar had come into the wood, but Cissy was sure she was not mistaken. The boar must have turned at the bottom of the hill, she said, and gathering up their paint-boxes, brushes, and pictures, the girls started to walk back to Barbizon, to be overtaken when about half-way by Morton and Etta, who bade Madame de Malmédy good-bye and walked home with them, telling that the quarry had been taken close to the central *carrefour* ; but the huntsmen did not come up in time, and several hounds were disabled before Comte Gaston de Malmédy managed to give the *coup de grâce*. Whereupon the eatable value

of boar's head was discussed till Etta mentioned that the
Comtesse was going to give a ball. Going to give a ball !
cried Cissy and Elsie, and if the words : Shall we be asked ?
were not on their lips, they were plainly written in the
girls' eyes, sending a smile curling round Etta's thin lips.
Etta is a little beast, who would like to have the whole ball
to herself, Cissy said to Elsie as soon as Etta was out of
hearing, a judgment that was unjust, for when the Comte
and Comtesse came to Barbizon to lunch at Lunions (the
horses, the carriages, the liveries, the dresses, and the great
title making a fine stir in the village), Etta introduced Elsie
and Cissy to the Comtesse, saying that the Comte must
see Elsie's rocks and Cissy's birch trees. She isn't such
a bad sort after all, Cissy said afterwards. Her triumph
wouldn't be complete if we didn't attend the ball, Elsie
answered. Etta must have an audience always. She 'll
get her dress from Paris, and a fine sum her brother Harold
will have to pay for it. She is determined to outshine us.
What shall we look like in our poor little frocks ?

You always try to see the black side of everything, Elsie.
She will get her pleasure out of the ball, and we will get
ours. Live and let live, that 's my maxim.

But did you see that Etta paid very little attention to
Morton ? She never left the Comte's side.

Yes ; I noticed that she seemed a good deal occupied with
the Comte. But after all, she is the Comte's guest. The
Comte is the great man and she must do him homage.

And did you notice how poorly the Comtesse looked ?
It is said that she is in the very worst health and is not
expected to live very long.

Oh, Elsie, you don't mean to say that Etta is already
thinking of dropping Morton in the hope of stepping into
the Comtesse's shoes later on ? That really would be too
far-fetched !

Far-fetched it may be, but Etta is always far-fetched.
I can't make her out. She is always talking about her virtue ;

but I hardly think that Morton would be as devoted to her as he is if he weren't her lover. She tells a lot of lies—of that I 'm certain.

Elsie's face changed expression suddenly, becoming so grave that Cissy knew she was thinking of what she should wear at the ball; and Cissy's thoughts taking flight from Etta, settled upon pale blue for herself. She looked well in blue; but she had worn the colour so often that it seemed to her she would do well to try her luck in pink on so historic an occasion as a ball given by the Comte and Comtesse de Malmédy in the palace that Henri quatre had built for *la belle Gabrielle*.

XII

The hairdresser had come from Fontainebleau, and while he tested his tongs, which were not yet hot enough, Elsie said : I think Morton is beginning to regret that he introduced her to the Malmédys, and it wouldn't surprise me if he were beginning to feel that it 's as likely as not she will throw him over for one of the grand people she is now living with. If mademoiselle is now ready, said the hairdresser. Cissy abandoned her hair to his hands and irons, and Elsie continued to dress and undress. I asked him, Elsie said, for some dances, but he told me that he never engaged himself beforehand. Perhaps she has thrown him over and will not dance with him. Or it may be, Cissy replied, that Morton has not engaged himself for dances because he wished to see if she would keep any for him.

Cissy's was the better guess, it being Morton's plan not to engage himself for any dances so that he might watch Etta. Clever as she is, he said to himself, as he walked up the staircase to the ballroom, she 'll not be able to hide from me the number of dances she has with the Comte and the number she sits out with him. And having shaken hands with his hostess, he sought a corner; and what he saw from his corner was all his heart's desire—a brown,

merry face and soft, fluffy hair. An Etta, he said, in white
tulle laid upon white silk, in a bodice of silver fish scales,
shimmering like a moonbeam when she lays her hand upon
her partner's shoulder, moving forward with a motion that
permeates her whole body. . . . A silver shoe appeared,
and Morton thought : What a vanity ! Only a vanity, but
what a delicious and beautiful vanity ! The waltz ended,
some dancers passed out of the ballroom, and Etta was
surrounded. It looked as if her card would be filled before
Morton could get near her. But she stood on tiptoe and,
looking over the surrounding shoulders, cried that she would
keep the fourteenth for him. Why did you not come before ?
she asked smiling, and went out of the room on the arm of a
young man. At that moment Comte Gaston de Malmédy
took Morton's arm and asked when the picture he had
ordered would be finished. Morton hoped by the end of
next week, and the men walked through the room talking
of pictures. On the way back they met Etta, who told
Morton she had promised the Comte the next dance, and
that he must now go and talk to Madame de Malmédy.

Madame de Malmédy sat in a high chair within the doorway, out of reach of any draught that might happen on the
staircase, her blonde hair drawn up and elaborately curled,
her head-dress recalling a cameo or an old coin. She spoke
in a high, clear voice, and Morton began to wonder on what
terms she lived with her husband ; and to find out, he spoke
of Etta as the prettiest woman in the room. Madame de
Malmédy did not contest the point, but said : Les deux
belles Anglaises, when Cissy and Elsie came whirling by,
Cissy white, large and bare, Elsie small and brown. Morton
regretted that he would have to ask them to dance, but he
could not do else ; and when he had danced with them, and
the three young ladies to whom Madame de Malmédy
introduced him, and had taken a comtesse into supper, he
found that the fourteenth waltz was over. But Etta bade
him not to look so depressed—she had kept the cotillion for

him. It was going to begin very soon ; he had better look
for chairs. He did as he was told, tying his handkerchief
round a couple, and the cotillion proved as unsatisfactory
as he expected it would. Etta was always dancing, but
rarely with him. Dancers retired from the dancing-room,
to return in masks and dominoes ; a paper imitation of a
sixteenth-century house was brought in, ladies showed
themselves at the lattice and were serenaded ; and when
at the end of his inventions the leader fell back on the hand-
glass and the cushion, Etta refused dance after dance. At
last the leader called to Morton, who came up certain of
triumph ; but Etta passed the handkerchief over the glass
and drew the cushion from his knee. She danced both
figures with the Comte de Malmédy, and was covered with
flowers and ribbons at the end of the cotillion ; and though
a little woman, she looked very handsome in a triumph that
Morton hated. But he hid his jealousy as he would his
hand in a game of cards, and when the last guests were
going, he bade her good-night with a calm face. Madame
de Malmédy had gone to her room ; she had felt so tired
that she could sit up no longer, and had begged her husband
to excuse her. And as Etta went upstairs, three or four
steps in front of the Comte, Morton saw her so clearly that
the thought struck him that he had never seen her before.
She appeared in that instant as a toy, a trivial toy made of
coloured glass, and he wondered why he had been attracted
by this bit of coloured glass.

He laughed at his folly and went home, certain that he
could lose her without pain, but visions of Etta and the
Comte haunted his pillow. He did not know whether he
slept or waked, and rose from his bed to meet her on the
terrace at Fontainebleau. But why at Fontainebleau ? he
asked. Her visit to the Malmédys having come to an end,
why did she not return to Barbizon ? And why had she
given him a tryst on the terrace by the fish ponds ? Was
she lodging at Fontainebleau because meetings with the

Comte would be easier there than at Barbizon? Was that it? And on his way to the fish ponds he considered the questions with which he would trap her. But these were forgotten as soon as he saw her coming towards him along the pathway, and talking to her he became so happy that he feared to imperil his happiness by reproaches. He was glad to speak instead of the fabled carp in whose noses rings had been put in the time of Louis the fifteenth. The statues on their pedestals, high up in the clear, bright air, were singularly beautiful, and he tried to speak of the red castle and the display of terraces reaching to the edge of the withering forest.

Morton, dear, don't be angry with me for not having asked you to dance as often as I should have done. I had to dance with the Comte, for I was his guest, but he means nothing to me.

But why have you left Barbizon? Why are you here?

Lunions is not a place for any woman who values her reputation.

If you cared for me, you would think very little——

Of my reputation? All the same, you would be sorry afterwards if I gave myself to you at Lunions in an inn full of cocottes.

Have you come here to give yourself to me?

What, in the Hotel de France? And friends are calling to see me all the afternoon! And servants coming upstairs! One has to undress.

It doesn't take long to undress. Besides, it isn't necessary. And then, feeling that he had said something foolish, he tried to laugh it off. If you really loved me, you wouldn't think of cocottes or the trouble of undressing.

Perhaps one of these days.

When will that day come? Is it near or afar? he asked hastily.

I won't promise, she answered, swinging her parasol in a way that seemed to him characteristic of her, for when

L

I promise, I like to keep my promise. You ask too much. You don't realise what it means to a woman to give herself. Have you never had a scruple about anything ?

Scruple about anything ! I don't know what you mean. What scruple can you have ? You 're not a religious woman.

It isn't religion at all, it is—well, something. . . . I don't know.

This has gone on too long. If I don't get you now I shall lose you   You are a bundle of falsehoods, Etta. All you see and hear and think is false. You said you 'd marry me, but you didn't mean it. You said it to gain time, that was all. Whereas I have always been truthful, never pretending to you that I was something I was not.

You have been true to yourself, Morton.

Which means, he cried, that I have been true to my base sensual nature. I asked you to be my mistress, and then, at your suggestion, I asked you to be my wife. I don't see what more I can do. You say you 're very fond of me, and yet you want to be neither mistress nor wife. Are you going to marry me, or are you not ? When ?

Don't ask me. I cannot say when. Besides, you don't want to marry me. If I am as false as you say—your falsehood being my truth, and vice versa—you cannot want to marry me. Think what the marriage would be of such an ill-assorted couple.

You would save me from myself ? he sneered. Of all the characters in comedy, the altruist suits you the least.

She did not answer, and he began to wonder if she hated him. At the end of the pause he asked her if she had taken rooms at the Hotel de France, and learnt that she had, but was returning to Barbizon. But why return to Barbizon if you have taken rooms at the Hotel de France ? he enquired. I am going to say good-bye to Cissy and Elsie. And you are returning to Fontainebleau to-night ? he asked. She was not sure ; and what happened was that she retained her

rooms at Lunions, and drove back and forth, sleeping sometimes in the village, sometimes in the town, perplexing
Morton, who sought vainly a reason for her simultaneous
patronage of the hotel and the inn. Letters come here for
her, he said, and letters come to the Hotel de France for
her. There must be a reason. There always is one. No,
Morton, there needn't be a reason, Elsie answered, but
there is a cause always. Perhaps, Morton replied ; a cause
that may elude us, an undiscoverable cause. Has she come
to hate me, Cissy ? She can't hate, Morton, for she can't
love. I wouldn't go so far as to say that, Cissy, said Elsie.
She may strike only on one box. I 'm sure she hates Davau,
for he saw through her. I think she must be a little mad,
answered Cissy ; her mother was, of a certainty, if half the
stories about her are true.

A few days later Etta appeared nervously calm, her face
set in a definite and gathering expression of resolution.
Elsie could see that something serious had happened, but
Etta, while admitting that something had happened, declined
to go into particulars. Morton had behaved badly, so much
she would admit, and after a little pressing she confessed
that his behaviour was the cause of her departure. She
must leave before he came down ; and as if unable to bear
the delay any longer, she asked Cissy and Elsie to walk a
little way with her. I cannot stay after what happened last
night. Oh, dear ! she exclaimed, my hat nearly went that
time. I 'm afraid I shall have a rough drive. You will
indeed, said Elsie ; you 'd better stay. I cannot ; it would
be impossible for me to see him again. We can't talk in
this wind, screamed Cissy, we 'd better go back. At that
moment a young pine crashed across the road not very far
from where they were standing, and the girls looked round
for shelter. Those rocks ! cried Cissy. We shan't get there
in time ; the trees will fall upon us, answered Elsie. There 's
not a minute to lose, said Etta ; come ! As they ran the
earth gave forth a rumbling sound and was lifted beneath

their feet. It seemed as if subterranean had joined with aerial forces, for the rumbling sound increased. The roots of the trees are giving way! cried Etta, and as she spoke the pines bent, wavered, and were strewn. It was hard to escape the falling trees, but they reached the rocks and found a safe shelter in an almost cave, where they lay hearkening to the storm. Now it seemed to have taken the forest in violent and passionate grasp, like a giant, determined to destroy it utterly. Sometimes the wind was far away, and as it approached they could hear it trumpeting, careering, springing forward; it paused, rushed, leaped, paused again, and the girls crept closer to each other, not daring to leave the cave, afraid lest the storm should return unexpectedly and overtake them in the avenue, now nearly impassable. You 'll not be able to go to Fontainebleau to-day, said Elsie. Then I 'll go to Melun, Etta answered, and meeting a carriage on their way thither, Etta jumped in, leaving Cissy saying: If it hadn't been for the storm she would have told us what happened last night. I 'm not certain that anything happened, Elsie answered; she just wished us to believe that Morton forced his way into her bedroom. And you don't believe he did? asked Cissy. My experiences do not help me to understand her, nor do yours, Cissy.

XIII

The next news of Etta was that she had gone to Algiers with the Comte, and the Comtesse, of course, who, contrary to all expectations, had decided to accompany her husband, bringing her children with her. Gabrielle's house would therefore be deserted till the early summer, till June. The Comte would be there in July and August, and where the Comte was Etta would be. Such was the news, and Morton, who had returned to Fontainebleau from Paris, fell to thinking of Brittany, where he would find subjects more consonant with his talent than Fontainebleau forest, which Diaz and

Rousseau had made somewhat trite and commonplace. Millet, too, had familiarised the public with long plains and shepherdesses following sheep. Jacques had painted sheep by day and night so often that one couldn't think of a sheep-fold except in Jacques's terms. But if he (Morton) were to spend his summer in Brittany, he would never see Etta again. And at the thought of never seeing her again he rose to his feet and walked up and down the studio, uncertain if he could go on living without seeing her. She would make the Comte miserable, unhappy, as she had made him ; but he would prefer to be unhappy with her than happy with any other woman. Life in this lonely studio, mending landscapes, is terrible. I will begin a figure, he said, and went out in search of a model and found one, a happy, rosy-cheeked little servant, out of a place, who was glad to sit to him, and whom he made almost as unhappy as himself, for she very soon guessed that he was in love with another woman. But despite the help of his little model, Morton found the forgetting of Etta to be a long and bitter business ; sometimes he thought it was all over, that he was free from her, but he knew he was not, and that if she held up her little finger he would go back to her. To be made unhappy, he said. Even so, I should go back to her. And when June came round and he prepared for his summer outing, the thought of seeing her again still held him in an unrelaxing grip ; and to see her he must go to Barbizon, however much he might hate to see the old, ill-paven street, the inn garden, and the inn parlour covered with pictures. I can never paint there again, he said to himself ; painting is happiness, and there's no happiness for me in Barbizon. Wherever we have been unhappy is a dead place to us. And his thoughts turning to last year's motives, he continued : My spirit dries up at the very thought of them ! But there's much else in the forest of Fontainebleau. And if she doesn't appear in June, she will not return, and I'll go to Brittany, where everything will be new, the earth, the skies, and the people. If I had the courage to start to-morrow for Brittany !

But he had not that courage and returned to Barbizon to wait for her, certain of pain and unhappiness, sorry for his pictures and sorry for himself, but unable to do otherwise than wait for news of Etta. Cissy and Elsie will bring me news of her, he said. But for Elsie and Cissy he had to wait several weeks, and his life seemed to burn up like autumn weeds when they told him she had not written to them during the winter. If she returns, it will be in another month, he said to himself, and regretting that he had left Paris, or thinking he did, he cursed the forest, saying that it kept alive his memory of her, till one morning Cissy came round to his studio with a letter that she had just received from Etta, who told that she was back in London, or rather in Sutton, and was coming to Fontainebleau a little later. Coming after the Malmédys, I suppose, said Morton, and looking through Cissy he saw Etta in his thought. She may be coming back to paint, Cissy answered, but Morton did not think that she would ever take up painting again. You see, she doesn't speak of returning to Barbizon, but to Fontainebleau, to be nearer the Malmédys. She hasn't forgotten you, Morton ; if you read on, you 'll see. Morton read on ; he swore and called her names, but he was pleased that he was not forgotten.

A few days later Etta wrote to Elsie ; her letter contained a cutting from a newspaper in which he was spoken of favourably, and at this expression of goodwill, Morton's resolution to stand aloof broke down, and he began to think of the letter he might write without letting her see that all she had to do was to hold up her little finger to bring her lover back to her. I thought, he wrote, that after this journey to Algeria there would be a turning out of pockets. She won't like that, he said, and chuckled over his sarcasm as he went to his subject in the forest. It was not long, however, before he began to regret his sarcasm, for Etta

did not answer his letter, and he attributed her silence to
his words. He was wrong again; Etta's answer, when it
came, contained no reference to the turning out of pockets,
and he said : A sense of humour in a woman is a great help
to a lost admirer. The words caused him a pang and then
a sinking of the heart. A lost admirer! I couldn't have
expressed myself better. And then hope began to revive.
She is coming back, and why should she write to me unless——
He did not dare to finish the sentence; and a week later
a note came saying that she was driving over from Fontainebleau and would call at his studio in the afternoon about
three o'clock.

On opening the door, it seemed to him that he was receiving
somebody out of a picture, so beautifully was Etta dressed;
a terra-cotta silk was unusual and certainly incongruous
in Barbizon, and in his rough way Morton expressed his
surprise : You look as if you were just about to step into
one of Watteau's ships bound for Cythera. Etta laughed,
saying that Watteau's ships never reached Cythera, doing
no more than to sail round its coasts, a remark that so thor-
oughly roused all Morton's old animosities, that Etta spoke
of Courbet, Corot, Daubigny, Diaz and Rousseau, without
being able to engage him in conversation, it seeming to
Morton that all her questions were designed to make fun
of him. Or is all this talk about Courbet and Corot merely
a beating to windward ? he asked himself, his gloom increasing every moment. And perceiving that she was
annoying him, Etta said : Well, tell me with whom you
have been in love. I met somebody who tried to undo the
mischief you did me, he answered, and she encouraged him
to talk about this new love of his, an encouragement that he
appreciated, for it relieved him of his love of her to tell
her of the benefit that this new love had been to him; and
to move her to repentance, he related that at one time he
was very near to suicide. And you, he said, when he came
to the end of his story, what have you been doing all this

while ? Tell me about the Comte. Did he make love to you ? We saw a great deal of each other, she answered, and as for making love, it all depends upon the man and the woman. Love differs with every one of us, she continued, and he asked her if she had found the Comte's love superior to his in practice and theory. She turned her brown eyes upon him and said, he thought somewhat sententiously, that he and the Comte were very different. You were true to yourself, she added.

And you to yourself ! he rapped out. I am always that, she replied, her thoughtful and decisive voice exasperating Morton, who asked her bluntly whether the Comte was her lover, a question that brought a look of pleasure into her face.

You may just as well tell me the truth, Etta ; it would be a relief to know that there was some trace, some spark of humanity in you.

No, he was not my lover in the sense that you mean, and I don't think I could give myself to a man with any conviction unless I was going to have a child by him.

I fear that we are as antagonistic as ever.

It may be, but as long as we are not untruthful to each other——

Oh, damn truth ! Tell me about the Comte, and if you are going to marry him. His wife is ill, very ill, and a permanent recovery is not likely.

I would not wish anything to happen to Marie, but if anything should happen—well, there 's no saying.

I should like to see you settled, Etta, Morton said paternally, whereupon Etta became discursive, and rattled off a story. The Comte's attentions to her in Algiers had caused much jealousy in the Government House, the other women not liking to see her put next to the Comte at dinner. She was invariably placed next to him. And thought catching fire from thought, she began to speak of the Comtesse's friendships, telling that one day, on overlooking the invitations sent out, the Comte noticed a certain name, and sending for his orderly, he walked to and fro, asking himself how it was that the name appeared on the list in spite of his having given strict orders that it should be omitted.

My orders to you were that Mr. Villars was not to receive invitations to the Government House, but despite my orders I see his name among my guests. What explanation have you to offer ?

That I am not answerable for the inclusion of Mr. Villars's name at dinner, sir. Mr. Villars received his invitation from the Comtesse.

The Comtesse did not know of my interdiction.

Pardon me, sir, but I mentioned your interdiction to the Comtesse.

Gaston turned aside speechless, Etta said, and I heard afterwards——

But, Etta, the Comtesse's lying-in was announced in the newspapers.

That third child was not his, as is well known. The Comte's health precludes the possibility ; and she spoke of a disease of the spine which obliged the Comte to wear iron supports. A sort of stays, Morton interjected. Etta answered : Yes, without perceiving the sarcasm, so deep was she in her own concernments. She broke the pause suddenly to tell of a journey that she and the Comte, and others, of course, had made, going as far into the desert as Biskra. You will be surprised to hear, she said, that I have returned to art.

I am not in the least surprised.

Not to painting, but to drawing.

Better still. Show me your drawings. Etta opened her sketch-book ; it had been in her lap all the while, but Morton had not noticed it. Before I show you any, she said, I would like to say that I look upon my scribbles as material for half a dozen drawings or more—— For a book you have written ? interjected Morton. Yes, she answered, how quick you are. I have written some articles, and while writing and thinking of them I made a few drawings, and

I think it would be unkind to separate the drawings from the text and the text from the drawings. But drawings done for reproduction require a little revision, Morton said. Yes, she replied ; and I thought that I might look to you for revision and advice.

Tea was brought in, and during the drinking of it, Etta's drawings were announced by Morton to be very clever ; and after tea, till the bell sounded for dinner, Morton listened to Etta reading her narrative of her travels in the land in which summer is always.

XIV

For the next few weeks Etta seemed to spend her time driving with a clergyman through the forest of Fontaine-bleau, visiting its various towns and villages, arriving at Barbizon nearly every day for luncheon or for afternoon tea—arriving in a carriage drawn not by one but by two horses, driven by a coachman in livery who wore a cockaded hat, and attended upon by a footman, also in a cockaded hat. A splendid creature he was standing by the carriage door, representing force and dignity, and a dainty spectacle was Etta, stepping in and out in her Watteau dresses, followed by her clergyman carrying a shawl and a parasol—a spectacle that provided Cissy and Elsie with an almost endless subject for conversation, each exciting the other to fresh sallies and acrimonious remarks. Etta always likes to do things in fine style, said Cissy, and Elsie answered : It is strange that Etta, who is so quick to laugh at others, sees nothing ridiculous in her own conduct. You 'll hardly believe it, but she has again taken a room at Lunions ! When did you hear that ? Cissy asked. Only this morning. And now she has her letters addressed here ; I saw one just now waiting for her. The room she requires, for she changes her gowns three times a day, exchanging her morning dress for one more suitable for the afternoon—— With stockings to match, for sure, interjected Cissy. But why does she come here with her parson ? asked Morton. I tried to persuade her out of this new wickedness ; for though you fooled me and made me very miserable, I said, we are evenly matched ; but this poor young man. . . . What did she say ? asked Elsie. She said he had come over in the hope of a curacy in Paris, and that if he did not get it, he was prepared to go to India on the Mission. But, being a man of great talent, she would like him to remain in Europe. He is staying at Fontainebleau, she said, and what more natural than that I should drive over to Barbizon with him ? And change her dress three times a day, remarked Cissy. I 've often thought she was a little mad, said Morton, looking questioningly at Elsie, who answered : She is certainly not normal. But what makes you think so ? She often comes to my studio with the drawings she did in the desert, Morton replied, and once we had a talk about the clergyman. It appears that Mr. Barrett is very High Church, and she would have him go over to Rome, if he does not get the appointment, on the grounds that Rome favours converts. There 's nothing Etta likes so much as a Catholic church, said Cissy. But, Morton, have we told you that letters come for her to Lunions ? Living at the Hotel de France and having letters addressed to Lunions seems very strange. It is certainly unusual, Morton answered, and the constant change of attire. And all for no purpose.

The painters separated, each to his or her special subject, and when they returned weary from the forest with their canvases the first thing they saw was the barouche with its horses, coachman, and footman, in front of the hotel. Waiting for Madame la Pompadour ! said Cissy. Madame Recamier returning from driving with Chateaubriand, answered Elsie, and they fell into the perennial discussion whether Madame Recamier had lived and died in strict singleness. After hearing all the evidence and Morton's conjectures, Elsie said : We shall only just have time to

M

make ourselves tidy for dinner ; and the girls went upstairs
wondering what richly coloured gown Etta would wear
so that she might fool the parson to the top of her bent.
The strangely assorted twain dined at a corner table,
Etta's gown and the parson's coat and collar distracting
everybody's attention from his and her neighbour. It was
always thus when they dined at Lunions, and on this day
dinner was half over when a servant brought in a letter and
stood whispering at the door, Morton and Cissy and Elsie
guessing that the letter contained evil news for Etta. So
they said afterwards in the garden when they talked together, telling each other how Etta's face had brightened
at the sight of the handwriting and how quickly a change
had appeared in her, the first lines of the letter affecting
her so much that the parson jumped to his feet to help her,
thinking that she was about to faint. She would have
fainted, said Elsie, if it hadn't been for the glass of water
that he forced her to drink. And did you see her face afterwards, Morton, as she strove to gain control over herself ?
Yes, indeed I did, Cissy ; and what powers of will she must
have to have carried on as she did. She sent the parson to
the piano with orders to do more than his usual splashing.

She must have suffered agony, said Elsie ; but determined
to deceive us, to prove to us that nothing had happened
worth speaking about, she got up to dance, and waltzed
about the floor with herself. It was out of politeness I
asked her to dance with me, but she refused, you remember.
Morton's face drooped into meditation, and Elsie answered :
If she had danced with you, the parson might have stopped
playing. Cissy continued the conversation, telling how soon
after Etta had called the Reverend Barrett over to her,
saying that she felt tired and would like to return to Fontainebleau. She showed pluck, said Morton, for while the horses
were being put to she stood talking to us and bade us good-
night in quite a cheerful mood, or seemingly. Now what
news can she have received ? The news she received,

answered Elsie, did not come from London.   Harold is not
dead, though the Comte may be.

The Comte!   Yes, it may be that.   Or it may be the
Comtesse.   She spoke of Marie as her great friend, saying
that she did not wish anything to happen to Marie, but if——

Oh yes, I know, interjected Elsie, clearing the decks!
clearing the decks!

XV

It was in the afternoon next day, as Morton was setting
out for Melun to fetch his mistress and model, that a letter
came from the hotel-keeper at Fontainebleau, saying that
Miss Marr had left word that she was not to be called in
the morning, and it was not till midday that a housemaid
entered the room and gave the alarm.   The doctor was
sent for, and after an examination of the body, he reported
that Miss Marr had died probably from heart failure.   Morton
handed the letter to Elsie and Cissy, who were returning
from their painting.   Good heavens!   cried Elsie, and at
Morton's bidding she and Cissy jumped into the carriage,
whilst Morton followed, saying: It was the letter that she
got last night.   And all the way to Fontainebleau they
asked each other questions: What did she do it for?   But
did she do it?   Was it an accident?   Or was it an over-
dose?   We shall never know, Morton said as they drove
into the long, straggling street of Fontainebleau, for she
has destroyed the letter, no doubt.   But did she show the
letter to Mr. Barrett?   Elsie asked.   Morton shrugged his
shoulders, and the carriage stopped before the Hotel de
France.

The hotel-keeper told them that he had sent round to
Mr. Barrett's hotel, but Mr. Barrett had taken the eight
o'clock to Paris.   He mentioned that visitors did not like
to sleep in a house in which there was a dead body, certainly
not on the same floor.   He had refrained, however, from
calling in the police, who would have taken the body to

the morgue, for he had known Miss Marr for some time, and she was a friend of the Comte de Malmédy. Morton told the man that he need not fear any loss for not having sent for the police and that a reasonable compensation would be paid by Mr. Harold Marr—Who will be here tomorrow morning, he said. As I have his address I will write the telegram at once. May we go upstairs, said Cissy, to bid good-bye to our friend ? We haven't brought any flowers, added Elsie, there was no time ; but we 'll send some. The hotel-keeper answered that a chambermaid would show them to the room.

Timorous, abashed they crossed the threshold. Like a piece of marble, said Cissy. And how unlike herself, answered Elsie, and the girls began to wonder if death reveals or hides the truth, or if truth and falsehood end with life. It seems only natural that the untruthful in life should be untruthful in death, said Cissy. Elsie did not answer, the moment not seeming to her one for criticism of their dead friend. All the same, it was dreadful to die like this, and laying aside their thoughts of the end that might await them, their eyes went round the room in search of the Watteau dress that she had danced in last night, and not finding it, Cissy said : She has hung up her dress in the wardrobe.

She has put away everything. Her parasol is in the corner and her hat is in its box.

She evidently thought it all out.

Not a drawer is open ; yet she must have opened many seeking the drug.

You think it was a drug ? Cissy whispered, and returning from the bed, she said : It was a drug, for there 's no blood. She put on a fresh nightgown ; how like her !

Ah, here is the veronal, said Elsie, and the bottle half empty. If it was full last night, she has taken enough to kill twenty.

And here is the letter she received at Lunions last night, on the toilet table, in full view. Ought we to read it ?

If she hadn't wanted us to read it, she would have destroyed it, answered Elsie, and they read the letter together, lifting their eyes from time to time to make sure that the dead girl was not watching them. If she shouldn't be dead, Cissy whispered, and should open her eyes and see us reading her letter! She will never open her eyes again, answered Elsie, and looking over Elsie's shoulder Cissy continued reading the letter that the Comte had written to Etta in answer to a letter of condolence she had written to him, full of pathetic sentiments about his dead wife, ending up by reminding him he had promised her that if ever he was free he would marry her. It was stupid of her, said Cissy, to write such a letter at such a moment. But he needn't have answered her so roughly.

His letter killed her. All her hopes were set on this grand marriage, all her vanity. The mystery is explained, Morton.

Morton closed the door. What mystery? he asked. She left the letter she got last night on the toilet table.

And you have read it?

If she hadn't wanted us to read it, she wouldn't have left it on the toilet table.

That 's true, said Morton, and Elsie handed him the letter. Read it, she said.

No, I couldn't read it in front of her. It was the cause of her death, I presume?

Elsie told him the contents of the letter, referring to it from time to time, reading out the words with which the Comte bade Etta good-bye. You see, said Elsie, that this letter put an end to all her hopes of ever getting him back.

So she took her life in a fit of spleen, Morton answered. How did she do it?

With a dose of veronal, Cissy replied.

To revenge herself on the Comte, said Elsie. I can think of nothing else.

Don't be so harsh, Elsie! Morton answered sharply. Now that she's dead it would be well to think of her as kindly as we can.

She always struck me as being a little crazed, Cissy interjected. Cut off from a good deal in life, Elsie added, and they went downstairs talking of the parson. Sent away to Paris, Elsie conjectured, to save him the sorrow of learning that she intended to throw him over for the Comte.

But he'll learn that from the letter, said Morton.

In his grief for her he'll forget the Comte, Elsie answered.

And will throw himself at her bedside, Morton continued, weeping and praying, and I hope that Harold will not find him here when he arrives. A painful and embarrassing scene it will be for both of them if he does. He reaches the Gare du Nord before six; it will take him an hour to drive from the Gare du Nord to the Gare de Lyons, perhaps more than that, and there may not be a train, or a very slow one. I doubt if he will reach Fontainebleau before ten at the very earliest.

SARAH GWYNN

On returning from the study door, whither he had accompanied the last patient, the doctor cast a glance of approbation at the two piles of gold and silver on his table, the gold slightly overtopping the silver ; and considering them as a very adequate remuneration for his afternoon's work, Dr. O'Reardon dropped into his great Chippendale armchair (the very one that Sir Stanley used to sit in—it had returned to Ely Place after a brief sojourn in Taylor's shop in Liffey Street), and ensconced amid its carvings, his thoughts ran on a tiresome woman for whose everlasting megrim he had written a prescription : five grains of carbonate of soda— a neighbour, an acquaintance, a garrulous woman, who never would take a hint but would go on talking, however many people were in the waiting-room ; she paid her guinea, but rarely failed to waste two guineas' worth of his time, putting him past his complacency. He regretted these accesses of temper by the burnished brass of the fire-irons and the multi-coloured marble chimney-piece, and continued to recall his patients. Another woman engaged his thoughts ; her rheumatoid arthritis perplexed him ; she didn't seem to improve under his treatment and he was afraid he would have to try inoculations. These cases, he said, go commonly from bad to worse. A moment after he was thinking of a child he had examined that morning for heart, still uncertain whether the murmur that had come to his ear through the stethoscope meant specific disease or whether it might be attributed to poverty of blood. Another, a still more serious case, was remembered ; and so that he might think better he closed his eyes, but began very soon to lose control over his thoughts, a veil seeming to rise and another to descend. He strove against sleep, but it was too late to rouse, and he must have slept for a long or a short time, which he could not say, but he must have slept deeply, for when the knocker of the front door awoke him he stared round the room, not recognising it as his own, returning to consciousness of himself through recollections of the parlourmaid who had run out of the house that morning without saying a word to anybody (she had her wages yesterday). From the parlourmaid his thoughts turned to the cook, who must be upstairs, else she would have gone to the front door. Now who could the visitor be ? A patient, most likely, though it was past four o'clock. For a doctor of his position to let a patient in was a breach of etiquette, but circumstance——— Another knock startled him from his meditation, and he returned from the front door followed by a sparely dressed woman, standing not much higher than his elbow.

All men and women resemble some animal, a friend had said one evening, and when he had pointed out many likenesses to cats and dogs, horses and hyenas, among his acquaintances, somebody said : And O'Reardon—what is he like ? The answer came at once : A camel, and immediately everybody saw the resemblance : the small head, high nose, long lip, wide, drooping mouth. The story was an old one, almost out of currency, but the little starveling the doctor had just let into his house recalled it. If I am like a camel, he said to himself, what is this woman like ? A squirrel ? No ; a squirrel is a gay boy. Before he could think again the little woman by his side began to tell that she had heard from Miss Lynch that he required a cook, and he listened, already won by a voice so pure and clear that his curiosity was stirred to see his visitor ; and the little, blonde face, the upturned nose, and clear, eager eyes that appeared when the lamp was lighted seemed to be the girl he might have guessed if he had laid his mind to guessing—a tiny, thread-paper girl in a straw hat, an alpaca jacket, and a thin skirt that did not hide her broken boots, a starveling, and remembering what Miss Lynch had told him, he said : The cook must be in the house somewhere ; she 'll get you a cup of tea.

No, thank you, sir. I came here thinking you wanted a cook. The doctor answered that it was the parlourmaid who had left. Then you 'll not be wanting a cook, sir ? she broke in, without a trace of disappointment in her voice ; she even seemed to the doctor relieved to hear that she was not required. I remember now, the doctor said. You were in a convent in Wales, weren't you ?

Yes, sir.

Miss Lynch told me about you ; but when you knocked I was asleep and must have slept heavily, for I didn't know my own room when I awoke.

I am sorry I woke you, sir.

There 's no need for you to be sorry. I 'm glad you did, and that I went to the door. You were in a convent for nearly ten years, and because you answered the Sub-Prioress, or maybe the Prioress herself, sharply, they bundled you out, clapping a straw hat on your head and an alpaca jacket on your shoulders, giving you but your bare fare to Dublin, not caring——

Oh, but you mustn't talk like that, sir ! It was all my fault. I spoke to our Sub-Prioress in a way that I shouldn't have. I lost my temper, and all the blame is with me. They did quite right to send me away, for they couldn't have kept me. You must believe what I say ; indeed, I am speaking the truth, and no more than it. The doctor did not answer, and at the end of the pause the nun said : I doubt very much if I should suit you. I think I 'll go.

You shall go, if you wish to go, in a minute or two, but I 'd like to say a few words first. Miss Lynch mentioned that you would not hear a word said against the nuns, and advised me not to speak about the convent ; but, as I have said, your knock awoke me, and I came to the door unable to collect my thoughts. That's how it happened, else I should not have spoken about the nuns. So, you see, there's no real reason for you to run away.

You want a cook, sir? The doctor answered that his cook had decided to stay, but the parlourmaid had left, and that if she would care to accept the situation he would be glad to engage her. I go out in the mornings, he continued, to my hospital or to visit my patients, and in the afternoons I receive patients from two till four. The wages are twenty-four pounds a year. I don't know your name.

My name is Sarah Gwynn, sir; and during the pause Dr. O'Reardon was again attracted by the tiny face, lit by blue-grey nervous eyes. I hope you'll not refuse the situation, he said, for if you do Miss Lynch will be very angry with me for my indiscretion.

I should not like you to have it on your mind, sir, that the nuns behaved otherwise than rightly, and would sooner lose the situation than——

Miss Lynch, who is a Roman Catholic, doesn't take that view, but we need not trouble ourselves about the rights and wrongs. You may have been overworked and tired; your nerves may have given way.

Yes, sir, that was it.

Sarah's vehement defence of her former friends and sisters in the Lord Jesus Christ had evoked the doctor's sympathy, and smitten by her originality, he determined not to lose her. You will require some clothes, he said, assuming that she had agreed to stay, and he went to his writing-table and took five pounds from the pile of gold. At the sight of so much money Sarah drew back, as if afraid. I should like you to buy the things you want before the shops close, he continued. Miss Lynch will advise you, perhaps accompany you, as you have only just arrived in Dublin.

I know Dublin, sir. I was here before.

Ah, so much the better. Well, I shall expect to see you when I return home for luncheon to-morrow.

You may be sure I 'll come, sir, she answered from the door ; and then remembering that the lock was a double one, he said : Allow me. The two handles must be turned at the same time.

Sarah passed out, and Dr. O'Reardon had barely reseated himself in his chair before he began to regret the impulsive mood that had impelled him to take five pounds from the pile by his writing-pad and give them to a woman he might never see again. But she came recommended by Helena, a level-headed woman, and the doubt that had arisen was swept away, and its place was taken by a sudden and awful dread of breakages. For the woman who had left him had been ten years in a convent, where the concrete is nothing and the abstract everything, and to-morrow, if she returned (which she would, for Helena Lynch would not have sent her to him if she were not sure of her honesty), his cabinets filled with Bow and Chelsea would be in her charge ; and the project of running after her with another five pounds, the price of a breach of agreement, started up in his mind. It was cowardice that kept him in his chair ; and that night he slept but little, leaving the house for his hospital filled with misgivings of what would happen between ten and eleven, the time she would arrive. He felt that when he returned for luncheon at one o'clock he would be told that she had filled a cut-glass decanter with hot water, with the usual consequences, or that a Chelsea figure had been swept from the chimney-piece into the fender. And the oriental vases and the birds ! He shuddered. The carved mirrors above the chimney-pieces she could not touch, but she might easily knock a carved garland from a side table with a sweeping brush.

His carriage continued to take him further and further from his cherished possessions, and if a capital operation had not been awaiting him, he would have turned back to leave a note saying that she was not to attempt any work, cleaning above all, before seeing him. As the carriage crossed Carlisle Bridge, he thought of his pictures, his collection and his own water-colours. A might-have-been lives on in the heart, almost a reproach, and the memories of the art that he had abandoned and that could never now be his, put the ex-nun out of the doctor's mind (it was thus that he now thought of her) till he arrived at the hospital.

II

At one o'clock O'Reardon returned along the quays, forgetful of the old shop in Liffey Street, deep in thoughts of an accident, one that every doctor dreads : death under an operation. The patient had not recovered consciousness, and Dr. O'Reardon crossed Carlisle Bridge, passed Trinity College, reaching home without seeing or hearing, so absorbed that he did not recognise the smart young woman in cap and apron who met him in the passage. He asked her if luncheon was ready, and she answered that it would be in a few minutes ; and it was not till she began to tell him that several had called to see him that morning, that he roused a little and began to ask himself who the young woman was that remembered so clearly the messages given to her. On looking under the white cap he recognised the anxious face of the vagrant nun whom he had seen overnight, asking himself again what animal she resembled, if it was the white and red that had put a weasel into his head. But a weasel is white underneath and red above. Or was it her gait ? She seemed to run forward and to stop suddenly, just like a weasel. Have you broken anything, Sarah ?

Broken anything, sir ? What makes you think that ? Sarah resented the insinuation so sharply that the doctor had to plead that his thoughts were away, and he related the unfortunate operation, the failure of which he knew could not be laid to his charge, nor to that of the anaesthetist or the nurses. The man ought to have been operated upon earlier, he said.

And as with time his mind freed itself from qualms of conscience, he began to notice that life was passing pleasantly, a great deal of its smoothness seemingly owing to the diligence and care of his new parlourmaid. Since she came into his service plates ceased to be chipped ; no Waterford glass had been broken, nor was his eye ever caught by a piece of ornamental carving knocked from a carven armchair. Nor did a cessation of breakages comprise all her qualities ; she was now the parlourmaid that every doctor desires and never finds. Her service at table was excellent, though she had never attended at table before she came into his service. In six months she was more learned than the best of her predecessors. Everybody envied him. A dinner of twelve doctors could not be managed by two servants ; another housemaid was called in, and Sarah's administration of the service was admirable. The plates were not put in the oven ; they were heated by hot water ; the entrées came out hot ; the claret was neither hot nor cold but kept warm to just the right temperature. She reminded him that Mr. —— did not drink champagne; and when the doctor went into the country every Saturday to paint, and forgot to wash his brushes, when he remembered them they were washed. He had never had a parlourmaid to wash his brushes before. His palette was cleaned, too, and without disturbing the colours that he had set. Messages were delivered and appointments made that he could keep. Every month he discovered new qualities ; economies were effected, and how she managed to supervise the household books without enraging the cook, he did not know, nor did he dare to enquire, but he noticed improvements everywhere, and also a change in Sarah herself.

She was a starveling when she came, shy and perplexed ; now she had put on a little flesh and recovered her strength, and though her face could not be said to be as merry as a squirrel's, it was alive and pleasant. He noticed the neatness with which she wore her cap, her carefully brushed hair, and that when her attention wandered, which it did sometimes, a far-away look came into her pale grey eyes; and so he was moved to ask her if she was happy in her situation and had ceased to regret the convent, to think well of the nuns, but remembering the rebuff he had received on the first occasion, he refrained from putting any questions to her. From these absences she would return suddenly, and he often wondered if she was aware of her absent-mindedness; he thought she was not, and that she came and went unwittingly. Her face lighted up when he spoke to her; she would continue the dropped conversation and go out of the room, a little more abruptly, he thought, than at other times. Sarah is much improved in health, he said to himself, and fell to thinking what her secret might be, without doubting that all Sarah had told him of herself was true; but there was much in her life beyond the facts that she had been in a Welsh convent for ten years and had been turned out at a moment's notice for rudeness to her superiors. Her accent told him that she came from the County Down, and for a Down girl to find her way to a Welsh convent was queer enough to set the least curious wondering how she had wriggled out of her Protestantism to begin with, and subsequently into a convent in Wales.

It had come to his ears that Sarah missed Mass, which was strange, unless indeed she had changed in mind as much or more than she had physically, and he remembered her words in defence of the outrageous nuns, and her abrupt rising from her chair with the intention of refusing the situation he had offered her. That time may have revealed to her how cruelly she had been treated was quite possible. She had never spoken of it again. It was true that the opportunity had not occurred. But the other reports! His friends had seen Sarah late at night in Sackville Street and Grafton Street and round Trinity College; nor was she passing quickly through these streets on her way home, but loitering, peering into the faces of the passers-by like

one in search of somebody. That his friends had met Sarah,
or somebody they had mistaken for Sarah, was certain ;
but the thought that the reaction from the convent had
driven her to lead a double life—his parlourmaid during
the day, a whore on her evenings out—was a belief that
none who knew her could entertain, for to know Sarah was
to believe every word she said. Her exalted moods, her
clear, pure voice—— No, it is not possible, he said ; moreover, Helena would not have sent her here if she were not
sure of her character, knowing how important it is to me.
. . . His thoughts passed into a reverie of the days when
Helena had decided to work for her own living, and the
excellent Health Inspector that had come out of this determination. But how had she come upon Sarah ? All he
knew was that they had met the day after Sarah arrived
in Dublin in the straw hat and the alpaca jacket. It might
be that Helena knew only Sarah's story ; but it is not easy
for one Catholic to deceive another with a tale of expulsion
from a convent, and sharp-witted Helena, though a Catholic,
was no fool, and he would learn Sarah's secret from Helena
when she returned to Dublin.

The words came into his mind : She 'll hardly recognise
Sarah, so much improved is she, almost a good-looking girl ;
and hearing her laughing—her laughter came through the
window with many sweet-scented airs from the garden—
Sarah laughing with Michael ! he said, and seeing her
standing by the tall, lilac bushes, gathering purple bloom
for his dinner-table, Michael, the gardener, drawing down
the high branches with his rake, he began a letter to Helena,
telling her of the coming of spring in his garden, the lilac
in bloom, the buds swelling in the apple trees, waiting for
the May-time. All the world, he said, yields to the gentle
season, and it may be that it will find its way into Sarah's
heart ; her feet are certainly on the lilac path, and I should
not be surprised overmuch (though I should be surprised),
if you were to find her married to Michael when you return,

a merry look in her eyes replacing the yearning look for
something beyond the world, which you have not forgotten,
so characteristic is it of her. . . . In the letter he was writing
he would tell, too, of the secret which he was sure that
Sarah was hiding from him—hiding, perhaps, from Helena.
His thoughts were brought to an end by the arrival of a
patient, and it was not till many days after that he discovered the half-written letter among some papers on his
writing-table.

III

I cannot thank you enough, he wrote, for sending me
Sarah, a most excellent, far-seeing servant, holding all the
threads, managing everything, interested apparently in me
and in me only; but behind this impersonal externality
she lives her personal life, of which we know nothing. She
has been with me now nearly a year, yet my knowledge of
her is not greater to-day than it was before I saw her. I
have learned, it is true, that she came originally from the
north of Ireland; she didn't tell me, her accent told me,
and I have been wondering if her bringing-up was Protestant
and if she became a Catholic from caprice. Newman, I
believe, went over for theological reasons, but theology
cannot have been the motive that seduced Sarah, whose
attendance at Mass is casual, uncertain, so I am told. Be
this a lie or truth, she is no longer religious; indeed I doubt
if she ever was religious. Then why did she, a Protestant
presumably, become a Catholic and enter a convent? And
why is she so silent about herself? The door opened behind
him, and without turning round the doctor answered Sarah,
who asked if he was busy: I am writing a letter to Miss
Lynch; and he continued writing till his attention was
attracted by the silence behind him. You heard me say
that I was writing to Miss Lynch? Now, Sarah, if you
have any message—— No, sir, I have no message. I
have come to ask you for her address. You see, it was

she who sent me to you, and may be able to get me another place, for I 've come to tell you that I shall be leaving you at the end of the month. But if you would let me go sooner——

Leaving me, Sarah, at the end of the month! What do you mean? I understood that you were satisfied with your situation——

Yes, sir; the situation is all right and I am grateful, but it can't be helped.

Can't be helped! the doctor repeated. Everything can be helped. Tell me why you 're leaving—why you 're thinking of leaving. Is it wages? Tell me; there must be a reason, and when I know the reason I shall be able to arrange.

There are things that cannot be arranged, sir, and this is one of them. As she spoke the words she moved towards the door, but the doctor rushed past her, saying: No, Sarah, no; you cannot leave the room until I hear why you want to leave me. It is not fair, nor is it right, for you to walk out of my house without giving a reason, like the parlour-maid you superseded. Are you going to be married, for if you are that will be a sufficient reason?

No, sir; I am not going to get married.

He watched her face, and she returned to the writing-table with him. Now, sit down, Sarah, and tell me why you 're leaving.

Well, sir, it is because the gardener wants to marry me.

But he hasn't interfered with you in any way?

No, sir; I 've got no fault to find with him.

No fault to find except that he asked you to marry him?

But I can't marry him, sir. It would be better if you didn't ask me any more questions, indeed it would.

Am I to understand that you like the gardener?

He is all right, sir; I shouldn't mind if things were different. Tell me, Sarah.

You wouldn't understand, sir; it would seem a lot of nonsense to you.

N

But everybody is nonsense to the next one. I would like to hear first of all why you left the north and why you became a Catholic.

I was always a Catholic, sir ; my mother was a Catholic.

And your father ?

Father was a Protestant, and mother went over when she married him. You see, in the County Down a Protestant can't marry a Catholic, for everybody would be against her. Mother wanted to bring me over with her, but I wouldn't go over, and that was the beginning of it.

Sarah stopped suddenly, and a little perplexed doctor and maid-servant stared at each other. I can't see, sir, how all this can interest you ; but if you wish to hear it, I 'll tell you the story, for I have been very happy here and am grateful to you, and, as you said, I can't leave without giving a reason. When mother went over I was twelve, and out in the fields at five o'clock in the morning pulling swedes and mangel-wurzels ; the wurzels are the worst, for they have roots a foot long, and it was terribly hard work getting them up, for I wasn't as strong as the other girls. They all thought it hard work ; our backs ached dreadfully when we went home to breakfast at eight o'clock.

And after breakfast ?

After breakfast I had to go to school ; and when school was over we began to feel the dread of next morning creeping over us, at least I did.

And to escape from the pulling of mangel-wurzels you came to Dublin ?

No, it wasn't that, sir. After a bit my stepfather was out of his luck ; ten sheep died on him, the mare cast her foal ; and we did not keep the bad luck to ourselves, for we shared it with the farmers round our way, and the talk began that somebody had put a curse on the County. If anything goes wrong in County Down it 's the fault of the Catholics. I was the only Catholic there, and as I passed by some boys on a gate, one of them said : There goes the papish, and another picked it up and cried : To hell with the Pope and his witches. I took fright in case the story should get about and my feet be put in the fire till I confessed that I had sold my soul to the Devil. So I saved up a few pence every week till I had enough to bring me to Dublin, and one day after my morning's work on the farm, instead of coming in for dinner I walked into Belfast. It was a brave long walk, more than seven miles, so I had to buy some meat, and this left me with only a shilling above my railway fare. I was afraid to break into my shilling in Dublin, but by ten o'clock it was that cold I had to have a cup of tea. I hung round the coffee-stall, thinking I might hear where I could look for work in the morning, and then the stall-keeper closed for the night. A drizzle was coming on, and the policeman I spoke to told me I had better go to the workhouse. But I didn't know the road, and if they didn't take me in (and why should they ? for I didn't belong to Dublin), I 'd have to come all the way back again. Why back again ? the doctor asked, and she said that she expected more luck about the parks. Than where ? queried the doctor. Than in the streets round a workhouse, she answered. The late hour and the word luck put the thought of prostitution and begging into the doctor's mind, and it was with a sort of relief that he heard her say that on that night luck would have meant to her a bench where she could sit till daybreak. I was looking for one, she said, when a girl spoke to me. I think I heard you ask the policeman where you could get a lodging, said she ; those were her very words ; but I told her I had no money to pay for one, only a few pence. She asked me if I was from Dublin and I answered I was not, that I was from the County Down and had taken the train from Belfast that night. We walked on together. I said : You are out late, and she told me that she was out to meet somebody. But it 's getting late, she said, and the rain is coming on again ; if you stay out all night you 'll be soaked. I told her I couldn't help that, for I had only a few pence

and was afraid to go to a doss-house where the beds are
threepence a night. She didn't answer me and I could see
she was turning something over in her head. It was then
that I began to take notice of her; I noticed her umbrella,
for I had never had one myself, and wondered why she had
spoken to me and let me walk by her side. She had a veil,
too. Quite the lady, said I to myself, and no ill-looking
girl either. She told me her name was Phyllis Hoey and that
she worked in the daytime in a biscuit factory, and if I came
with her in the morning I could get work there, not work
that would be well paid for, but enough to pay for my lodging.
As for food and clothes, well, that was another thing, she
said. She told me to come in under her umbrella out of
the rain, and I came up close, afraid at first to take her arm.
We 'll be fellow-workers in the morning, she said, and you
can sleep with me to-night. I didn't know where she was
taking me to. It was a long way, and it was all I could do
to hold out till the end, and I can't tell you, sir, what a relief
it was to get out of the darkness, to see her light a candle,
and to catch sight of the bed. We slept soundly enough,
and in the morning she took me to the factory. The manager
wanted an extra girl, as it happened, and I would get eight
shillings a week. As I only got three-and-six a week for
pulling mangel-wurzels, eight shillings seemed like a fortune.
Why, said I to Phyllis as we went to the workroom, if you
let me live with you we 'll have sixteen shillings a week.
We won't have all that, said Phyllis, for there are always
fines; they generally manage to get a shilling a week out
of us. Well, fifteen shillings, said I, and it was disheartening
to hear her say that we 'd have to pay more for the room
now there were the two in it.

The day passed from eight o'clock in the morning until
twelve, packing the biscuits in tin boxes, with every layer
separated by paper, and they told us we mustn't let it get
crumpled; if the Inspector found the least wrinkle in the
paper, we had to unpack the box again, and as we were paid

by piece-work I soon saw that like this we wouldn't get even
six shillings a week maybe. At twelve there was an hour
for dinner; as I'd had no breakfast I didn't know how I'd
get through to the end of the day, and I wouldn't have if
Phyllis hadn't taken me to a grub-shop, where she said most
of the girls went for their food, the ones that wasn't living
at home, and Phyllis paid for me, for I'd have no money
till the end of the week. But, said I, our dinners alone will
cost us all we earn. Phyllis laughed and said that there
were always extras; I thought she meant overtime, and
we went back to the factory. It closed at seven. And on
our way home I asked if we couldn't buy our food and cook
it ourselves, and save half of what we spent in the grub-
shop. But Phyllis was afraid that we'd not get back to
the factory in time, and any saving we'd make would be
lost in a fine. And so talking we got back to our room,
where Phyllis began to dress herself out just as I'd seen
her the night before, hat, umbrella and gloves, and as she
didn't offer to take me with her, I stayed at home, waiting
up till midnight. You mustn't wait up for me, she said,
for if you do you'll be too tired to go to work. And what
about you? said I, and waited for an answer, which I didn't
get. She just went on undressing herself, taking out of her
pocket more money than I knew she had gone out with.

It was that night as we lay down together that she said
to me: Well, Sarah, you may just as well hear it now as
later. A girl can't get a living out of the factory; it just
keeps us employed in the daytime, and then the girls go
out into Sackville Street, and there, or round about the
Bank or in Grafton Street, the money's good—you can
pick up half a sovereign or maybe a sovereign. But you
don't find them along the pavement, said I. Our gentlemen
friends give as much, ninny, she said, and I quickly understood that the factory girls, all the young ones at least,
made their living, or the best part of it, on the streets, and
that I'd have to do the same, for I couldn't thole going on

sponging on Phyllis, who only fell away from the right course because there was no other way for a girl to get her living in Dublin, none that she knew of. I heard Phyllis fall asleep, but I couldn't sleep that night for thinking, it not seeming to me that I could go on the streets nor that I could stay at home while she did, for that would be like taunting her, living a lady's life at home and she walking out round and round, up one street and down another. That's how I saw her in my head all the night, afraid to come back without half a sovereign, and to take money earned her way seemed no better than earning it that way myself. Phyllis didn't try to persuade me ; she said that every girl must do the best she can for herself. She had often heard of girls marrying in the end off the streets, but she didn't want to say a word that might lead me where I didn't want to go. She said she quite understood, but that there wouldn't be enough money for both of us if I didn't go, and in the end I might have been pushed into it, for I'm no better than Phyllis ; and there never was a kinder soul, and maybe it's kindness that counts in the end.

And how was it that you escaped the streets, Sarah ?

No more than an accident, sir. We were at work all day in the factory, as I've told you, and while Phyllis was out from seven o'clock till half-past eleven or twelve, I used to sit sewing, trying to make a little money that way, and as it was summer time the nuns were out every evening in their garden. I forgot to tell you that our window overlooked a convent garden, a lovely garden, with big trees and green plots, and it was lovelier when the nuns came out and walked in twos and threes through the shadows. I had only known religion as a quarrelsome thing that set men throwing stones and beating each other with sticks, breaking windows and cursing each other, and I said : If I had time, I'd like to know more of the nuns, they seem so quiet and happy. But we were, as I've said, at work all day, and it wasn't till there was a strike in the factory that the days were our own, with no bell ringing and nobody to take our names as we went in. We could go and come as we liked, only there was the money ; but as most of the girls got their living as I told you, sir, we could hold out. It was whilst the strike lasted that I went to the nuns' chapel to attend Mass, a thing we seldom had—on Sundays we had to sleep it out. The strike lasted a fortnight, and I heard a little more of the Catholic religion than was spoken about in the County Down. Phyllis said : If you have a feeling that way, tell the priest who hears your confession that you 'd like instruction in the Catholic religion ; he 'll give it to you and jumping. So I did, and entered the Church just about when the strike was to end.

But, Sarah, I thought you were always a Catholic.

My mother was a Catholic and I was baptized one, as I 've told you, but mother went over when I was a child ; between twelve and thirteen I was at the time, so you see I had had no instruction, or very little, in my religion. I 'd been a month in Dublin by this time and owed Phyllis more money than I would ever be able to pay her back, and I was thinking of going into service, which I ought to have done long before, but I knew nobody that would recommend me. Father Roland (that was the priest who instructed me) said he would recommend me, but he was a long time about it and things were going from bad to worse. It seemed that I would have to do in the end as Phyllis did, and it might have been like that if Father Roland hadn't said one day : Some nuns in Wales are looking out for lay sisters, but they are very poor and cannot afford to send you the price of your passage over ; and you 'll want money to buy the clothes you 'll wear during your probationship. But where am I to get the money ? I asked, and he spoke of putting by a little week by week ; and I was going to tell him how I was living, but the story didn't seem one for a gentleman like him to hear. And it all seemed more hopeless than ever. Phyllis said nothing, but I knew she was thinking that I 'd better come out with her of an evening. She was down on her luck ; for nearly a week she had not met with any money, and we were as poor as we could be, but still I clung on to hope. I seemed very selfish to myself, but you see, I was only eighteen and knew nobody except Phyllis and the girls at the factory. If I had known then what I know now, I could have gone to an agent and got some charring, maybe a situation. But I 'm making a long story out of it, and the telling of it will make no difference. I must leave you, sir.

I 'll be able to tell you, Sarah, if you 'll have to leave me when I have heard your story.

Well, sir, one night Phyllis came home in great spirits. She had met a gentleman who had been very kind to her and given her two pounds. We talked about him a long while, and Phyllis was to meet him next day. And when she came back about half-past eleven, that was her time, she said : I told him about you, and he says that he 'll pay the money for the convent if you 'll come to meet him. It wasn't for sin that he needed me ; the man was really a very religious man and knew that he was doing wrong in lying with Phyllis, but he couldn't help himself ; and that was why he told her he would give the money to get me into the convent. I was to pray for him in return.

And did you go to meet him, Sarah ?

No, sir ; for the next time Phyllis saw him he said that Phyllis's word was good enough for him, and that he 'd give her the money, taking in return for it my promise to pray for him. Tell him, I said to Phyllis, that I will never cease to pray for him, and for you, too, dear Phyllis, though indeed it should be you to pray for me, so much does it seem that I 'm the wicked one. And we spoke of the wages of sin. But Phyllis said : Dear, you wouldn't do it well ; you 're not suited to the life. It 's well that you didn't.

She seems to be a very good girl, your Phyllis, the doctor said.

Yes, Phyllis is a good girl. There never was a better

one, so good that it seemed to me, as I was saying, sir, that I was the wicked girl and Phyllis the good one. But that couldn't be, for the Church says different. Then I seemed to understand that every day I stayed in Dublin I was putting Phyllis into sins that she wouldn't commit if I wasn't with her. The night she went out to meet the gentleman again I prayed for them both all the time, and the money seemed hateful money she brought back. But there it was ; it was earned, it was gotten, it would have to be spent, and it was better it should be spent on a good purpose than on a bad, so it seemed to me ; and the next day we bought the clothes. Father Roland wrote to the nuns. A telegram came, and we went down to the boat together, crying all the way, for we were very sorry to part. Sir, I don't think I can go on telling you. It broke my heart to part with that girl ; she 'd been so good to me and we were such friends, and there was nothing for it now but we be to part for ever. I felt I was never going to see her again, and I think she felt the same about me.

Have you never tried to find her, Sarah ?

Oh, sir, all my evenings out have been spent hunting for her round Merrion Square and round about College Green, up Sackville Street as far as the Rotunda, looking for her in the crowd. Now and again it seemed to me that I saw somebody like her, and I ran and looked into her face, but it was not Phyllis. I can't go on telling you the story, sir. I can't, indeed I can't. She laid her face in her hands and fell across the doctor's writing-table, her sobs alarming him, the big tears rolling from her eyelids down her swollen cheeks, even to her chin. If anybody were to call ! The doctor waited, saying nothing, relying on silence to calm the girl's grief. At last he said : Let me hear the rest of the story. You went on board the boat and arrived at the convent—when ?

In the late afternoon, sir, towards evening. I don't think I can tell you any more of it.

Yes, you can, Sarah. I cannot tell you whether you are to stay or go till I 've heard the end.

Well, I don't know that there 's much more to tell, sir. You can guess the rest, that I was very miserable at leaving Phyllis, and felt more and more as time went on that in God's sight there could not be much to choose between us, and at last I went with my story to the Mother Prioress.

To the Mother Prioress ! the doctor repeated.

You see, I wanted to leave the convent and go back to Phyllis and tell her that I 'd lead her life. In great grief one hasn't one's right thoughts. And when I came to the Prioress to tell her that I wasn't happy and what I had left behind, she said : My child, you can't go to a life of sin. Well, what can I do ? I asked her, and she told me that there was one remedy for it all, and that was prayer. You see, she said, you are without money, without friends ; you can't save Phyllis from the life she is leading, but you can pray for her. All things are in the hands of God ; he alone can help. So I took the Prioress's advice and prayed. . . . After a time I was a postulant and then a novice, and when I had taken the final vows I seemed stronger. But there was always in my heart the pain that I had left Phyllis to a life of sin and gone away myself to a life of comfort and ease, with the hope of heaven at the end. I couldn't get it out of my head, and I wouldn't have been able to bear it if it hadn't been for the Mother Prioress, who was very good to me and understood that the lay sisters had as much right to hear Mass as the choir sisters. But her time came, as it will come to all of us, and the Prioress that came after her was quite different from the one that had gone.

It was she who turned you out of the convent, wasn't it ? Sarah answered : Yes, sir, and continued her story drearily, telling that several lay sisters in the convent had died, and that many of those who remained were old women who had come to the end of their time, infirm, bed-ridden women : We had to attend on them in their cells and wheel

them up and down the Broad Walk when there was a little
sun. These old sisters were a great burden on the funds
of the convent; I think the choir sisters felt it. And then
two lay sisters died, young women who were not strong
enough for the work. That was about three years ago, sir.
So the convent was short of workers, and the choir sisters
had to shift for themselves, and not being used to work
they soon tired. So the Mother Prioress wrote to all the
priests she knew for postulants, but the ones that answered
her letters wanted to be choir sisters; none of them had
fortunes, and the convent couldn't afford to take them without. So all the work fell upon us, and many days we didn't
even get Mass. There was no time for private prayer;
it was drudge, drudge, all the day, and if half an hour or ten
minutes did come, I was too tired to pray, and there seemed
to be no hope for me to make up my arrears. My health,
too, began to fail, and I was distracted by thoughts that I
was failing in my duty towards Phyllis. The Prioress had
told me I could only help Phyllis by my prayers, and in the
last years there was no time. And what with bad health
and thinking that I was remiss in my duty towards her and
the man who had given me the money, one of the big dishes
dropped out of my hand one day in the kitchen. The noise
and the clatter of the pieces brought in the Sub-Prioress,
who told me I wasn't worth my keep. I didn't answer
her, but she brought the Prioress to see the kitchen, and
everything was found fault with: it wasn't swept, and the
crockery was chipped and broken—all through my carelessness. I don't know what they didn't find fault with
that day, and they thrieped on me till at the last the blood
went to my head and I spoke without knowing what I was
saying, telling them that while they were walking idly in
the garden we were working our lives away. Yes, I think
I said that two nuns had died already of hard work and bad
food, and that we had no time for prayer; that the nunnery
was no house of prayer but just a sweaters' den, and that

I 'd sooner go back to a biscuit factory, where at all events I had the evenings to myself for prayer. I said many wrong things, but however wrong I was the Prioress shouldn't have turned me out of the convent after ten years of work. I stood up for her when I came here first, sir, when you spoke against her ; but perhaps I am wrong now and was right then. And now you have had the whole story.

Not all the story, Sarah.

Well, I know no more of it, sir.

You have not told me why you 're leaving my service.

My duty is towards Phyllis, sir ; I have promised her my prayers, and there 's the man that paid for me, too, to be considered. If I married I would be having children and I 'd have to look after them, and Phyllis would be forgotten ; I couldn't be remembering her always except in a convent.

You 've never told me, Sarah, how you met Miss Lynch. You must have met her the day you arrived in Dublin.

No, sir ; it was the next day. I arrived in Dublin late in the evening, and after walking about Sackville Street, Bond Street, and round Trinity College, searching for Phyllis——

But you were ten years in the Welsh convent, and in ten years——

She may have married ; she always looked to marry, I know that, but being in Dublin I had to look, for one never knows. I was just back where I was before, with this difference, that I had a sovereign. The nuns at the last moment said they 'd let me have that much——

For ten years' work ! chimed in Dr. O'Reardon, but without noticing the interruption Sarah continued : It was all over again what it was before, myself asking the policeman to direct me, and when he heard I had money he said there was a woman in the street he lived in who would take me in. He directed me. There was in her house a child put out to nurse——

And Miss Lynch being a Health Inspector ! said the doctor. I see it all !

But I wouldn't want you to think ill of the Welsh nuns, sir. You see, it was hard for them to keep me and I after saying to the Prioress that she was answerable for the lives of the lay sisters, and much of that sort. They couldn't have kept me, and I have reason to think they have suffered in their consciences ever since, for when I wrote to them to tell them where I was and that I 'd like to enter another convent if they 'd give me a brief, they wrote, leaving out many of the bad things I 'd said, for they were in the wrong too themselves, and they felt it, I 'm sure of it. I am leaving you, sir, with sorrow in my heart, for I cannot find Phyllis, though I have looked everywhere for her.

Phyllis may be dead.

Even so, sir, I must pray for her; we must pray for the dead. I know you Protestants don't, but we Catholics do. And I hope you 'll forgive me, sir, if I 've deceived you in anything, an' indeed I have that, for I only came into your service to earn enough money——

To go into another convent, the doctor interrupted.

Yes; that was at the back of my mind always.

Well, if that be your conviction, Sarah, you must go.

Now will it be putting you to an inconvenience if I don't stay my month?

It will, Sarah, but I haven't the heart to detain you. Peace of mind comes before everything else; and I dare say that I shall be able to get another parlourmaid within the next three days. And we part then, Sarah, for eternity.

Not for eternity, sir. We shall all meet in heaven, Catholics and Protestants alike.

And what about the broken-hearted man on the ladder clipping the ivy on the wall of my house?

Throwing out the sparrows' nests, sir. He said you told him to.

What is to be done, Sarah? Sweet-peas and sparrows are incompatible.

He 's sorry to do it, sir. He showed me a nest with four

little ones, and the moment I touched their beaks they opened them, thinking their father and mother were bringing them food.

You think more of the sparrows than of Michael, Sarah.

I 'd think of him ready enough if it wasn't for my prayers.

The door closed. The doctor was alone again, and he continued his letter to Helena Lynch, hearing Michael's shears among the ivy.